Whatever It Takes

a Bonfire Circle Story

By

Quint Emm Ellis

ISBN-13: 9798771923437
Independently published

Cover design by:
Raquel M. (@raquel98rm on Fiverr)
Library of Congress Control Number: 2018675309
Printed in the United States of America

Table of Contents

Chapter 1: the End.

"Every day is the start of a new year."

- unknown

The montage of images halted at the scene of a crowd chanting as a disco ball made its languid descent along a pole. But it was the beaming smile directed into the camera that had snagged Ta'Mara's attention. Despite the chaos of last night's NYE celebration, the host's stare screamed loudest of all; his lips stretched from ear to ear, the glint of his bright, white teeth outshining the lights of Times Square, itself; the corners of his mouth as sharp as daggers. The grin didn't engender a sense of gaiety for Ta'Mara. It conjured an image of predators catching sight of doomed prey.

Stupid, stupid, stupid prey.

She switched the channel. But a few clicks of the remote continued her disappointing tour of what cable channels had to offer. Finally, with pursed lips, Ta'Mara Taylor Lawson silenced her most obvious form of entertainment with a frustrated jab; and tossed the remote on the sofa cushion beside where she sat curled up with her favorite blanket.

Glaring at the darkened screen she lamented that her television had failed her when she needed it the most.

"The t.v. must be male", she muttered, only thinly-amused as she leaned against the arm of the sofa and began chewing her bottom lip. Impressions crowded her mind; too many to discern one from another. Too many for her to entertain the idea that she might figure out something — anything — she might do to distract herself today.

Quiet hung heavy and dense throughout her apartment. The sun, however, seemed determined to penetrate its curtain. Shining boldly through the windows she'd finally uncovered, its light washed over her face and caressed the area of her chest that lay exposed beneath her robe. Perhaps it was the sun's fault, then, that the thoughts she'd frozen in time began to soften and melt and ooze out between the cracks found in her carefully constructed layers of distractions. Now, she would have to face the day after New Year's Eve—the day off that everyone looked forward to but that she'd dreaded because it'd meant nothing but time to think about the one thing she was trying to avoid.

And so it was, for Ta'Mara, that the first day of the year began with tears and continued with the inevitable messiness of snot, tissues and piteous binges of very good, but very bad food. By the end of her last carton of ice cream, an equally messy decision was made.

❋ ❋ ❋

...later that evening, a few blocks away.

Jared Iona looked forlornly at the twenty-pound dumbbell in his right and then his left hand. With a sigh and roll of the eyes he placed them back into the pile of exercise equipment that rested in a jumbled pile on one side of his closet. Sliding the closet door shut Jared shuffled toward the kitchen, envisioning himself opening the freezer door and eventually gnawing on the last ice cream sandwich.

Within ten minutes all his fantasies had come true; including the part where he felt like a complete failure. But the ending surprised him this time—because he'd never sobbed this hard before.

~ Quint Emm Ellis ~

4

Chapter 2: the Beginning.

After just a block Jared had to halt his jogging and brace himself, bent over with hands on knees and gut ballooning and retreating. He didn't dare consider what he must look like to onlookers; that'd get him nowhere. Standing up and taking a deep breath, he closed his eyes and mentally prepared to launch himself into tackling the last two blocks. Behind him he caught the faint sound of rapid footsteps approaching him. Taking a cautious look backwards he felt his heart skip like it always did when he saw her, the woman he'd named 'Lady-Speed-Walker'— the woman who'd inspired him to start taking his workout seriously.

Since the beginning of spring he'd noted her and her quick steps and swaying hips as she sped-walked by his duplex around the same times on Monday, Wednesday and Friday evenings. He recalled wondering if this was a new routine for her; Jared had been pretty sure he would have noticed her well before then had that not been the case. Not only for the rare form of exercise and the way it forced her body to move; but also for the fact that she was so consistent—not to mention adorable.

Admittedly, part of the impetus for initiating his own jogging routine was in the hopes that he might run into her. Curiosity hounded him about his mystery crush. And now, she was running into *him*. He'd only barely opened his mouth as she zoomed right by him, her eyes straight ahead and overhead earphones firmly in place to shield her from intrusions.

Clearly, Jared thought, he'd have to do better than that. His brain only caused him to hesitate for a second with the rebuke regarding exactly what his goal was—and then he was off. Even at a jog he found himself keeping a fairly challenging pace in order to—casually—catch up with her at the next corner where she awaited a green light. Now, if he could only manage a word or two in-between catching his breath.

Arms on hips and chest rising rapidly, he swallowed hard and prepared to greet her as she jogged in place, but as soon as the green light flickered on Jared was left in her dust once more. And this time, he ceded defeat as he watched her figure grow smaller and smaller.

Taking up a more leisurely pace he achieved his consolation goal of jogging one more block to his local cafe where he treated himself to their smallest, plainest frappuccino. Occupying one of the seats at the counter, he nursed his drink and avoided thinking about the jog back home. Instead he considered what he might say to the mystery woman should they meet again. "Great day for a run, er, walk!" No. "I'm not creepy, I promise!" Hmmm, that'd likely have the opposite effect. "Hey, I saw you out my window!" Definitely. Not.

Or maybe he should just say it wasn't meant to be. Afterall, he's overweight and under-confident and maybe that's where he should steer his attention. Of course, he was also a man. And she was definitely a woman. Not skinny or even thin, but all the right shapes were stacked in all the right places; she had that kind of feminine roundness that he could definitely appreciate...and he was honest enough to admit that he wondered if that often under-appreciated fact might actually give a guy like him a chance. Her style of dress was not flashy but felt practical and thoughtfully composed. She seemed—approachable. And cute. He wondered what kind of music she was listening to. Wondered what kind of guys she was into—and at that he shook his head; there he went again, thinking about things that don't help him.

Taking the remnants of his drink with him he hopped off the chair and out of his reverie. With single-minded determination—he barrelled toward his fateful meeting with the pavement—only to find her walking in just as he was about to exit. Their eyes met. And did her gaze linger on his? Was that a slight smile on her face? Should he take that as an invitation, or was she just the friendly type?

Something halted his thoughts and his forward motion.

Or rather someone.

A soft cry came from a woman he'd just run into and onto whom he'd spilled what little had been left of his plain frappuccino.

"Oh dude, I'm so sorry," he belted out.

She looked up at him in shock, shaking her head as she continued to calculate what had just happened to her. Finally, she paused, blinked, and exhaled the breath she'd inhaled sharply and hadn't realized she'd still held. Allowing for a slight chuckle, she sighed and then waved him off in dismissal; "It's fine," she said shortly but without malice. Moving to the drink station that was near the door, she grabbed a handful of napkins to begin blotting at the large, tan stain that marked her shirt right above her right breast.

"Seriously?" her friend balked at him. "Are you blind?"

Jared's mouth opened wordlessly before the words tumbled out: "No—I—was just distracted, I guess." At that he couldn't help but glance around, his eyes seeking the source of his distraction, but he halted, embarrassed at the scene he must have made right in front of Lady-Speed-Walker. Instead he turned his attention back to the woman he'd unceremoniously branded. "Look, I'm genuinely sorry. How can I help?"

"I think you're good. Please—don't do anything else," she stated, wryly.

~ Quint Emm Ellis ~

9

"Maybe I could pay for you and your friend's drinks? I'm really sorry."

She paused from her dabbing to look up at him as if assessing something. He saw her shoulders visibly relax before she shook her head, declining his offer. "Don't worry about it," she added with a smirk that surprised Jared. "Sometimes coffee happens, right?"

Jared noticed, then, that she was pretty; beautiful actually. In the midst of everything he hadn't noticed until she'd really looked at him. He hazarded a smile, relieved to hear the humor in her comment. "That's a very grounded response." He grinned, proud of himself: "Get it? Coffee. Grounds?"

She smirked and looked at her friend who looked quizzically back and forth from her and him.

"Too soon?"

Chuckling, she nodded. "Yeah, give it a couple more minutes and that'll be hilarious. Or not."

Jared laughed with her. The woman's friend made an annoyed face. Jared ignored her. "Look, it's the least I can do. Let me treat you both and hopefully that'll mark the beginning of a better day going forward," Jared insisted.

She blinked at him, once again seeming to consider him, then she shrugged and proceeded to the counter.

As Jared followed the two ladies he looked around the cafe and was glad to have spotted Lady-Speed-Walker waiting for her drink among the small crowd gathered at the pick-up station. He thought he caught her quickly glancing away from his direction before she began nibbling on her bottom lip, seeming to stare at nothing in particular.

When the cashier rang up the order Jared hurriedly handed over his card and declined the receipt. The woman's friend went over to the pick-up station to await their orders. Meanwhile, Jared hadn't even realized he'd continued his idle chat with the woman he'd spilled his drink on until she stopped the conversation to ask the cashier for the receipt. On the back, she wrote down something and handed it to Jared with a twinkle in her eye. His brows furrowed as he took the small paper and mentally processed that he was reading a phone number on the back. *Her* phone number.

She shrugged in a surprisingly bashful move, "Just in case you ever want to run into each other again sometime," she explained, "Get it?" she teased, a bashful smile pulling at the corner of her lips as she walked away to join her friend at the pick-up station.

Wait, what?!

He might've imagined what he must've looked like, his mouth forming an "O" on his face; but just then Jared noticed Lady-Speed-Walker heading for the door. He looked back at the woman who'd just given him her number; the woman glanced over at him expectantly, even while being chatted up ferociously by her friend who eyed him with apparent confusion. And yet, he found himself gesturing to the woman with an incredulous smile and a weak wave of the hand in which he held her number—before rushing toward the exit.

What the heck was he doing? He thought to himself as the sounds of traffic met him outdoors. Was he crazy? He continued to consider, even as his heart sped up at the sight of Lady-Speed-Walker's figure headed back in the direction from which they'd both come. Hot, nice, funny women do not exist in his world, let-alone give him their contact info. But when one does he chases after a cute woman who he's never even spoken with and didn't even notice him when he was standing right in front of her?! Was he just a glutton for punishment?

The thoughts raced through his head, berating him as he fought to catch up to the woman he'd first noticed so many months ago as he'd happened to glance out the window of his duplex. Oh, crap—maybe he *was* that creepy guy. Maybe he should back off.

But then he was beside her at a corner, again. And this time he said, "Hi". And this time, she heard him and, with a curious look behind her at the cafe they'd just left, she cautiously offered a "Hello" back.

"I had wanted to say something back there in the cafe but then...I..."

"I saw," she responded, a look of curiosity on her face.

"Yeah, well," he spoke in the ensuing awkward silence. "Not my finest moment."

She chuckled at that and shrugged, "You handled it well." She opened her mouth and then seemed to think better of it, turning her attention back onto the light. He did the same, wishing he was a bit more practiced in the art of talking up a woman. "Most of us might've professed our genuine apologies for several minutes," she seemed to force out, "and then left it at that." She licked her lips before admitting and turning her head to look at him, "It's—always nice to see someone go the extra mile. It's so rare, you know? Very considerate of you, despite her friend being a bit of a jerk about it all."

He shrugged. "Aw, I get her friend—she looks withered but maybe she's got good flavor. She's showing loyalty. You gotta respect that."

"Hmm," she murmured with a thoughtful smile. "I guess I can't disagree with that. Who doesn't appreciate a bit of loyalty from those who claim to care about you." Her brows creased. "But what do you mean by 'she looks withered'? She didn't look that old to me."

Jared laughed and rubbed the back of his neck, feeling a blush creep up his olive-toned face. "Oh, it's kind of one of the Hawaiian phrases my family has

---

gotten used to. I just forget sometimes that they're not common sayings."

At her inquiring look he went on. "My dad's Hawaiian, well, he was born in Hawaii but he grew up here for most of his life after my grandparents moved. Anyway, we just all got used to different proverbs he'd say, like 'The banana looks withered, but it has excellent flavor.' Stuff like that."

Ta'Mara's expression became thoughtful as she parsed out the logic of the saying. Then she smiled, nodding her head. "Hmmm, that makes sense. Yeah, she did seem pretty withered, actually. So that must mean she was sweet as pie."

They both laughed at that. "Well, at least you got her friend's number out of it," Ta'Mara commented, then stopped laughing, realizing she'd just outed herself. "I mean, it looked like you did, as I was walking out, I just glanced and saw." She clamped her mouth shut before it embarrassed herself any further.

"*That*, I wasn't expecting," he admitted with a chuckle.

A small smile appeared on her face in response and he could note the moment her eyes caught on something, causing even that to waver and her demeanor to lose some of the repose that had begun to flow into her during their conversation. He followed the direction of her gaze and realized he still grasped the now-infamous receipt in his hand.

She turned her attention to the streetlight. "Oh, the light. It's changed. I—I better get going, nice chatting with you!"

"Wait! I, uh..." She stopped in mid-stride and looked back at him, a question on his face. Now what in the world would he say to her to justify that dramatic request. He looked at her and she looked at him; and he promptly crumpled the receipt and tossed it in the nearby trash can.

His mind railed at him. But the thoughts quieted at the smile that seemed to reluctantly spread across her lips, which she pointed toward the sidewalk before returning his gaze. And all of a sudden, he felt unreasonably certain that she'd be more than worth a million such numbers.

"You—uhm—headed this direction?" she asked.

"Yeah, I actually live a few blocks from here. Just started jogging. Trying to get in shape, you know?"

She nodded. "I've been speed walking for a while now. Heard it's better for your joints." She shrugged. "But then research will probably change regarding that at some point, too."

"Then I guess we better take advantage of the findings while they're still valid, huh?"

She laughed, "Exactly."

"Maybe I should try speed walking. At least to start. But," he nodded to her drink in hand, "do you usually speed walk with a hot coffee in hand?"

Ta'Mara laughed. "I always ask them to just fill it halfway. And add a little whipped cream...you know, as a buffer to make sure the liquid that's in there can't spill out."

"Of course," Jared agreed with a grin. "As a buffer. Good idea. Brilliant idea."

Ta'Mara laughed, "Thanks for playing along." Shrugging, she continued. "It's still better for me, overall. Less sugar than what I would typically order. But it still allows me to indulge a bit."

"Makes sense," Jared said, looking up, "Light's green, again. Maybe we can speed walk together?"

She grinned at him, raising one brow before playfully tossing over her shoulder, "Sure, if you can keep up." Before he knew it he was several feet behind her.

"I can't wait to try," he said to himself, laughing as he jogged to catch her

Chapter 3

✳ ✳ ✳

Over the next couple of weeks Jared and Ta'Mara's intermittent "accidental" meetups gradually turned into something intentional. It was agreed upon that Jared could use the motivation to shed the pounds he so desperately wanted to lose, and she could use the company. "I'm tired of being the same person I was all throughout school," he'd explained to Ta'Mara. "Something's gotta change."

They'd made the cafe their turning point, until Jared could work his way up to Ta'Mara's current marker, which was one block past the cafe. That day, they sat discussing one another's motivation for getting serious about their workouts.

Ta'Mara knew she was no model—and would never be—but she did feel great about the transformation she'd seen in her lifestyle and body so far and looked forward to seeing more to come. Since her one friend who lived nearby was not remotely interested in making the drastic changes to food intake and exercise that she had, it was a blessing to find a like-mind and a shared sense of purpose in Jared.

And she found herself very easily adapting to the new routine with Jared, which included brief interludes where they found themselves gushing about dreams, memes and fears.

"For me, it was my health," Ta'Mara had admitted. "Diabetes runs in my family, unfortunately, as well as high blood pressure. My doctor said I was becoming dangerously close to falling prey to the former. And if that happened, the latter disease wouldn't be far behind." She grimaced. "Visions of pill popping and dialysis machines was the dose of reality I needed, so to speak." It'd taken months of calorie counting and dedication to get her body moving to see positive changes happen, but she was slowly seeing the results—not only in dress sizes but, more importantly, in her health diagnostics.

Jared nodded, sharing that he admired her determination. "I feel like you'd accomplish just about anything you set your mind to, Ta'Mara. The world is your oyster, so to speak."

Ta'Mara only shrugged in response.

"What? You don't think so?" Jared had prodded.

"Well, I'd like to see things that way...and I certainly don't place limitations on myself. But sometimes the world around us places limitations on us, you know? I mean—forget about it. I don't want to get too intense. Thanks, though."

"Oh no, not 'forget about it'. What were you gonna say?"

Ta'Mara bit her lip—should she dare risk what was turning out to be a very lucrative friendship for both of them? Shouldn't she just be happy with this superficial level? And it struck her that, to her surprise, she had some hope that maybe there was more depth to this friendship than the casual acquaintanceships she'd become accustomed to at work, at church and in every other social environment where company was mixed. Oh well, here goes.

"Look, I don't expect you to understand or sympathize, but the thing is that, as a black person and as a woman, I'm acutely aware that the storyline has not been, nor is it still so cut and dry. I believe that an individual can work hard and achieve much. But that doesn't mean that the road to success doesn't still include obstacles that wouldn't be there if ethnicity, gender and weight didn't factor into one's standing in our society. And even in terms of how people relate to one another on a general level. Relationships can often be steered by preconceptions and implicit bias, not to mention the experience of the educational system and the application of justice being influenced by those same factors."

She paused, trying to gauge his response before continuing. "I'm not trying to play the violin here, but tryna' give a bit of perspective—my determination stems from me learning to be real about a situation. I've got to be realistic; otherwise I could be blindsided by setbacks vs. strategic about them. Or I could miss a gem-of-a-piece of insight, just because I prefer a delusion. I'm not gonna let myself become a victim of disappointment, I won't self-sabotage, I won't let my fears be my own enemy when there are already unwarranted strikes against me—I like myself too much for that, and I owe too much to those who've gone before me who didn't have the same opportunities I have.

"But even with all of my effort, well, I mean, part of being realistic is realizing that healthy people know how to ask for help—and I have to be okay with admitting that everybody needs help at times—not a handout but 'a hand-up', as they say. I'd like a hand-up, sometimes. I'd like to not feel like I have to fight against so much useless stuff that has nothing to do with my potential. It just gets tiring, trying to live up to an expectation that I can do this alone; that I can keep pushing back at all the walls and still make it through to the other side with my sanity in check." She blinked, having momentarily forgotten that she was talking to a man she'd only met a couple weeks ago. A man who, though of mixed heritage, would likely be perceived as a tawny skinned white male. She pressed her lips together to stem the tide and watched him, readying herself for the awkward silence to follow.

"Damn." Jared said, looking at her with astonishment. "That's what I'm talking about!" He said a little too loudly for the cafe. "You're freakin' amazing." He subdued a bit, unapologetic about his outburst, but more sober as he observed, "And look, you're right...I can't ever understand—I can't walk in your shoes. But thank you for giving me a chance to listen. And to think about some things, too, that I'm sure I take for granted. Yeah, none of us are an island, right?" He paused, seeming to think about something. Then turned back to her, seeming to stare into her soul for moments. "Look, I realize that all of that couldn't have been easy to share. Thank you. And I know we've only just met, but I hope that maybe I can somehow be a part of your support system. I believe in you, from just the little I've seen so far I know you're capable of anything; particularly if given a fair opportunity."

Now it was Ta'Mara's turn to be astonished. "Uhm, yeah, sure you're...welcome. Thanks for, you know, hearing me." She took a sip of her frapp, "There's a lot more where that comes from," she mumbled around her straw, suddenly self-conscious about entrusting him with that tender part of her worldview. On one hand his response was a relief, but on another she feared continued forays into honesty would eventually push this man away...or worse: establish a relationship on her being the "black friend". The last thing she wanted to become was someone's "Wikipedia for the 'black experience' " or "woke" person's trophy-friend. She'd been there.

Jared chuckled, acknowledging he'd heard the comment she'd made pre-sip. "Ta'Mara, I figure we could all manage to learn a lot more than what we already know; not everything is learned from a textbook. If we're gonna be our best selves we need to be willing to learn from one another—especially when it challenges us." He made a "come here" gesture with both hands, "So, bring it."

The muscles in her cheek hearkened a smile. "Are you a glutton for punishment or an idealist, Jared?"

Jared patted his stomach, "Well, a glutton...obviously, but not for punishment. And an idealist," Jared seemed to sincerely ponder that, "Never saw myself like that, really. I think I just like hearing your thoughts; I like how you express them, I like—" you. "—Learning about people," he finished lamely. "I mean, I guess I've kinda been trying to learn to listen better. So I don't miss what's important." He looked back down at his drink and busied himself with taking sips from his straw.

.

"Well— I really like that I felt comfortable enough to share that with you, so honestly I mean," she found herself saying in response to his earnestness.

To that, Jared beamed.

As they left the cafe that day Ta'Mara noticed him humming the melody to Matthew Wilder's "Break My Stride". She began singing the words as they stood beside the cafe door, readying themselves for their fast walk back home.

Jared joined in so that they were singing the chorus together, eliciting curious looks from passersby.

Ta'Mara chuckled. Jared beamed at her and with a proud look on his face proclaimed, "That's your theme song—at least in my head, that's your theme song, Ta'Mara. If anybody can overcome the obstacles placed in their path, I'm confident you can. And if I can ever help you, with anything—well I hope you'll give me that chance."

"Thanks Jared," she said, a wide warm smile emanating from her lips, eyes and heart.

They both hummed her song, off and on, as they struggled to keep their breath on the long walk home.

Chapter 4

***

Within a few weeks both she and Jared were able to extend their distance to two blocks beyond the cafe. On their way back home, they made their usual stop at the cafe. And to celebrate Jared's accomplishment Ta'Mara treated him to his favorite "plain" frappuccino and toasted with him on their way to an empty table.

"So why do you get the same drink every time we come here?"

Jared shrugged. "It was my dad's fav when he'd come to visit and we'd stop by this place. Was the closest he'd get to diverging from plain coffee. I'd always tease him about it and he'd take it with good fun, dishing it out as good as he got, too, even after the stroke." He stopped abruptly.

Ta'Mara looked at Jared, offering a small, inviting smile and silence that beckoned to be filled.

"Our dad was a janitor—a facilities manager— until he'd had to retire," he blurted, speaking about himself, his younger brother and their younger sister, "the baby".

"He had a stroke just before his 53rd birthday. I think losing the job hurt him more than losing some of the mobility in the left side of his body, to be honest." Jared was pensive for a moment, before a smirk crept into the corner of his lips, "He used to take my brother and I to work with him on Friday nights — never my sister because, of course, she was his princess who shouldn't be exposed to such drudgery," he rolled his eyes. "The same sister, who as we speak, is celebrating her graduation from college by working as a novice teacher at a pretty tough school located in a state she's never been to, and doing so for the next year as she finishes out the stint she'd signed up for with Americorps." Jared shook his head, and Ta'Mara could see and feel the pride he had in her.

He continued sharing about his father, "Anyway, our dad. Yeah, he'd have so much pride in showing us how to remove any and every stain. How to be sure that the space you left behind was better than the one you entered. Because, even if nobody else noticed, you would...and being able to take pride in your own efforts mattered more than any accolades." Jared shook his head, nostalgically, "I swore that after I grew up I would never swing another mop or wet rag or toilet bowl brush in my life. I would be the richest son-of-gun there ever was and I'd have an army of people to do my cleaning for me."

He sipped a long time on the straw of his drink before continuing. Ta'Mara waited, somehow feeling the weight of what was to come before it was even realized.

"He died last year. And..." Jared shook his head, "I don't know, I'd been working in corporate, had started an MBA program, just so much to not be like him. And all of a sudden I realized I missed him. Like he'd been there in front of me all that time, but I hadn't really seen him for the amazing man that he was. I knew he was an amazing dad...but I hadn't fully comprehended him as the person he was that lent itself to that role. And I was so desperate to really know him, you know? Before I knew it I'd applied for a janitor position at his old company. I was overqualified but I had a friend there that—after trying to coerce me out of it—helped me land the job. Can you imagine that...pulling strings for a custodial job. Not fair, I know—"

He glanced at her guiltily then, before looking away to continue. "I get that there were probably candidates who needed the job more—" His lips tightened at the new awareness of how his actions may have impacted others. Finally, he inhaled and exhaled, realizing that nothing can change the past. "What's crazy is that everything he taught came rushing back. And I began to feel this amazing sense of pride in my work that I'd never felt in corporate america. And I felt closer to my dad, too. Like he was right there, showing me the ropes, all over again. 'Cept I finally started to realize he wasn't just teaching us how to clean; he was teaching us how to, just, be."

Ta'Mara nodded, trying to imagine the man that raised Jared, imagining a smaller, younger Jared by his side, along with a similarly dark-haired brother, impatient and teasing one another as their father repeatedly demonstrated a task; or their dad standing back with a gleam of pride in his eyes after viewing the work that he and his sons had accomplished together.

During their walks together, Ta'Mara had never let on that she'd noticed Jared before. On occasion she would see him walk from his car to home. And she'd noticed how he'd sometimes place coins in the nearby meter of someone else's car who didn't have a neighborhood parking permit. Or how he would pick up trash that had found its way to the front of the duplex he lived in—he'd pick up the litter whether it'd fallen on his side of the property or that of his neighbor. She'd noticed how he'd carefully park his car close to the curb to allow room for traffic to flow down the narrow lanes. All such small things, but they all pointed to someone who noticed others and cared enough not to neglect them.

After a while, Ta'Mara ventured, "And your brother?" Jared looked up at her, pulled out of his reverie by her voice. "What did your brother say when he heard about your decision?"

Jared grinned. "Oh, he told me I was crazy, of course. And I couldn't help but agree." His grin stretched farther, "But he also understood more than anyone else, even more than mom. Guess who's started assisting me from time to time, now?" He winked at her. He looked away, smiling. "We both needed the reminder."

"Of what?"

"Of who dad was. Who he wanted us to be. And who we are, no matter what else is going on. 'Mālama'. 'Mālama' is a Hawaiian value, it means to care for, to protect. Its meaning extends toward our land as well as toward people. And that's our dad and our mom. That's who they are. And that's everything they wanted us to be."

Like Ta'Mara, Jared wasn't a model, either. Though tall, he wore his inky hair so closely cropped that you would never know it had a tendency to curl were it not for the rare periods of time that he let it grow just a smidge longer—and even then he had a habit of topping it with a short list of his favorite worn, soft, fabric ballcaps. His jaw sported an ever-present after-five that peppered his olive skin, and his rounded belly mirrored rounded glasses that completed his nonchalant geek persona. He seemed to wear shorts and plain t-shirts as much as possible. He was one of those guys that you immediately just liked. Before even getting to know him Ta'Mara's first impression caused her to wager that he was the kind that was helpful at work and everybody loved him. That even the women found him cute, in a safe and dorky way. That guys found him to be a relatable, masculine, non-judgmental and a surprisingly insightful confidante. As a matter of fact, she'd've wagered that most people found him easy to talk with.

More than anything, Ta'Mara was glad to have found that her assumptions seemed true—at least so far.

And maybe, against her own better judgement because she really should be focusing on herself right now—-but maybe she had a crush on him.

Chapter 5: the Love...

What are you thinking about?" he asked a few days later, right before grabbing a potato wedge from her stash and popping it in his mouth. They were sitting outdoors at a local Mediterranean cafe that served the best garlic fries. Ta'Mara wondered if it'd been a mistake to introduce Jared to her spot; he'd fallen in love with the fries and was all too willing to split his order with her. "Come on," he'd say, "It's a few fries and you're doing amazing. Treat yer'self...on me! And don't worry, you know I'll help you eat them." They'd begun hanging out outside of their walks. And by now, he knew that food was her love language... thankfully, he never asked to come here more than once a month; and he was an enthusiastic partner in her never-ending search for healthy food that actually tastes good, too.

Picking up one of the fries she'd scooped onto her napkin from his plate, she admitted as nonchalantly as she could, "I was just wondering if I'm ready for a relationship—I mean, I feel like I am." She looked down at her dwindling pile of wedges and took a bite of the one she held. Then shrugged, looking away, "Like, maybe a romantic one." She looked back at him with a small smile that quickly faded.

Jared had stopped chewing and stared at her with a look of wide-eyed terror. He'd seen her far off stare and serious expression and had figured she was working out some kink or challenge in whatever she'd meticulously planned for her agenda the following day. And like a million times before he'd wanted, for all the world, to be able to lean over the table, take her chin in his and kiss her until all of the gears that constantly whir in her mind ground to a screeching halt.

He cleared his throat, realizing he'd missed his cue to respond. "Oh, well. Okay." He looked away, afraid that his feelings would show in his eyes. Was she thinking about someone in particular, he wondered? Was she thinking of him? "Were you thinking of someone in particular?" he inwardly winced at how his voice rose to a near squeak near the end of his question, but his curiosity bulldozed its way out of his mouth before he'd had the chance to manage himself.

Ta'Mara shook her head, not sure how to interpret his halting response and flushed cheeks. She'd thought that she'd seen signs that he was interested in her, too. They'd seemed so clear; yet he'd never overtly said anything to indicate his interest in her beyond an exercise buddy. And she was far from an expert in these things. So maybe she'd been completely overlaying his feelings with her own. She opened, then closed her mouth. Why couldn't she ever come up with the right words at the right time? She inhaled deeply and just shook her head a second time as she focused on the obviously fascinating pile of potato wedges clustered on the white napkin in front of her.

"I mean, what I meant to say," Jared offered, feeling all thumbs but knowing he'd already messed up the moment pretty royally if there'd been any hope that he had been in consideration, "Is that I was thinking the same thing." He added, belatedly, "Too."

"Right," she said feebly, still quite enamored with rearranging the spuds in front of her, though she'd placed the half eaten one down beside them.

Was he still being too vague? Man, he's such a wuss, why couldn't he just tell her how he felt about her, from the very beginning? He looked at her and, pushing away his plate of fries, he sat forward with his forearms resting on the tabletop and his heart thumping a million miles a minute, silently willing her to look at him.

When she did, he plowed ahead before his words had a chance of being drowned under the weight of his fears. "I've been thinking about you, Ta'Mara. A lot, actually." The smile that slowly lit up her face and warmed her eyes made his heart jump into his throat. Compelled, he let his words continue to fall from his mouth. "From the day we first met, actually." And even before then, he mentally added.

He hadn't noticed the tenseness in her shoulders until he saw them relax along with the rest of her body; and yet, the air was charged. Were they really doing this?

"Jared, I really like you. Like, like you." she chuckled at how immature that must sound. "I wasn't sure...I thought that maybe it was just me—"

Jared vehemently shook his head as he leaned in farther to clasp the hand she'd placed on the table. "Oh, no, no, not just you." Her skin was so soft. She turned her hand over to clasp his—palm to palm—and he felt something click into place within him. This was so good, so right, so everything. "I guess I should have made my move sooner? I wasn't sure you'd be interested in a big lug like me; I mean I'm a janitor, for goodness sake—not the most prestigious career in the world, you know." With his other hand he rubbed his neck, self-consciously. "I think part of what I'd hoped to gain during our walks was the courage to do something about the feelings I've had for you. I guess I still have a way to go to grow in the confidence department."

Ta'Mara unconsciously rubbed the pad of her thumb over the skin that stretched over the back of his hand. "I feel like that applies to both of us," she chuckled. "But am glad we managed to fumble into this, despite ourselves."

He watched their hands entwined, her skin a dark, brown maple and his golden pecan, contrasting and complementing, just like them. She watched as her other hand came to rest on top of his, her fingers gently tracing patterns on his skin. He licked his lips and caught her gaze. She leaned forward so that she could more comfortably grab his hand in hers, lifting them so that she could place a kiss on his fingers. "I love these hands, Jared. They do such good things for so many. They belong to a man I admire, who is honest, takes pride in his work and has the best work ethic I've ever seen; someone who is genuine, thoughtful, consistent, respectful and respected just because of who he is; this man enjoys me for me. These hands belong to the person who I want to be more like."

And right then, Jared almost let slip the fact that he more than liked Ta'Mara...he loved her. And the realization shook him.

He found himself blurting, "I don't want to move us too fast."

She blinked, his hand feeling a bit weighter in her hand, a bit more foreign. "What do you mean?"

He gently extricated his hand from hers. "I mean, I can't tell you how long I've been wanting this—with you. And how much I want it. It's just, now that it's here—" I realize I need to get my feelings in check before I scare you away, he wanted to say.

Ta'Mara looked away, finishing for him. "Right, I see. Yeah, sure, let's not rush things." And by "not rush things" she meant, "forget about it, you're obviously not interested now that you've caught your game."

"Hey, Listen, I uhm—" she began gathering up her napkin, haphazardly swaddling the remaining fries so she could discard the whole lot. "I think we should just—"

"I don't want you to change your mind about me!" he blurted again as she began to rise from her chair. She paused in mid-motion, then slowly reclaimed her seat.

He went on, hoping the words about to tumble from his heart came out exactly the way he felt. "And I don't want to move you—us—into something that we're both not fully ready for. You think so highly of me; and I'm beyond honored. You're so amazing to me, too, Ta'Mara." In a hushed exhale of air he added, "More than you know."

Reaching over to enclose her hands in both of his, french fries and all, he explained "I'm so scared I'll mess this up. I don't want you to change your mind about me. And I know we haven't known each other so long, yet, but I see something real, here, and important. And I also respect your beliefs and just want to make sure we pursue things in a way where you won't ever have regrets or anything. I don't want to lose the relationship we're building together just because my eagerness prevents me from treating it with the care that it deserves. I want you to get to know me more—I guess I want more time to slowly reveal the depths of my weirdness" he chuckled. "That way you can't say you were duped into anything." He smiled, shyly, hopefully at her.

Ta'Mara's small smile mirrored his as she nodded, understanding. Impressed that he cared enough to share so honestly with her.

Jared leaned forward to brush his hand against her cheek; and with her own hand she pressed his palm against her skin and leaned her face into his caress, the warmth of his hand spreading from up to her temple and down her neck and shoulder.

She was a woman who grew up in the church. And though she hadn't attended in quite some time she still held on to the values and beliefs, which transcended any brick-and-mortar facility. Still, when it came to love, she'd found it hard to deny her wandering heart. Jared wasn't a believer, yet he'd aligned more with Christian values than a number of people she'd encountered at places of worship she'd attended—and as much as his touch made her want otherwise, she welcomed his respect for her and consideration of both of them in the pace he expressed wanting to set.

Even so, the thoughts she read in his eyes mirrored her own: honoring one another in this way would be a challenge for them both.

Chapter 6

✳ ✳ ✳

Before that fateful day when they'd revealed their feelings to one another, one of their most pivotal conversations had centered around their shared relational experiences—or lack thereof. Though they were both in their mid-twenties, neither Jared or Ta'Mara had had a long-term or even short-term serious relationship to speak of—both having enjoyed the "friend-zone" far more often then either would have liked.

"Not to mention that it's pretty hard to meet a guy who loves Jesus, isn't married, enjoys sci-fi as much as I do and doesn't creep me out. All necessities, as far as I'm concerned." She chuckled.

For them, it made the prospect of a genuine romantic relationship weightier; they both knew that there would be no such thing as an introductory fling as far as their hearts were concerned—they'd be all in—so hopefully the other person was, too.

"I figure it's like measles." Ta'Mara had said. Jared had begun walking her home after their excursions, claiming that it gave him a chance to cool down. "If you've been exposed when you're young, then when you get older you don't have to worry about it. But if you've never had it, then as an adult it'll kill you." Ta'Mara had stated, decisively.

"So, getting into a serious relationship as an adult might kill us?" Jared teased.

Ta'Mara shrugged and held back a grin. "Well, 'love' and 'war' aren't placed in the same sentence for nothin'!"

"Also, it's chicken pox." Jared corrected.

"What? Oh!" Ta'Mara rolled her eyes. "Whatever. You know what I mean."

"Yes. You're saying love is like a disease."

At that, Ta'Mara burst out laughing, playfully nudging him with her shoulder, Jared dutifully feigned being knocked off balance as she continued the walk toward her apartment's front entrance.

"Aye!" he'd exclaimed with mock offense. His expression transformed into a huge grin as he resumed his balance and quickly made up the few paces needed to catch up to her.

As they walked, both grinning, Ta'Mara couldn't help but note the older white gentleman and his wife slowly making their way down the block together. She'd seen this couple from her window often, and always found it so endearing to witness the display of long-term commitment and love.
She felt buoyed by the thought that today she, too, was enjoying the company of someone who was becoming more and more special to her. A mix of hope, understanding and even longing warmed her smile as she offered a nod of acknowledgement to the approaching couple; the older man merely nodded; while his wife seemed to stare just a little longer than was kosher, a look of utter curiosity blanketing her face as her eyes darted first from Jared then to Ta'Mara then to Jared again. A line then appeared, pressed between her lips as she turned her face resolutely forward, failing to acknowledge either of them beyond that.

Ta'Mara frowned and inwardly shook her head, glancing up at Jared who had been completely oblivious. She considered bringing it up, but wondered how he would respond. Would he think she was being overly-sensitive? Would he just not know how to respond out of helplessness and cluelessness? So instead, she inhaled deeply as she intentionally steered her focus on the bulk of their camaraderie, on this sweet walk home and how good it felt to be with someone who "got" her—in a lot of important ways, at least.

✱✱✱

Jared had managed to hold on to a small group of buddies from highschool and college; but his best buddy had been a senior when he was a freshmen and they'd been fast-friends. Lawrence had taken Jared under his wing that last year, and he and Jared moved in together following Lawrence's graduation. Lawrence was a thinker, soft-spoken and solid. A man of integrity, almost father-like even at a young age, he'd experienced loss at an early age—and the experience brought out a wisdom that Jared had come to rely on. Lawrence had been a rock that Jared was able to look up to, especially during the loss of his father. While Jared had been the oldest of his siblings he'd found a big brother in Lawrence and a confidante. And Lawrence was now getting married to his long-time fiance, Darla—and sought out Jared to be his best man.

"So you'll be bringing Ta'Mara." Lawrence stated, not asked.

Jared grinned broadly, a flush beginning to darken his cheeks. It'd been a pretty big deal for him and Ta'Mara to have gone on a double-date with his best friend and his bestfriend's then-girlfriend-now-fiance. At first, he'd turned down his best friend's offer, reiterating that he and Ta'Mara were still trying to figure out how to navigate the feelings they'd professed.

To which his best friend had replied, "Cuz you're both scared shitless. You even more than her, I'd wager." Lawrence always knew just how to push Jared's buttons. And he loved him for it. As a result he, Ta'Mara, Darla and Lawrence had had a great evening together playing board games, watching a Netflix movie and treating themselves to standard fare of pizza and popcorn.

Jared still remembered the way it'd felt to have Ta'Mara's head rested on his shoulder and Lawrence and Darla settled on the couch with Darla's legs propped up on Lawrence's lap as he absentmindedly massaged her feet. Jared had kissed the top of Ta'Mara's head and then found himself licking the residue of the sweet-tasting oils she used to moisturize her strands. She'd looked up at him and rubbed the oil into his lips with the pad of thumb, smiling up at him with a look of contentment and...more. He'd kissed her lips, then, sharing the sweetness with her.

The moment was so simple and natural that it was shocking. And by the pleased looks on both Lawrence and Darla's face, Jared and Ta'Mara hadn't been the only ones moved by the moment.

Jared brought his thoughts back to the present. "Yeah, Lawrence, of course. I mean, we're both pretty inexperienced in the whole real relationship department. We don't want to rush things—so, you know, don't get any ideas just yet or anything."

"Or, it might put the right idea in both your heads."

"Whoa, whoa, whoa! Man, are you kidding me? We just started dating! Let's give her a few minutes before we scare her off with a ring, maybe."

"Jared, I've seen less chemistry between Emmy-winning on-screen actors. What you two have—it's real. I can see it. And I know what I'm talking about. I've seen you with the other women in your life—"

"You mean all two of my girlfriends?"

"Okay, I'm including your friend-zones and crushes, too."

"Very generous of you."

"What I'm trying to say is that, for the first time, I see an adult having a real relationship with another adult. Something tangible enough that it's pushing you, motivating you. Not just with physical exercise—which alone is seriously amazing."

"Thanks, Friend."

"Hey, I'm no gym rat myself—so I admire you! I just pray Darla doesn't decide to put herself—and thus me—on some kind of regimen. Might make for a short marriage."

Jared rolled his eyes. They both knew that Lawrence would cut off appendages for Darla if she could give even a halfway reasonable justification for it.

"But, what I was getting at is that I also see you growing in confidence, affection and openness outside of your inner circle. It's like she's shining a light on you so that everyone else can see you for who you are. I imagine you're doing something similar for her, Jared. So yeah, I just don't think people have to wait forever when they've found the right person for them."

"I don't know. I guess I just feel like a mess...I just want to get some things in order."
"You think anyone's ever ready for intimacy? Look, I love my fiance, but she's not perfect. I certainly am not, either."

" 'But you're perfect together', " Jared sing-songed, batting his eyes.

Lawrence rolled his eyes, "No, but we're better together. She brings out the best in me...I do the same. Sometimes we bring out the worst, too. But we work through it...grow closer. Hopefully grow better as individuals, too. That's the strength of a relationship that's worth having. Not two people who've got it together...just two people willing to invest the work, patience and humility needed to keep growing as individuals while also working to grow closer together. Just think about it, that's all. I love you; and I'd hate to see your fear make you miss out on something and someone that could be the best thing that's ever happened to you."

Jared couldn't help but feel a little overwhelmed by that thought. His fear of losing Ta'Mara is what had prompted him to suggest they move slowly. But could moving too slow result in the same thing?

Chapter 7: the Oopsies.

The night of the wedding, Jared was so proud to have Ta'Mara on his arm. Her pale-yellow maxi dress was snug at the bosom and billowed in soft folds down to the floor, seeming to glow against her dark skin tone. It took his breath away—she took his breath away. She'd always been attractive to him, but he recognized now how months of consistent workouts had continued transforming her figure into a firmer version of the mounds and curves that'd initially caught his attention.

Jared wanted Ta'Mara, in every way. And he had from the moment he'd met her. But that night was the first time he felt compelled to forget his own insecurities and take the chance that he was the right man for her.

Jared didn't miss the double-takes during the reception when he'd introduced his beautiful date to old college acquaintances. And he couldn't help but wonder if it was because of their different ethnicities, or because she was so obviously out of his league. Or both. But he realized he didn't care about the reason; he only cared about taking care of the woman who had grown to become the best part of his day. He wanted to care for her today, tonight and everyday that she'd let him.

He and Ta'Mara were seated at the head table with the wedding party. They watched as Darla and her father took to the dance floor for their father-daughter dance, both with tears streaming down their faces. And Jared envied them. Darla was a vivacious woman who's eyes glowed when they fell upon her fiance. Her kinetic energy filled the room, and were it not for Lawrence's steadiness to balance her out, could even be a bit overpowering. And apparently like others in her family, she emoted easily, freely. It inspired him.

He felt a nudge on his arm to find Ta'Mara looking at him with a question in her eyes. He smiled and got up from his chair as the song ended and a faster paced song began. With a smirk and a waggle of his eyebrows he held out his hand and kissed Ta'Mara's fingers when she'd placed her hand in his in response. Rising from her seat she followed him to the dancefloor and had the best time just moving with her man. It didn't hurt that Jared was putting on quite the show, intent on making her belly laugh as hard and as often as possible. Finally she decided to join him and they both danced as silly as they could muster, enjoying one another as if they were the only two in the room.

When the songs transitioned into a slow melody, Jared slowly drew Ta'Mara toward him, expertly guiding her hands to his shoulder and his chest. As inexperienced as he was at relationships, he was thankful that his first girlfriend had loved to slow dance and had willingly suffered many a trampled foot to get him to the level of proficiency about which he could now boast. Placing one hand on the curve of Ta'Mara's hip and his other firmly against her back, he pulled her close to him and kissed her on her forehead before she nestled her head against his chest. And with that he led her, moved their bodies to the slow beat of the music and reveled in the feel of the woman he loved, soft and warm against him. "I could stay like this with you forever, Ta'Mara" he admitted in a whisper near her ear. He felt her soft "mm-hmm" against his chest, and felt her hand slide up his chest to meet her other hand around the nape of his neck. She leaned back, her eyes boring into his. "Jared," was all she could manage.

The voice right beside them startled them both. It was Darla, but a somewhat tipsier version. "You two," she hooked her thumb behind her, "Go. Get a room." She smiled, a happy bride pleased with the night and the love of her life. Jared's jaw dropped open and he looked at Ta'Mara who just shrugged. "Look," Darla continued, pausing to finish off what was left in her wine glass, "I'm the bride and the queen for the night. And I decree that you two are too hot-to-trot to spend the rest of your evening here. It is my decree," she said solemnly, pointing one well manicured pointer finger in the air, "that thouest shalt get out of this 'stablishment and go bonk the night away!"

One of the bridesmaids seemed to appear out of nowhere and, with a smile, gently led the queen back to her royal companion, who seemed to be well on his way to tipsy-ville himself. Ta'Mara and Jared's gazes followed Darla's journey back to her husband and watched as the two kissed passionately and began dancing together. Then Jared and Ta'Mara turned to look at each other quizzically—before bursting out laughing.

Later while filling up at the food bar, one of Jared's old college buddies sidled up beside him, slapping him on the back. "Jared! Wow man, it's great to see you doing so well. You look good! And I have to say, you are doing mighty well in the ladies department. How did you and her get together?"

"Don't sound so surprised, Colin."

Colin balked. "Surprised? No, not what I meant. We were just saying—"

"We?" Jared looked back at the table where he and Lawrence's old college buddies sat with some of their dates.

"I mean—I—was just saying how, well, I noticed that you didn't seem to date much in college. But even when you did date it's not like they were…" Colin trailed off, having at least enough awareness to have spotted the trajectory of his foot. He coughed and focused on filling his plate. "Anyway, man. Yeah—uh—you definitely—" But Jared had decided to leave before the guy could finish whatever awkwardness would continue to gush from his lips.

That night, they stood together just beyond her apartment door, kissing their goodnights. Before Jared could turn to leave Ta'Mara held onto his jacket lapels. "Come in?" she invited, looking up into his eyes. He nuzzled his nose against hers and nodded, whispering, "Okay."

Once inside she gestured him over to his couch as she threw her small clutch on the small table beside the door, where it'd be visible for her in the morning and would prompt her to transfer her cards and cash into her everyday purse. "Water or anything? I can make some tea, or coffee."

Jared sat, his heart thumping the beat of some crazy song. "No, thanks. Wait, yes, I think cold water would be great. Very cold." She blinked at him, but nodded and proceeded into the kitchen. He could hear the clink of glasses and the faucet. The opening of her freezer and the clink of several ice cubes. The "click" of the stove rang out, and the sound of the kettle landing on the stove's grate so that she could warm the water for her tea. Soon she was heading toward him, placing a glass of chilled water on a coaster she had placed out for him. Then she sat beside him. He reached for the glass and drank most of it down in several long gulps.

Once he placed the glass down he looked up at her. She watched him and she raised up her hand to rub the bottom of his wet lip with the pad of her thumb. He loved how she did that; and he could feel the weight of his eyelids grow heavy. She leaned closer and kissed him, and he responded, increasing the demand in their kiss and leaning her back against the sofa until he felt her shift beneath him so that her body could flatten beneath his. "Jared" she whispered, her hands rubbing his back, welcoming the pressure of his body on hers.

And then, suddenly, Jared was struggling into an upright position, disentangling himself from her arms to stand away from her, closer to the door. His hands in his pockets. Ta'Mara could hear herself whimper—whimper!—at the sudden loss of his weight and warmth.

"What's wrong," she asked, pushing herself up into a reclining position with her arms, the soft fabric of her skirt that'd bunched up on the sofa slowly gave in to gravity, cascading romantically off of the sofa.

"Nothing!" Jared almost barked. "I mean," he continued in a softer tone and a tortured expression. "This, I want this so much, too. But if I know you the way I think I do—" He paused as he looked at her, to gauge the truth of his next words, "I think you'll regret this decision. Your faith, I mean. I don't want you to regret making love with me tonight. Or any night, for that matter."

And in a roundabout way, that was the first time the word "love" had entered their audible vocabulary.

"Baby," he continued, stepping only slightly forward. "If you tell me that you're okay with this, that we'll be good, then I'm all in. I want you. I..." His chest rose and fell rapidly, as if he were exerting great effort.

She looked away. And that was all the answer he needed. Stepping back, he nodded and said, "It's okay."

"Wait, I—I want to be okay with it. I want to make love with you, too." she added quietly, her eyes searching for the understanding that she knew he felt. "I wish you hadn't asked, though," she admitted with an empty chuckle. She sighed deeply and rubbed her forehead.

"I'd better go." Jared said. But his feet wouldn't move until he got confirmation. She looked up at him, bit her bottom lip and surrendered a nearly imperceptible nod.

He nodded back. "Mālama pono," he said quietly, before exiting her apartment as quickly as he could. And wondering if he was an idiot for the right reasons, or just a plain, garden-variety fool.

Chapter 8

✳ ✳ ✳

Over the next week Jared made an effort to speak with Ta'Mara but she always found a reason to avoid meeting up with him. Finally, he resorted to waiting outside of her workplace in the hopes of catching her—and that she'd actually want to see him.

When he saw her his heart flip-flopped, like it always did. And when she noticed him he observed the smile that appeared on her face but his relief was short-lived. Her expression quickly shifted to something unreadable.

She extended a farewell to the co-worker she'd walked out with and parted from them so that she could make her way to where he stood with hands in pocket, looking as awkward as he had their last night together. The sight made her heart sink. She really hated that this is what she'd compelled him to do—to feel.

"Hey," she said, suddenly shy and unsure.

"Hey," he said back. He opened his mouth to say more but then closed it. He tried again, "I just thought maybe we could grab something to eat real quick. Talk?" He added in a sigh, "I miss you".

She walked to him then, and he welcomed her in an embrace, just like she knew he would. "I'm sorry," she mumbled into his chest. "I—"

"Hey, you don't have to explain anything. If you need to process stuff, I understand. I'm not tryna push you or crowd you or anything. I just want us to be okay."

She pulled back a bit, her hands still on his hips. And she nodded. "Yeah, we're okay. I mean, I'm kinda a wreck, but, you know," she sighed and chuckled.

"Ah, sweetheart," he said, placing his palm against her cheek.

She closed her eyes and raised her hand to his, enjoying his warmth. "I do want to explain, though. I think I need to...it's just hard to face some things, sometimes."

Jared nodded his understanding.

"It's just…I'm not mad at you, really," she continued. "I looked up what 'Mālama pono' means," she said, her pronunciation only somewhat halted. "It's that extension of Mālama you talked about. Extending the meaning to encompass care for people. It's like bidding someone well; to bid them protection, or something like that, right?" Jared nodded.

Ta'Mara grimaced. "Yeah. And that's what you did for me. I know that. And I—I think I'm mad at myself, maybe? Here I am, the Christian and it's you that had to put the breaks on things. And maybe I'm kinda wondering what's the point of it all. I mean, I was willing to ignore my beliefs long enough to…well, I mean why not just ignore them all together? It's what other people do and I'd be less of a hypocrite. I mean, the only thing that stopped us from being with each other is a belief system that I didn't even adhere to."

Jared looked at her and stroked her cheek again, the soft skin gliding beneath his fingers. "Ta'Mara, there are a whole lot of people having sex right now, in all kinds of ways, expressing the freedom they feel to do so. But as far as I can see, it's not actually making people feel more fulfilled. I mean, depression is on the rise, despite the fact that screwing is on the rise, as well—not to be crass. So for me, from what I've seen, your faith brings you joy, hope, peace, fulfillment. Seems like it's worth all the sex in the world. And I'd never, ever, want you to lose it. Because it's been the backbone of your tenderness and resilience and willingness to give a knucklehead like me a chance. It's been my strength, too, vicariously through you."

"One day, it will be the right day for us to express how we feel about each other—physically and with every bit of ourselves. And oh my good Lord I'm looking forward to that day!" He exclaimed. "But outside of His timing," Jared pointed toward the skies above, "It just wouldn't work for us—you and me. And I knew it, I know it. And I already told you I'm not messing this up," he grinned. "I plan on your being stuck with me for a good long while," he paused and captured her hand in his, bringing her fingers to his lips. "If you want."

She grasped his hand tight and nodded, "I want." Then, tilting her head and peering at him she said, "Are we...saying something here?"

He smiled and began tugging her closer to him. "Yeah, I think we are saying something, here." When she was close enough to him he leaned down and touched his forehead to hers.

She hit him, smiling, then nested her head against his chest and wrapped her arms around his waist. "You're such a tease, Jared," she murmured into the fabric of his t-shirt. She felt the rumble of his chuckle beneath her cheek.

"Not trying to be a tease, Love." He paused, letting the word sink in for them both. He felt her arms tighten around him and her nuzzle even more against him. And he found himself wondering, for the millionth time if he'd made the right decision last night. He continued, his voice gravelly with emotion, "I'd...just had something else in mind for the moment I asked you to marry me." His voice had neared a reverent whisper as he'd stated the last few words.

He felt her body stiffen and his breath stilled. Daring to look down at her as she arched back to gaze at him, he found himself buoyed by the wide, bright smile and glistening eyes that greeted him.

"Jared Xavier Iona, are you asking me to marry you?" Ta'Mara asked, cheeks rounded by a wide grin, her tongue peeking momentarily between her teeth in anticipation.

Jared pulled her tighter, if that was even possible. "It's not the way I'd hoped, I mean, I don't have anything to give you, yet—including a ring."

"Well, I'm not pressuring you to ask me, either. But if you were to ask me, Jared," she paused, "I'd say, 'Yes'".

Jared grinned, and dropped to one knee in front of her. "I don't have a ring, or much else for that matter. But..." and he took both her hands. "It would make me the happiest man that ever lived if you would do me the honor of taking my," he swung the clasped hands up before them, "hands in marriage." With that he took one set of of thier joined hands and kissed her fingers; then proceeded to repeat the gesture with the fingers held in his other hand. He then brought their hands to his lips, giving each set of her fingers one more kiss before raising his gaze to hers.

To his surprise, Ta'Mara got on her knees and mirrored his actions. Repositioning her hands in his, she pressed her lips to his fingers, first one hand and then the other, closing her eyes with a smile and a nod. Opening her eyes she said, with a shrug, "Jared, you're all I need. Yes, I'll marry you."

With that, Jared whooped and raised their hands above their heads: "We're getting married!!" he exclaimed, standing. Soon as he'd helped Ta'Mara to her feet she found herself hoisted into his arms, and being twirled around to the tune of both their laughter.

It was then, as they heard a spattering of clapping, that Ta'Mara remembered that they had portrayed their personal dramedy outside of her workplace, to the benefit of the remaining stragglers who happened to be making their way to their car.

Ta'Mara waved shyly to their audience from the bed of Jared's arms and could feel her fiance's beaming grin directed toward the small but growing crowd. She looked up at his face and he returned his gaze to hers. And it dawned on her that—unlike her usual self—she wasn't embarrassed in the least by the attention they'd garnered. The journey to get to this place had been long and lonely in its distinction for each of them. So yeah, this warranted some celebration.

Chapter 9: the Life that followed.

Ta'Mara woke up to the sound of her phone's alarm. It blared in the background as she lay in her bed, eyes boring into the ceiling. Slowly, she raised her finger to her cheeks, and swiped at the wet trail of tears that always followed the nightmares which forced her to relive her happiest moments with Jared.

Jared.

A swell of anger, grief and confusion threatened to awaken the body of tears that had quieted. With practiced, deep breaths she willed the tides to subside just long enough for her to sit up and retrain her focus on preparing for another work day. But even as she went through the motions an exhibition of her past life's painful events twirled, shimmied and danced around in her mind:

The week of giddiness that'd followed their agreement to commit their whole lives to loving one another. The weeks that followed of Jared growing more and more distant, until that fateful FriendsGiving gathering where everything disintegrated between them. The following days in her apartment during which tears, doubts, misery, ice cream and food delivery people served as her only frequent companions. And the awkwardness of returning to a workplace where she was flooded with questions about her marriage plans. The Christmas holiday she'd spent alone despite her parents pleading for her to join them back home in the midwest; but she'd refused to run home, she'd refused the idea that she'd been broken and needed help with the repairs. But even now, the thoughts that'd run through her mind during that time scare her. It wasn't until New Year's Day that'd she'd admitted defeat, broken her lease and committed to start over back in her home town.

It'd felt cowardly to decide to change everything around her, to up and move back into the embrace of her parents. But that's what she'd done. She'd fled.

And she didn't regret it.

After moving back home to live with her parents in Kansas City, Ta'Mara enlisted a couple different staffing agencies that ensured she never lacked a clerical job and its meager income. Thankfully, while at her local library, she'd stumbled upon a booth set up there advertising an opportunity to gain a scholarship to a local programming bootcamp.

She'd applied. And after taking an online test, followed by a brief interview to assess her goals, she'd been astonished to receive word of having been selected as one of the scholarship recipients. Immediately, Ta'Mara sought out and found part-time work that would allow her to work evenings and remain available for the bootcamp's daytime classes. Still, she would not have been capable of affording to truncate her hours so dramatically had it not been for her parents who had graciously welcomed her back into her childhood home with them. Following graduation she'd managed to garner a spot at a tech-oriented employment agency that was able to provide her with diverse opportunities where she could gain entry-level experience as a software developer. Eventually, she'd felt confident enough to attempt small free-lance jobs that didn't pay her much but gave her additional experience. It'd taken over a year of doing both temp work and her occasional freelance work before she'd felt prepared to apply for a Junior Software Developer position And it'd taken nearly six more months before she'd secured her first full-time job in that role.

From there, it'd been a slow but steady climb to grow in the profession, only to find that she missed the creativity and humor found in developing other things. That had led her to design her first app, N3rdAlert!!!, a platform where fans could share news about software development, online and irl games, science-fiction and fantasy books and "you know you're a nerd if you relate to this" humor. It had garnered a relatively small but loyal following and she'd kept it up for a few years before eventually transitioning the app into an open source project and committing to just approving community-designed changes on occasion. But it'd been an amazing experience to have built something on her own, and have the t-shirts to prove it! She had even more ideas for future applications, but had yet to pursue them.

Thankfully, her career as a Software Engineer yielded a reliable paycheck that had helped her pay off the large credit card debt she'd racked up when she'd upped and moved out of LA with little cash, except for "cash-back". After erasing that debt, she'd tackled her car loan. And after wiping that slate clean, she'd set her sights on her student loans from eons ago. She'd started chipping away at that last mountain of debt two years ago and, at the rate she was going, she estimated she'd be able to put it to rest by the end of this year.

Her next goal was to add even more aggressively to the savings she'd allotted to go toward the down-payment on her very own house. She craved the day when she could customize her living space in any way she pleased; and when she could begin to build the level of equity that could never be realized while renting.

It's goals like these that really motivated Ta'Mara. She loved to process and execute a plan.

And she also loved ignoring the thoughts about the man for which she'd been so willing to throw her beliefs, plans and processes out the door.

"Stupid," she chided the woman staring back at her from the mirror, toothbrush in hand. "No, not stupid."

she corrected, regretting that sentiment. "You're not stupid," she stated to the woman peering at her. "You're a person, a woman, a human who took a chance. And that's okay." Her eyes then narrowed and her lips tightened briefly before she stressed her final thoughts, "Just learn from it, Ta'Mara. Fool me once..." she reminded herself with the start of the old adage.

It was a saying she recited to herself regularly, especially during the times she'd entertained the prospect of a relationship. The few men that'd managed to get past her roadblocks never seemed to make it too far before her self-preservation skills kicked in, and they'd run like hurt puppies. Or they would reveal themselves to be Christians-when-convenient; impatient with her when she didn't let their advances advance them into her bedroom.

Or they just made her feel safe; like she was the most beautiful gift a man could ever dream to have, only to tear apart everything they'd shared and discard it without a backwards glance.

Ta'Mara inhaled a shaky breath, slowly releasing it, open-mouthed.

Yeah, as far as she was concerned, men were an option. And the options weren't very good, supposedly Christian or not.

The woman in the mirror nodded her head in agreement.

Ta'Mara watched herself as she took one more deep breath while pulling herself to stand at her full five foot four inches of height. Chin up, she assumed the straight posture Ta'Mara had worked so hard to reclaim over the years.

With a small smile, she was satisfied that she was ready to begin her morning preparations. Like every morning, Ta'Mara studied herself in the mirror, both critical of and coming to terms with the shape that had filled out so quickly following the end of her and Jared. She wondered how much of her—now non-existent— credit card debt had been directly related to comfort food. Smirking, she found herself wishing that she could rid herself of the debt she'd racked up in calories as easily; but neither her body nor her appetite seemed inclined to decline. And the sedentary job she held only contributed to how easily her body kept weight on.

It was also likely that she was just far less motivated now; she'd long switched her eating habits to focus on healthier versions of the foods she loved (with room for fun), so she was full-figured, but healthy and still had a very feminine shape that could be highlighted as long as she dressed mindfully. And her doctor had confirmed that she was doing well, though she was still careful to stress that Ta'Mara still had to be vigilant and that a bit of physical activity wouldn't hurt. But work in the IT field was exhausting, a mental drain that extended into the bones. Add being a woman in a world that is still dominated by men oblivious to their man-splaining, "I-don't-hear-female-voices" tendencies, and you add a whole other layer of stress.

She dropped her towel and surveyed the peaks and ridges, hills, swells, mounds of her rounded, soft shape. At over forty years of age, she felt like she looked pretty good. Truth be told, though, she sometimes didn't know how she felt about her body. She could appreciate the warmth of her deep, brown tone, the soft mound of her belly that led into the plush curve of her hips and thigh. She could also find herself resenting the creases and rolls that fell outside the perimeter of what many deem to be attractive—a fact of life, but a hard pill to swallow.

And sometimes, at her worst times, she couldn't help but think, "If Jared didn't want me back then, what would he think of me now?"

And then she'd remember that he was an asshole, and that would break the spell for the moment.

Once dressed, she unwound one of the handful of short, thick braids that graced her head each night, preventing her 4b tresses from becoming an instance of trauma-inducing knots while she slept. Starting in the front, she began the messy process of wetting, moisturizing and finger combing one section at a time. Once done, she admired the look of the inky, tightly wound coils that haloed her face, each natural curl sparkling, winking under the bathroom's light. If she'd possessed the courage, she'd wear her hair down like this everyday. But she groaned at the thought of facing a reckoning every evening as she worked to separate the entwined lovers her locks loved to become. So she did what she'd always done: gave herself a side part for a hint of intentionality, grabbed a soft, stretchy band and gently but deftly gathered her damp curls into a high pony-poof before using a second hair band to wrangle the glistening soft ball of coils into a soft bun. Adding a pair of hoop earrings finished the look.

She'd adopted the technique of standardizing her wardrobe for work. Perhaps one expression of her introverted nature was a preference for giving her mind more room to mull over things she felt more important than what she wore. So today, like every workday, she wore solid colored, high-waisted yoga-like pants that closely followed the curve of her hips and thighs and flared slightly below the knee. Along with that she donned a matching tank and one of the many long blouses whose ends she'd either tuck in loosely, allow to hang free or would tie together in a low, loose knot, depending on her mood. The overall ensemble emphasized the curves of her thighs while de-emphasizing the curves of her tummy. It was not only easy, elegant and attractive, but it was comfortable, too. And best of all, it was one less thing to have to worry about—she could feel great about her appearance with barely a thought.

When she wasn't in the office, she'd usually be in pajama pants and one of the gray "N3rdAlert!!!" tee shirts she'd had made up for herself shortly after having launched the app.

Jeans and a t-shirt were the norm for folks in her field. But she'd learned that one way to help her have a better day was for her to feel good about how she was presenting herself to the world around her; it made even bad days a little easier to handle. But she also liked reminding herself that she was working for someone else during those hours—so in essence this was her uniform. With her own software out in the world doing its thing for a bit she'd discovered an urge to be her own boss—and that she could accomplish that via the development of multiple streams of income. She envisioned her future self doing contract Software Engineer jobs while simultaneously building small apps that'd bring in a bit of supplemental income.

She wasn't trying to be rich or anything like that. For Ta'Mara, "success" equated to being free to do the things that make you happy, while being debt-free, able to pay your bills, having a reasonably sized rainy-day fund and the ability to indulge in a basic level of wants vs needs on a somewhat regular basis. Having experienced the opposite so often after she'd left college and home, she'd understood that "comfort" was a privilege.

Suited up, Ta'Mara nodded in approval, graced her reflection with a little smile and left the sanctuary of her small cottage to catch the tram and begin another work day.

As she walked past the other rental cottages that made up the small community she resided in, she already couldn't wait to get back home. Last night she'd taken a huge leap of faith by having responded to a potential client with her intention to bid on their project. So she was anxious to continue working on the proposal that could lead to the first contract job she'd had since she'd started working as a full-time Software Developer. And maybe she'd pick up a romance novel or two from the library on her way home. Fake romances, the stuff of dreams and of little reality...yeah, those she could handle.

It'd been three years since Ta'Mara had transitioned into her role as a senior team member at her current place of employment. She enjoyed the opportunities that the company offered to work with various clients, different tech stacks and code bases and to learn new technology on company time. But her favorite thing about the company was its flex-work which allows employees to work two, and on occasion three, days a week at home—assuming the employee's annual review justified the continuance of that perk. There's nothing like being able to host a meeting (online) wearing hot pink plaid flannel pants. The only downside was how difficult it could be to disengage from a work-related project. She'd often found herself working late into the night.

This was a busy time of year so three remote work days a week were pretty much out of the question, but tomorrow was Friday and she was definitely going to take advantage of the opportunity for a pseudo-three-day weekend by making it a stay-at-home day.

When Ta'Mara had decided to move from Los Angeles those years ago she'd had no idea where she'd land. But the only place that'd made sense was the place she'd grown up. And here she'd remained, Kansas City, Missouri. Since the 2010's it'd developed a pretty hipster-esque vibe in its downtown area, particularly in the Crossroads sector and River Market area. It's in the latter that she'd finally settled, amidst the Farmers' Market, boutiques, shops, restaurants and, of course, right beside the Missouri River and the finely crafted pathways that'd been constructed for pedestrians to stroll alongside its—albeit muddy—waters.

One of her favorite things about living here was the ease of transportation. Outside of the River Market, public transportation was reasonable. But within the downtown area and just beyond it, public transportation was phenomenal.

Now standing at the streetcar stop situated outside of the cluster of cottages that made up her residential community, Ta'Mara didn't have to wait long for a KC Streetcar to make its appearance and slow to a halt before her. She greeted the driver and took her seat. She preferred this to taking her car because it saved her gas, was convenient for her and she actually enjoyed the few minutes before work where someone was taking care of her needs, allowing her to enjoy the attractive scenery which meandered past her window. Having grown up taking the public bus all around the city when her parents couldn't take her someplace themselves, it'd taken some time for her to adjust to the Streetcar's policy of not having to pay a fare. She couldn't help but note the irony of life as we know it: the River Market was inhabited by people who could afford the exorbitant prices and comfortable lifestyle it touted. And yet, for those who didn't have the option of a car, public transit came with a cost.

Ten minutes later Ta'Mara exited the streetcar and with a wave to the driver, began traversing the half a block that spanned from the streetcar's stop to her building.

"Hey Tay," greeted the office manager from her front desk as Ta'Mara made her entrance.

Ta'Mara smiled and waved at the pragmatic woman, who's shiny, dark curls remained much like hers, molded into a bun. Though a far neater bun. Unlike Ta'Mara, Jules Rayden's was impeccably coiffed, her edges were always smoothed and not a flyaway dared to make itself known. "G'morning, Jules. Happy Thursday." Ta'Mara offered, slowing her approach at the desk as she proceeded to the offices in the back.

Jules nodded her agreement as she turned her attention back to her computer, pushing up her black rimmed glasses with one hand, and with the other lifted her coffee mug—and the plastic tip of the metal straw extending from it—to her lips.

Ta'Mara waved "good mornings" and greeted several others before finally making it to the solace of her small office. The silence lasted but for so long.

"Got a minute?" Resnik asked, popping his head through the doors threshold. Her boss, Resnik Arnold IV, was around her age and preferred to try to keep a sense of equality among his staff. That often included in-person one-on-one conversations or his stopping by his staff's desk versus summoning them to his. It was a thoughtful gesture, but came across as awkward all the same; because at the end of the day, he was still the man in charge of your future at the office.

"Of course, Resnik," she replied, quickly straightening from the slouch she'd settled into upon sitting at her desk.

Resnik had already begun entering her office before she'd answered and was now settling into the seat opposite her.

"Thanks, Tay. First of all, good morning!"

"Good morning Resnik," Ta'Mara dutifully responded.

"So I've heard back from one of the clients," he continued, "and they'd like to see a few features added to their application." Resnik began, setting down the notepad from which he'd recount the details..

Twenty minutes later Resnik left Ta'Mara's office and she was finally able to relax a bit before getting her day started. With new tasks in hand, she broke down each task into practical, doable chunks so that she could discuss and distribute those tasks among her team members at the start of next week.

✳ ✳ ✳

"See ya' tomorrow, hon," Charlene waved on her way out of the office for the day.

Ta'Mara looked up and brightened despite feeling worn out. The mental stresses of the job could be draining, but fulfilling. "Oh, yes. Well, see you online, at least." Ta'Mara smiled widely. "I'll be working at home tomorrow. But definitely feel free to reach out if you need anything or if you wanna hop on a video chat."

Charlene was one of their newer employees. She'd graduated from a non-profit programming bootcamp just a few months prior with the intention of transitioning from her former career as an accountant. Ta'Mara had really pushed for the company she worked at to invest in the community and in growing local talent. Charlene had been one of their first recruits. She reminded Ta'Mara of herself not too long, a fresh grad from bootcamp just needing a chance to prove herself. Ta'Mara was also well aware of what it can be like working with a team that has few, if any, fellow devs who were women. Deemed "Bro-culture," the impediments and biases are real. And a real pain. If she could help another woman's introduction into the field be more welcoming than her own, she'd take the opportunity. And the not-so-young apprentice had not disappointed. Charlene was intelligent, diligent and open to learning. She worked hard to ensure that the work she contributed had been well tested to decrease the likelihood of her introducing bugs. Speed would come. But taking care in one's work, that's hard to teach.

Charlene would be turning forty in just a few months, but you wouldn't know it. Her olive skin was unlined but for the faintest of creases on her forehead derived from hours of mental exercise crunching numbers, and now, figuring out technical bugs. Her hair was cut short on the sides. The medium lengthed hair on top that formed the foundation of her pixie cut was currently formed into a chic, softened mohawk made up of naturally deep black strands that boasted occasional strands dyed a silvery gray, "to prepare for what must come," she'd say, before chuckling.

Ta'Mara might have wondered if the woman was experiencing an early start to a mid-life crisis of sorts, but quickly observed on both her resume and her demeanor that Charlene was just that rare blend of right and left brain. "My parents fit the stereotype for asian parents," she'd explain, "Being the daughter of immigrants meant I had few options regarding my career. Accounting seemed the least grueling of them all. I figured if I can give them that, then I should be able to give myself the freedom to express myself in other ways. It's an uneasy compromise, but one we've both lived with." Even in her dress, Charlene opted for fashion-forward versus the business casual (but more casual than business) wardrobe that permeated the software development world. Today, her petite frame was garbed in slim fitting doe colored slacks topped with a faux black corset that contrasted well with the long, puffy sleeves of the white shirt she wore tucked within.

"Ooh, working at home? That's a smart move. Mind if I borrow that next week?"

Ta'Mara chuckled. "Of course. Just place it on the calendar so we all know."

Charlene saluted, "Will do, boss-lady."

Ta'Mara playfully grimaced at the term, "Charlene".

"Oops, sorry Tay. It just slipped out. You're the woman in charge! The boss-lady. And I for one find it inspiring." Charlene winked and grinned as she turned to head out, "Tah, sweetheart, and don't stay too late," she said, the words trailing behind her as she lifted an arm over her head in a farewell wave.

Ta'Mara marveled. She was a year older than Charlene, was the woman's boss, and yet to see them interact you'd never know it.

After another half hour wrapping things up for the day, Ta'Mara packed up her laptop and the files she felt she might need tomorrow and left in time to catch the KC Streetcar back home.

Once home, she plated the leftover chinese food from last night's takeout and stuck it in the microwave. While it heated up she walked to her bedroom, undid her hair and quickly exchanged her work clothes for a large tshirt and fuzzy socks.

Man, did she love being home.

She allowed herself the luxury of enjoying her dinner while streaming one of her favorite sci-fi shows. It took superhuman strength to turn off the t.v. and avoid letting herself get invested in the next episode, but she managed the feat. After placing her empty plate in the sink and running a little water over it she left her dishes for Saturday chores. She revved up her coffee pot and proceeded into her home office.

"Your mission, should you choose to accept it," she proffered to herself as she settled into her seat and flicked on her computer, "is to draft an out-of-this-world proposal." Ta'Mara's mind itched with anticipation at being at the ground floor of a project. The client wanted a total revamp of both the website and its mobile functionality. So Ta'Mara would have the chance to be the architect—and she couldn't wait to get started.

The client had initiated contact via the freelance app on which Ta'Mara had created an account eons ago, though she'd never really done anything with it. She just hadn't felt ready to add on work as a contractor. But apparently the client had somehow spotted the N3rdAlert!!! logo, was familiar with the app and after confirming that Ta'Mara was the app's developer they'd been forthright in their desire to work with her. She'd still have to submit a proposal, and oh how Ta'Mara hated the bidding process. But the enthusiasm of the woman who'd contacted her shined through in their ongoing conversation and Ta'Mara was convinced that this was an opportunity she'd regret turning her back on. So tonight, her personal goal was that of drafting a plan, "Nay, a work of art" she corrected herself aloud, that would not only "Wow" her new client, but herself. She expected she'd be staying up late that night and Friday night polishing things off. If all went well, she'd be ready to submit her final composition some time on Saturday morning, well before the Monday deadline.

Faux cracking her fingers before the computer's screen, she began the work of developing the outline she'd sketched out the night before.

Lorna smiled, pretty pleased with herself in how things were progressing. The biggest unknown in the formula was taken care of.

"One down, one to go," she mused, swiveling to and fro in her office chair. Her grin broadened and her firsts shot straight up in the air as she allowed herself to twirl full circle in unabated glee. She could not wait to see how this all turned out!

Chapter 10

* * *

It was just another Saturday morning for Jared, as he lifted and slowly lowered the weights he held, completing the last rep of his thrice weekly workout regimen. He no longer needed to add bulk, and wasn't interested in the chiseled physique he'd had years ago. Now it was just about feeling good about his body and maintaining the discipline that helped him do so. Placing the dumbbells on the floor, he grabbed a sanitizer cloth from a nearby dispenser and cleaned off the weight's handles. Having done that he stood up, grabbed the towel that hung around his neck and quickly wiped off the sweat that dripped from his brow and ran down his neck. He felt a tap on his shoulder and stiffened in surprise before turning to face the red-head standing before him. He'd noticed her when he'd entered the gym today; who wouldn't? She frequented the gym, like so many of them, but she was a fairly new member.

"Hey," she began. "I was just wondering if you were done with those?" She pointed to the 80lb weights that Jared had just freed. He glanced down at the weights and smiled brightly back at her. "Sure, go right ahead," She smirked, her blue eyes twinkling and her nose scrunching as she and Jared stared at each other. "So," she said, "You know I didn't come all the way over here for an 80lb dumbbell," she chuckled.

Jared chuckled with her and whipped the towel back over his neck, grabbing its ends and allowing his arms to rest. "I'd be pretty impressed if you had."

"I've seen you around, and I—" she feigned shyness. By now, Jared could recognize a woman accustomed to getting what she wanted from men. Hell, he'd become the kind of man who could get what he'd wanted from women. He'd become the kind of man who could recognize the game from its many angles, and who'd enjoyed playing it with the variety of women who'd taught him and who'd been taught by him, along the way.

But he wasn't that boy anymore.

"What's your name?" he asked. The question seemed to catch her off guard. For the slightest of moments her expression revealed what Jared already knew: that she had already scripted how this encounter would go and he'd just veered from it. She quickly recovered, masking that moment of uncertainty with a smile that matched his own and softly tucking a perfectly placed errant lock behind her ear. "Maddie," she offered, with an outstretched hand.

"Short for Madeline?" he assumed.

She wrinkled her nose in a way that he knew she knew would typically be considered adorable. "Only if you're my mom. And you are definitely not my mom."

Chuckling, Jared let go of one end of the towel and took her hand, "Jared."

Her hand lightly squeezed his before pulling away, sliding her palm against his. "Short for Jared?"

"Sure," he said, deflecting the line he'd heard a million times at this point. He inhaled deeply before settling into a stance. He'd considered switching gyms several times over the past few years, because he'd become well known at this gym for his great interest in the opposite sex. And though, now, that reputation had made his life difficult at establishments he'd frequented, it was the dawning acceptance of his latest stance that really seemed to embolden both his past and would-be partners. It'd been hard to find a gym that he'd liked once he'd moved to Oceanside, California. But once he'd walked into this one he'd felt right at home. It'd felt so similar to the one where he'd first began his journey toward the level of fitness he enjoyed today. The one that was right across the street from the coffee shop that had held so many poignant memories. So Jared had decided to maintain his membership; and deal with the bed he'd made—so to speak—which entailed being upfront in situations like this, so as to dampen the likelihood of future ones. "Maddie, can I ask you something?"

She bit her lip and then grinned, "Well, sure, now that we're old friends, shoot."

"First off, I don't want to assume anything, Maddie. But-uhm-if you were looking to pick up a 210 lb dumbbell vs these 80 lb ones, you're better off sticking with the lighter versions." Self-deprecating humor was endearing to some women. But for women like Maddie, he knew that the hint of a lack of self-confidence would rule him out as a potential long-term mate. Which would then place him in the category of a boy-toy. Madeline nodded, and he watched her mentally place him in her phone directory under "booty-call". "But seriously," he continued, "my question is: do you know Jesus?"

Madeline went still, her eyes blinked as her brain tried to process this incalculable turn in their dialogue. She opened and closed her mouth, a blush rising up her neck and spreading across her cheeks. "You mean, Jesus—of the Bible, you mean?" At his nod, she responded, "Uh, well, I do go to Mass every now and again. I mean, I'm Christian, and all." Her words trailed off.

He nodded. "Tell you what, if you want to go out some time, I can tell you about my own journey and what led me to give my life to Christ. I'm not looking for a date, but I'd welcome a conversation."

"More like a conversion," she said through pursed lips in a low but intentionally audible voice. "You know what, I'm good. Thanks though." She looked him up and down and shook her head. "Damn shame to waste all of that," he heard her murmur as she turned to walk away.

Truth be told, he'd rarely gotten a 'yes' to that question. It was pointedly meant to turn off a hot-blooded woman who had one thing at the forefront of her mind. And he was glad it did its job. He was sincere in his profession of Christianity, but he also knew that he was a man experienced in fully appreciating the glory of the female body. So it was risky to invite opportunities where his own restraint might be tested. But so far, he hadn't had to face that possibility; both because few women had ever accepted his offer—and because it'd require an act of God for those who did to make it past the standard that Ta'Mara had left in her wake.

An ache pierced his chest at the thought of her. He shook his head and cleaned up the area he'd been in, knocking back the last of the water that'd been in his metal bottle before heading to the showers in the gym's locker room.

But once the thought of Ta'Mara appeared, it remained firmly put. Who was he kidding, the truth was that she has always remained at the top of his mind. Always. Even now, that fact is what made Jared have to will himself not to imagine his hands as being hers on his body while he cleansed himself of the days' grime. He turned the knob to cool the water's temperature for the remainder of the shower.

Once home from his morning workout, Jared fixed himself a sub sandwich, taking a healthy bite of it as he carried the plate into the room he used as his home office. At his desk, he set his plate down and reached over to adjust the picture of his family that sat within arms length. It was a picture of all of them together, Mom, Dad, his brother, his sister and him. That picture was taken nearly two decades ago.

After his mom passed four years ago, he and his siblings struggled to figure out what to do with the house that she and their father had made into a home for them. He'd recalled so many conversations he'd had where Ta'Mara had pointed out how limited opportunities could be for some versus for others. It's what had prompted him to give up his job as a janitor so that someone else who needed it more could assume it. That shift had left him open to really consider what his next steps would be in his career and in what other ways he might honor his parents' legacy of diligence in whatever work was set before and in how he demonstrated genuine care for others.

It's that same sentiment that prompted him to suggest that he and his siblings look to benefit a family who might not otherwise be able to afford a house in the same price range. And that's what they did. They didn't focus on the offer, but on the story of those who were seeking a home. Eventually, they sold the home far below market value to first-time home owners, a couple who were expecting their first child and were in the market for a house in a neighborhood with a good school. Jared and his siblings felt there'd be no better way to honor the love that their parents shared with one another, for their children and for people, in general.

They split the proceeds of the sale, and his brother and sister had decided that they had enjoyed the process well enough to pool their money into buying and renovating two smaller properties. Jared wasn't as much into the idea, but was more than willing to contribute his portion to their dream, while remaining a silent partner. Within a year, what had been a side job bloomed into a full-time gig for his siblings as they grew the number of properties that they had flipped for sale. But it was Jared who brought up the idea to honor their point of origin, too. His siblings had agreed without hesitance. So, when they could, they'd reserve a sale of a house for those applying through FHA or other assistance programs, though that usually meant a lot more tedious work than when dealing with buyers who had garnered traditional mortgages.

Their company's model had provided a little bit of direction for Jared. He'd admittedly lost a bit of that as he'd adjusted to a life filled with opportunities he'd never had before—but that lacked the one thing, the one person he needed.

Jared thought about all that had transpired up until this point.

Fifteen years ago he'd allowed his insecurities to compel him to push Ta'Mara away. He'd picked a stupid, inane fight with her while they'd been at Darla and Larry's FriendsGiving and broke off their engagement right there. And he watched her heart break before his eyes. She'd tried to talk with him, to reason with him but he couldn't hear her past his own fears; his fear of his feelings for her, of the idea that one day she would leave him and it'd destroy his entire world. By New Year's Eve he was a mess. So much so, that he'd shown up to his brother's house that morning already noticeably tipsy. He was supposed to have been there to help him prepare, but after helping himself to a bottle of champagne he'd passed out drunk in his living room by late afternoon. He'd managed to get Jared into the guest bedroom, where he snored in the New Year. The next morning his brother, Larry, Darla and even Lorna — via Zoom — were all piled into the bedroom to straighten Jared out, hangover or not. The tough love his friends and family had granted him, along with copious amounts of water and coffee, somehow penetrated the fog and helped Jared see how selfish he'd been, and how he'd allowed his own fears to produce a self-fulfilling prophecy.

After that day of reckoning, it'd taken some time for Jared to come to terms with the havoc he'd wreaked on both his and Ta'Mara's lives. And, indirectly, on the lives of those who loved them both. But by the time he'd come halfway to his senses and had gathered up the courage to face Ta'Mara, he'd gone to her apartment only to find that another tenant had taken her place. Ta'Mara had moved.

Reaching out her family was like reaching out to a brick wall. He'd understood. He understood loyalty. And he understood he'd been anything but. He'd been an idiot.

It was then that the full weight of what he'd done to her, to them, crashed down upon him. And for weeks he hadn't known what to do with himself. He felt himself descending under the weight of shame, self-hatred and regret associated with having unnecessarily wrought pain upon the only woman he'd ever fallen in love with, and who had loved him so deeply, just for who he was. That reality regularly haunted him, walking the halls of both his waking thoughts and his dreams—until he finally started visiting the gym that'd opened up directly across the cafe that had become their first hangout. Seeing that facade everyday motivated him to push himself, to get past the pain that threatened to swallow him whole. To maybe become the kind of man that was strong enough to not feel these feelings anymore.

After a while he'd begun to notice more women staring in his direction and even openly smiling his way. It wasn't long after that he began getting approached by women. It'd flustered him, for certain. But he found it easy to allow these ladies to take the wheel and try to help him forget the emptiness that lay beneath the surface.

And one day, he found that he could predict scenarios, he could repeat lines, gestures, looks. He found himself convincing himself that this was the life he'd wanted all along. That things were better off this way, which is why they'd turned out this way. He'd become great at lying to himself. And this time, there was no amount of conversation from his family that could change his mind.

His skill at picking up on both verbal and non-verbal cues translated well in his work life as well. Eventually, he found himself relocating to Oceanside, California to work at the marketing firm at which his friend, Larry, had been working for a while. With his career advancing, his love life anything but dull and his physical health at its peak, Jared had convinced himself that he was living the dream.

All it'd taken was a chance encounter at the grocery store with an old and particularly annoying college buddy to sober Jared.

An inward groan had emanated from Jared when he'd noticed Colin approaching him one day in the grocery store, a package of tampons unabashedly on display in the man's small handheld cart.

"Jared! Whoa, I didn't know you were in Oceanside! What a small world. Yeah, my wife and I are visiting some of her relatives. Was going to pop by and see Larry for a bit. But the wife needed me to get something for her. So, how are you and your girlfriend?" Colin had asked loudly, a wide grin stretched across his face. "The way you two looked at each other I just knew I'd be getting another wedding invitation soon. But don't worry, I won't hold it against you that I didn't receive an invite. One less present I had to buy." Colin laughed at his own joke.

"Naw, man, we—uh. It didn't work out." had been Jared's only response. He'd tried to turn away and busy himself with the selection of brussel sprouts in front of him. He hated brussel sprouts, but if Colin had gotten the clue Jared promised to give the nasty little things another chance.

"Ah man, sorry to hear that," had been Colin's reply, not budging one inch. "But from the looks of it you're probably doing alright for yourself in the ladies arena, huh? Maybe it's you who should be sorry for me." The guy had held up a ringed wedding finger far too close to Jared's face. "Yeah, I miss a lot about the single life." Then Colin shrugged, "But you gotta say 'no' to some things in order to be able to say 'yes' to others, right? My wife is the best thing that's happened to me. Still," he'd said, lowering his voice in a conspiratorial tone while leaning closer to Jared, "I wouldn't mind being able to go one day without seeing her pee with the door open. Keep the mystery alive, you know?"

The conversation had seemed never-ending. But worse than its tedium had been how successfully a single memory had flung Jared back to the best and worst times of his life.

After that conversation Jared had recognized the pain that arose, unabated, undiminished. And he didn't know what to do, because obviously there was no amount of exercise or lovers that could he could hide behind. He'd already tried that—and yet there he was, sensing the edges of an all to familiar abyss. It was then that he'd remembered one of the last loving conversations they'd had. "Seems to me that your love, joy and hope are worth more than all the sex in the world."

That Sunday he'd found himself sitting in his car in the parking lot of a local Christian congregation, watching people mill into the building. He had been so apprehensive. Religion wasn't his thing, but then again, he wouldn't have thought he'd ever become a gym rat. Or find that he had a knack for marketing that'd define his career. Nor would he have never —ever— thought that breaking the heart of the woman he loved was his thing; and tearing apart the one relationship that'd mattered most to him. Nor would he have ever foreseen his joining the ranks of tramps, hooking up with women on a regular basis and having only emptiness to show for it. Everything has a starting point, both the good things and the bad. Praying for courage he realized he did not have, he somehow found himself exiting his vehicle and entering the building where, weeks later, he would confess Jesus Christ as his Lord and Savior.

That's what'd marked the start of his second life and second career.

Chapter 11

※ ※ ※

Booting his computer at home, he logged into his account on the freelance site that his sister had signed their company up for. She'd approached him a couple days ago about needing him to take over talks with a recent contractor. She'd asked that he familiarize himself with the online conversation that she'd been having with the vendor over the past week before introducing himself.

The bid that'd been accepted was from a user named "TailorMadeFullStackDev". The first thing he noted was that the contractor's bid had been a bit pricey. Going to the vendor's profile he noted that it was pretty sparse, barring the optional photo which bore an unremarkable image of the word "N3rdAlert!!!". Though their profile indicated they'd joined the platform about two years prior, their portfolio was empty—there was no prior work to attest to their capabilities.

Jared scratched his head in confusion. He perused through the long list of other contractors who had bid and who had testimonials and examples to reinforce their rates. In just a matter of minutes he'd already spotted a couple contractors who seemed more proven, despite being in the same price range as Lorna's selected vendor.

He texted his sister:

> **Jared**: Hey, help me understand why you accepted the bid that you did. Am I looking at the right contractor? They don't have anything in their portfolio. On the other hand I'm seeing a couple other contractors that really seem to fit the bill. We should look a little further into them.

He received an immediate response:

> **Lorna**: I've seen what she can produce and trust me, you'll be in love with the final product.

Jared: Hmm, that's a bit enigmatic—and dramatic, sis...Are you doing someone a favor or something? Or is that assumption based on an invisible portfolio that I'll get to look at as well? You gotta give me something here, I can't handle this blind.

Lorna: Believe me, I'm doing us all a favor. If you had bothered to read any of our dialogue in the message center you'd've seen the proposal she'd attached to her bid and everything else you need to know. If you still have questions, ask her. But she's the right choice. Mark my words, Jared.

Jared could just imagine the exasperated expression on his younger sister's face. He shook his head, annoyed at her ability to make him feel like the bothersome little brother. She was letting him know that, approve or not, this was her arena; he was merely a gladiator. He loved his sister, but it's times like these that "daddy's little princess" seemed to show up in full authority.

He shook his head and gave up. He'd agreed to be a silent partner in their business. His part was to encourage them when needed and invest in their talent. And he did trust Lorna's judgement, she'd proven herself able to handle the nuance of negotiations better than either of her brothers. It was due to her ability to pretty accurately assess the value of whatever was on the table for both parties. But it still didn't sit right with him to hand over such a large project to a vendor who couldn't even bother to update their profile. Licking his lips he inhaled deeply and resigned himself to getting acquainted with their newest contractor via the online conversation initiated by his sister. Though he still couldn't figure out how his sister had convinced the "silent partner" to contribute even this much.

Oh yeah, blackmail. Once the business had taken off his two siblings had continued to split the profits equally with Jared, despite Jared's refusal. "Hey, I'm a product of our father, too, you know. I haven't made the inputs, I'm not expecting the rewards. I appreciate the thought but no I won't accept that. You've both earned these wins; and I celebrate that and support you."

"Well if you think you can ditch us like that you've got another thing coming," his brother had said.

"Yeah, we don't just share the hard things, Jared," his sister had chimed in. "We share the triumphs, too."

Jared tried to compromise, suggesting they just pay him back his initial investment. But they refused. "You're gonna take this money and enjoy it, whether you like it or not," Lorna had told him. So instead, Jared had just made it a practice to reinvest his share back into the company and didn't take "no" for an answer; he told them that it helps him to justify his ongoing role as their silent partner, and that was the truth.

And now, his sister was not-so-playfully telling him that his silent days were over, at least for now while she needed just the littlest bit of help from him to help her juggle everything else that's on her plate.

"I have no interest in real-estate, Lor, that's why I'm a silent partner."

"I know, I know. But there's all kinds of things that go into any business, and one of them is telling a good story; you've got that down pat. Jake is the sales guru. I'm the business guru. Between us we do alright. But neither of us have the skills in marketing needed to take this company to the next level. You do, big brother. And you know the story of us and this business and nobody can relay it like you. Heck, if you had programming skills we'd hire you to design our website and mobile app! Instead, I need someone who can take the time to help guide the person we're contracting in the right direction with all of that. It can't just look nice, it has to look like us. I really need you onboard for this. When have I ever asked you to do anything else—" at his pointed look she rushed to add on, "—for the company, I mean? Come on, be my hero, big bro. Pretty, pretty, please with a cherry on top?"

"Oh please that may work with your boyfriends," he started, with a hand up to hold off her attack.

And then she pouted and he was toast. "Fine."

✳ ✳ ✳

Jared was driving to work the next day still thinking about the prior day's events. He'd read through the conversation between Lorna and "TailorMade." He'd noted that neither his sister nor the contractor had ever signed off using their real name. He didn't mind, he understood how these freelance platforms work. But it did surprise him that his sister would be okay with such a lax setup. He knew how she enjoyed a good, solid contract.1

The second thing he'd noticed was how casual Lorna was with the contractor. He'd seen from their conversation that Lor had learned of the contractor's work from the woman's app. Surprising for him, since he'd never have thought Lorna to be a fan of a "nerd"-anything. Their conversation had meandered off of the topic of the job several times, to the point where he almost felt he was reading a conversation between two girlfriends. How would the vendor feel about him having read the prior conversation and establishing a more business-like rhythm? What was really interesting were the contractor's responses to his sister's broader-than-business line of conversation.

She'd confessed to preferring smaller appliances that were ideal for cooking for one person; that she enjoyed stay-cations and long drives accompanied by a good audiobook. She'd once lived in Los Angeles but was glad to get to experience all four seasons, now. So Jared gathered that she was a homebody, maybe a bit of a romantic and, from the sounds of it, single. She was also a fan of his books; or at least feigned to be so for the title that Lorna had forwarded a link to. At that sight, Jared had flushed and immediately texted his sister. He'd have preferred to not have been introduced as a male Christian romance writer.

Jared: Whyyy did you send our VENDOR a link to one of my books????

Lorna: I wanted her to understand why and to whom I was handing this project off! Your stories are great. Not my thing, of course, but there's no denying my brother's skill as a storyteller. A painter of pictures.

Jared: Flattery will get you nowhere.

Lorna: What's the big deal? You share your books with, like, a thousand other folks.

Jared: Yeah, but only a handful of them know my legal name. You included.

Jared: And by the way, it's thousandsss of other folks.

Lorna: Okay Stephen King. Anyway, well if that's the issue just don't exchange names or if need be stick to using your pen name in the convos. I never offered my name, really, during the convo and neither did she. Sometimes I'd sign off with my first name initial, like I do elsewhere. But usually she and I just

communicated under our
account's moniker. So there
you go, no biggie.

      Jared: Feels a bit distant.

Lorna: Well, it's not like
you're trying to marry her.

      Jared: You're just full of
      jokes today.

Lorna: Hey, we're the client
and this is an ad hoc
business transaction. As
long as both parties uphold
our ends of the bargain,
who cares what names are
behind it?

Jared thought about that and agreed. He wasn't
ashamed of his writing career, exactly; but he
recognized that, for some, that title might discredit
him more than reinforce his credentials. He also just
had found no good reason to announce to the world
of romance readers (and non-romance readers) that

he was Ryan Jamison, the up-and-coming king of clean, closed-door, cinnamon roll-mances.

Chapter 12: the Re-Introduction

Wow, was all Ta'Mara could think of as she removed her earbuds; only to slightly stiffen at the sound of the wistful sigh that escaped her lips, betraying her thoughts to the world around her. She was sitting in front of her computer. At work. And had gotten nowhere since the time she'd arrived because she'd been too preoccupied with finishing her third Ryan Jamison novel as an audiobook. She'd had to force herself to sleep the night before so that she might have a chance at being somewhat less zombie-like for the start of her work week. Monday, she'd "worked" at home, but most of that day had consisted of what she could get done in between her time consuming this latest read.

It'd been a bit of a whirlwind of a week: the Saturday before last Ta'Mara had awoken energized and eager to finalize the draft she'd completed the day before. After several re-writes she had pushed herself away from her final product and had sent it off with her bid that afternoon. The client had been surprisingly quick to respond, accepting Ta'Mara's bid and by that evening their online dialogue began regarding the company's goals. With most of the major details defined by the following Thursday the client had informed her that they would be handing off the direction of the project to one of their partners; one who was more adept in the area of communicating the sentiment that shaped their business. She'd figured that had meant a background in marketing, which the client had confirmed. But she had not foreseen that the client would also reveal their partner's moonlighting gig as a romance writer.

After following the link that'd been sent to her, Ta'Mara wrestled with the question of whether or not she should risk further investigation. The book's premise seemed interesting, but she dreaded confirming that she'd just agreed to be subject to the guidance of a man—and a company— who thought he was talented and insightful enough to speak on behalf of a woman.

Boy, had she been pleasantly surprised; and she'd spent the better part of the weekend and that Monday in the same state. Not only was this writer's style elegant, the storylines both fun and heart-tugging with hints of sexiness; the dialogue sincere and relatable—but it was his "closed-door" approach to romance and his tendency toward redemptive storylines that drew her the most. And on top of that the bulk of his stories involved interracial couples, too? Who was this man?

With a slight shake of her head she hoped to shoo away at least half of the fantasies that'd nested there over the past several days.

"Okay, boss lady, time to get to work," she admonished under her breath. With a wry grin at the moniker, Ta'Mara settled into her chair and leaned into her computer, ready to tackle the backlog that'd accumulated since the day before.

* * *

From: Their Legacy Real Estate
To: TailorMadeFullStackDev
"Hello, it's nice to 'e-meet' you. I understand that my partner has informed you that I will be assuming the lead role in this project. I've read over your proposal and agree with much of the direction you've suggested, however there are a few items that I believe would benefit from some re-consideration. See my notes attached and I look forward to hearing your thoughts."

From: TailorMadeFullStackDev
To: Their Legacy Real Estate
Hello, it's nice to 'e-meet' you as well; I will respond tomorrow evening once I've had a chance to review. Feel free to let me know if you have any questions or additional comments in the meantime.

* * *

Lorna: Have you reached out to the dev yet? The software developer.

> **Jared**: I know what 'dev' means and yes I have lol. Am currently expecting her response to the changes I'd noted. Now, do you mind if I handle this myself or did you intend on being a backseat driver the entire trip?

Lorna: Give ya one guess *wink emoji*

> **Jared**: *rolls eye emoji*

Chapter 13

* * *

Ta'Mara pulled into her company's parking lot. She'd decided to drive today to make it easier to pick up groceries on the way home. But truth be told, she'd driven every day this week so that she could enjoy her latest Ryan Jamison in surround sound on her way to and from work, blaring from her car speakers.

> *"The biggest mistake I've ever made was letting anybody get between us, including my own self," Matthew whispered, desperate for her to feel the truth of his words.*
>
> *Kayla allowed herself the luxury of selective memory, of leaning against him and allowing her body to remember how easy it was to mold to the plains and plateaus of his form. But her mind could only be fooled for the briefest of periods; it soon dredged up the past, and with it the last of the*

composure his words had almost eroded.

"You're right, Matthew" Kayla agreed, her voice strained and tired as she pulled away from him. "It was a mistake that cost us both dearly." Biting her lip, she shut her eyes in an attempt to stem the tears that already streamed down her face. "And I'm—just not eager to risk reliving the same tragedy—not with you. I'm sorry, I wish things were different somehow. But sometimes 'a second chance' is just..."

"...is just a fairytale," Matthew finished for her, his voice soft, low, smothered in regret and restrained sorrow.

"That's right, girl," Ta'Mara mused aloud before closing the audio book app running on her phone. Gathering her things she made her usual trek to her office with all the mandatory greetings, all the while considering the heroine of the story she'd just suspended. Ta'Mara hated that she could relate to the tale, to the woman so much. She hated even more that she'd gotten so invested in a romance novel—and particularly one written by her client. Boy, talk about awkward. But she couldn't help but respect the man's ability to build grounded, engaging characters, worlds and plots. And yet, like most romance novels—and, of course, unlike real life—you could rely on all of the bits of struggle, confusion and revelation to coalesce into a triumphant whole. There was a surprising amount of solace found in indulging in Kayla's well-deserved display of doubt, self-preservation and dignity. Even so, Ta'Mara allowed herself to admit that there was also solace in knowing that, at the very least, Kayla and Matthew were assured a happy ever after.

✳ ✳ ✳

The remainder of Ta'Mara's workday was pretty uneventful thanks to Ta'Mara's propensity for avoiding the need to put out fires. One of the main reasons she'd been promoted to this level was because of her ability to consider their applications' designs from different perspectives and foresee areas where the app could fall short of client's expectations. Ta'Mara enjoyed being able to exercise her A-type tendency to try to "cover all her bases". And though her least favorite part of her job was that of managing people, she was proud of the fact that her team had come to respect and even attempt to emulate that approach. It'd slowly become an instilled part of her small team's methodology, and was why her team had become among the most reliable among the developers.

In the past, she'd worked long hours both in the office and at home as she reorganized processes, worked to correct errors that had been causing small snags in their system and tried to get her team back to what she felt was a solid foundation. That work had paid off, and Ta'Mara found herself putting in those late nights less and less. Which is why she'd been able to consider contract work.

"Who would have thought I'd be working with a romance writer for my first gig," she thought, chuckling to herself as she turned off her laptop and began placing it in her computer bag. Long ago she'd committed to not using her own computer for company work, so she always brought her laptop home in case an emergency popped up that required her attention.

After reviewing the notes that her client had sent a few nights back she'd felt she'd had a good idea of the direction they were wanting to go and had worked on a draft revision of the proposal. She'd sent the final version to him the following morning along with a few questions to help her better define a couple areas where she'd noted gaps in his logic. She was already impressed with how he'd initiated things: seeming to actually invite her input vs. just dictating his own. His notes had been insightful, direct and creative—she especially appreciated the clarity and thoroughness with which he communicated. As they'd continued their dialogue she felt assured that their introduction had been an indicator of what the remainder of their working relationship might look like; and if so she'd consider herself blessed.

Noticing a new message notification via the freelance app she used, Ta'Mara quickly went to check it, only to encounter a pang of disappointment upon realizing that it was a message blast from the platform informing users of new features.

It'd been a couple days since she and her client had last spoken. And maybe Ta'Mara could allow herself to admit that the fan-girl part of her couldn't help but be thrilled at the idea that she was chatting with the author of books that she'd come to really enjoy—and that she'd learned had a significant fan base, considering the niche market he served. She found herself wondering if Ryan Jamison was his real name. She'd been tempted to bring up his books since their first exchange but hadn't been able to determine a course for doing so that didn't involve her sounding like, well, a fan-girl. Besides, it wasn't part of the job. And that's what she needed to focus on. Once this project was complete, and she received a stellar review, it'd be the first chapter in that leg of her career. So she needed to focus on that project and her plans on what to do following its completion.

She decided that, while she awaited a response from her client, she'd go ahead and redesign the wireframe for the website and mobile app based on what they'd determined so far, to ensure they were both still on the same page. She'd had some questions about the relationships between some of the data. So Ta'Mara would flesh out those questions, as well, so that she could more confidently design the software's backend. She could send those to him tonight or tomorrow morning to make sure they continued making progress and completed the project in a reasonable timeframe.

Before she started on that, though, she would take some time to outline her plan for expanding her contract work projects. Should she consider taking on a second, smaller freelance opportunity, for instance? That'd help build up her portfolio a little faster. But then again, she wanted to ensure that this one went excellently. If so, she could have a long-term client in terms of maintenance of the software and adding features as their company's needs grow. So many variables to consider, she thought to herself as she placed her gear in the passenger seat on top of her reusable grocery bags and then swung herself behind the wheel of her car.

She sighed the sigh of a person content with the prospects of planning something while also acknowledging the tedious nature of doing so. She'd leave all that for when she got home; but first she needed to grab her some groceries. Setting her radio to pick up her phone's bluetooth, Ta'Mara picked up her book where she left off before pulling out of the parking lot.

* * *

**From: TailorMadeFullStackDev
To: Their Legacy Real Estate**
Hello, attached you'll find revised
prototypes for the website and app that
reflect our most recent discussions. I
look forward to making your company's
vision a reality.

**From: Their Legacy Real Estate To:
TailorMadeFullStackDev Good evening.**
Wow, these are perfect! You are truly
talented. Thank you for being so
proactive with reaching out. I've had a
few things come up which made it
difficult for me to return my attention to
our project. But you've definitely got my
attention.

I also noticed that you've adjusted the
design a bit. Which is wonderful,
because that's the one other thing I was
considering commenting on. I like what
you've done; feels very welcoming and
that's exactly the sentiment I wanted to
convey.

May I ask what inspired that change?

From: TailorMadeFullStackDev
To: Their Legacy Real Estate
Good evening to you too! I hadn't
expected you'd still be up and available
to respond so quickly haha. I'm very
glad you like the changes. As far as my
inspiration, well, your partner had
mentioned your being an author. And, I
guess I was inspired by your writing.
Felt that, perhaps, a more romantic
approach could be appropriate given
the sentiment that serves as the
foundation for your company's efforts.

After reading that brief response Jared was grateful to
be alone; he'd hate to have had to explain the
grin—and the blush—he could feel rising up his
cheeks. He respected her forthrightness, and was also
flattered that she'd not only read one of his books,
but was moved to allow her impressions of it to
influence her work. That didn't mean that she had
liked it, of course, but he found himself hoping she
did. Because, at the very least, her work showed her
to be an astute observer who was not only passionate

about her work but intent on pinpointing and highlighting the characteristics that make her clients unique.

In other words, he might just have to admit that his sister was right; this person seemed like a definite keeper.

But he did wonder if she'd liked the book.

> **From: Their Legacy Real Estate**
> **To: TailorMadeFullStackDev**
> Yes, I'm a bit of a night owl like yourself. I have to say, I'm very impressed that you were able to intuit a redesign based on one of my books! Mind my asking which one you'd read?

Ta'Mara decided she'd go with a partial truth. No need to relay the total number of books she'd read and come across as a potential stalker or something.

> **From: TailorMadeFullStackDev**
> **To: Their Legacy Real Estate**
> I'm actually not really a night owl, but sometimes it can be hard for me to push away from the computer when I'm

working on something I enjoy. I'm sure you know how it is.

I've read "Ready, Set: Hello" and am finishing up "Lovers' Quarrel". I've really enjoyed them both.

She'd also enjoyed the other three she'd hungrily consumed, but he didn't need to know all of that.

From: Their Legacy Real Estate
To: TailorMadeFullStackDev
I hope I didn't make it obvious that I was fishing for that compliment. Thank you, I enjoy writing. It's not something I advertise in my professional life, in general, but I'm glad my partner thought to mention my work to you. She obviously knows what she's doing. But don't tell her I said that ;)

And yes, I completely understand how difficult it can be to balance life and work; particularly when you both enjoy what you do, and can take your work home with you.

From: TailorMadeFullStackDev
To: Their Legacy Real Estate
Exactly. But it's a great problem to have. I definitely consider myself blessed.

From: Their Legacy Real Estate
To: TailorMadeFullStackDev
I'd say that sums up my feelings, as well: Blessed.

Really good chatting with you. Goodnight.

* * *

Jared smiled as he shut down his computer that night. Though it'd been a brief and rather simple conversation, there'd been something really sweet about it—something akin to camaraderie. He couldn't remember the last time he'd had that kind of conversation with a woman, outside of church, who wasn't family or gay. And he recognized it wasn't because he was just so irresistible; but that he'd played his part, too, in inviting the innuendo and sexual undercurrents that'd he'd come to expect as part of his reparte in both business and casual social contexts. That pattern applied regularly with women; but it could even appear in conversations considered by today's standards as being enlightened jest amongst guy friends, whether straight or gay.

At the time, he'd considered it playful banter that didn't need to be taken seriously by either party. But with time, and with all that's changed in his life, he realized it was tiring and fruitless. And could even be harmful if either party took the game more seriously than the other. From the point at which he'd surrendered his life to Christ Jared had become much more conscious about how he communicated with people, and especially women. It's that seed of

understanding, repentance and a desire to grow in
that all-important area that'd prompted Jared to
begin writing. He'd begun with short stories that he'd
shared only with his computer screen. Just fleshing
out ideas of how a relationship might look like that
was very human, but also touched on the holy, the
revenant, the respectful.

Jared had figured that, though he may never live up to
that ideal, without a vision for how that'd look he'd
surely fail in the pursuit of it. He'd modeled stories off
of what he'd observed of a few romances, including
that of his parents', a few couples he knew from
church, and Lawrence and Darla. Though they
weren't all believers, he felt that they all expressed a
kind of love that was a reflection of the God he knew
in the Bible. While he couldn't say the same of every
couple he'd met at church, in the few he'd managed to
meet he witnessed how the mutual respect and
honor that he'd come to admire was made even
stronger by each spouse's shared devotion to, and
distinct relationship with, the Lord.

He'd read some romance novels prior to his writing;
and was surprised at how explicit they were. Not that
he minded, at all. But it hadn't helped his
commitment to learn to view his interactions and

view of women through a different lens. So he'd searched for other alternatives and stumbled upon Christian authors and non-Christian authors who wrote "closed door" romances. He couldn't help but note that these lines of novels held less instances of the "beast-with-a-heart-of-gold-who-just-needs-the-right-woman-to-tame-him" hero that pervaded many of the genre's more salacious offerings. Jared knew that guy...he'd played that guy, and on good days maybe he'd actually thought he was that guy. And now, he could see right through that guy. That guy didn't need a woman to change his ways, he needed a miracle.

A few short stories in, Jared had been curious to see what others might think of his little stories that featured fallible men and women, trying to do the right things but just getting some of those things wrong. He decided to upload the story on an IR short-story forum, under a pen name of course. The feedback had been overwhelming! He had not expected such positive reviews for his "clean" romance. He hadn't mentioned anything about God or Christianity, but he couldn't help but relay themes that involved catalysts and metamorphosis. And the fact that his characters hadn't even consummated their relationship until after they'd "accidently" married didn't seem to dampen the enjoyment of his readers.

After one reviewer prompted him to publish a more expanded version of the story, he decided to do just that. Delving once more into the lives of his characters, he allowed them to fill in the blanks and produce a novel that he felt rather proud of—and rather anxious about sharing with a wider public. But he did just that, self-publishing on a widely distributed online book platform that offered that avenue for independent authors. He'd priced his book at just $1.99. And had made sure to update his short story with the link to the newly published expanded novel.

Then nothing had happened. Months went by and Jared had seen only sporadic purchases, though his online author account did grow in followers. The disappointment he'd felt was impossible to deny, but he recalled he'd never written for the sake of popularity. Jared had begun writing because it helped him process and express his hopes and fears and a shaky but strengthening walk with God.

So he published another book. And another. And another. And another.

"Lovers Quarrel" had been his fifth novel published in just over a year, and it marked the first time he'd gained the courage to allow a book's pages to cradle the most meaningful relationship he'd had with a woman. It was a turning point for him, in many ways. He'd modified aspects to a degree, but the essence of the story of he and Ta'Mara held true. In his mind Jared had justified his choice as being one of practicality: simply following the industry-wide encouragement to "write what you know." But as he allowed the story to be revealed on paper, he grew to accept that he also wondered if the woman he'd loved might ever happen upon the book one day, and see herself in it. He'd wondered if she might hear him, hear all of the doubts that'd pushed him away; and all of the certainty that caused him to believe, even now, that she was his once-in-a-lifetime romance. He wondered if she'd think about him, miss him like he did her, yearn for him...even a little. He'd wondered if she'd consider loving him again, like Kayla had. He tried not to wonder if she was already married. And though the realization of how likely that possibility was had regularly, painfully, halted the beat of his heart, it hadn't halted his hand from writing.

Once published, the novel had somehow made it into circulation among black female book clubs, which produced his first hit and catapulted his work beyond those circles. Given that he was in a very niche market, he knew that "hit" was a relative designation. Still, the book was the first that'd began bringing in an assortment of reviews and a very meager but regular income to show for it. It also served as a means for introducing his other titles to a similar level of success; many of which shared the honor of circulating among the same, pivotal book clubs that'd buoyed his first offering.

Jared couldn't believe it and felt so honored to have had his writing be so readily received by women who both shared his beliefs and who did not. He wasn't surprised at the dotting of complaints that his books weren't risque enough for some, or that the inferred or overt references to Christianity weren't everyone's favorite. It didn't take away from the fact that, overall, a diverse group of women embraced the content, which served to increase his confidence and help him feel connected; less alone in his hurts, his hopes and the faith that bound him to share them with the highest level of integrity.

That was five years and 18 books ago and Jared saw no slowing in his imagination. He was experiencing a bit of a block lately, but that's happened before. With a little bit of writing everyday he knew the story would likely turn the corner at some point and find itself. Either Jared's characters would lead him the right way, or life would serve as the motivation he needed. Either way, Jared trusted the Lord to provide whatever was needed when—and if—he really needed it.

Just then, an idea came to mind and Jared smirked. Booting up the computer, he went over the storyline developing in his head and considered what, if any, of the existing story would fit.

Once the pages of his latest novel appeared on the screen, he blocked off the text just below the last paragraph with a horizontal line. Below that he wrote out the outline that had come to mind and some of the dialogue that was flying through his mind at warp speed. An hour later, he had rearranged some of his existing story where he could, aligning bits and pieces under bullet points that comprised this new story line's skeleton. The remainder he struck through before copying and pasting it below the new outline. He liked to keep content available in case the story called for it later on. Satisfied with the new start of his novel, Jared shut down his computer and prepared for bed. He let out a long, loud yawn, fully aware that it wouldn't be long before his alarm announced the start of a new day.

Chapter 14

✳ ✳ ✳

From: Their Legacy Real Estate
To: TailorMadeFullStackDev
Would you mind my asking what got you started in your career as a developer? Not to make things awkward or anything (haha, famous last words)—but I was just thinking how under-represented female software developers are in the literary world—was thinking it'd be cool to make that field a central aspect of my next character's career aspirations.

From: TailorMadeFullStackDev
To: Their Legacy Real Estate
Wow, no not awkward at all lol. I'm honored! I second that observation and hope you do that!

Well, it's a very long story that I won't get into the details about, but essentially I had one of those "aha" moments.

Much of my adult life I'd been uncertain of what I wanted to be "when I grew up". I realize not everyone can relate to that, but for some of us it takes a turning point to really give us the context needed to thoroughly reassess/re-learn who we are, what we want and how we want to invest our energy and time during this very brief life we have. That was the case for me.

So, one day, I just took the whole day to write down my strengths, weaknesses, likes, dislikes and all of that. And through that I saw patterns that helped me recognize a few things, including the kind of work that I enjoyed most. Once I realized that I like building, designing structures that help to automate work and that

I enjoyed working with Excel formulas, things started to click. I'd recently spotted an ad for a local coding bootcamp and so that prompted me to research bootcamps. Within a couple months I'd started classes at the bootcamp I'd first heard about...mostly because they, thankfully, also offered a handful of scholarships during each session to people who lived in the area. I know that some of my classmates were able to garner Jr. Dev positions immediately after graduation.

For me, it took about a year or so of part-time and freelance work to finally land my first permanent job. So everyone's road is different, but I'd say that my initial struggles made me that much more appreciative of the opportunity and made me that much more determined to succeed at it.

The rest is history, so to speak.

Does that help?

**From: Their Legacy Real Estate
To: TailorMadeFullStackDev**

Yes, that's perfect! And thank you for being so willing to share with me. I have an idea—would you be interested and willing to act as a kind of consultant as I move forward with my latest project? I know just enough about software engineering to be dangerous; but obviously know nothing about the experiences of women in that field—and I want to do my heroine justice on both fronts. I'd compensate you for your time and knowledge, of course. If that's an offer you'd consider, it could be a side project that's concurrent with this one, or I could wait until this project is completed; whichever works best for you.

Also, I can relate with having a moment, or moments, that demarcate a kind of "before" and "after" in our lives. I've had my own share of the kind of moments that can break a person, even while forming the foundation upon which something new and better can be built.

From: TailorMadeFullStackDev
To: Their Legacy Real Estate

~ Quint Emm Ellis ~
146

Wow, Yes! I would be very happy to act as a consultant regarding software development and a career in that field from one woman's perspective. In advance, thank you for wanting to be so nuanced in your portrayal of this person. If you want, I'd be happy to connect you with associates who can offer their perspective, as well.

I'm fine with working concurrently, though I'd advise perhaps you're using a different account? It'd make it easier for me to keep track of the subject matter I'm responding to.

From: Their Legacy Real Estate
To: TailorMadeFullStackDev
Wonderful. Thank you for your help, and for offering to connect me with other sources. I may take you up on that as I delve more into the character.

As far as using a different account, yes, that makes sense. I have an author's account on this platform which I've used to hire book cover illustrators, editors, etc as needed. I'll message you from there in just a moment.

From: RyanJamisonAuthor (official)
To: TailorMadeFullStackDev
Hi, it's me! Feel free to send me an idea regarding compensation for your consultant work, when you get the chance. Depending on how quickly my work progresses, I may be reaching out to you with questions on a daily basis. I'm very much looking forward to working with you on this project. Thank you, again, for agreeing.

From: TailorMadeFullStackDev
To: RyanJamisonAuthor (*official*)
Will do! And I'm really looking forward to working with you, as well. Thanks for asking.

Ta'Mara chuckled to herself, shaking her head at the thought that she might actually inspire the development of a romance novel heroine. How crazy was that?

***

Lorna: Hey, I really liked the updates to the design and proposal. Thanks bro! See, this is why we need you.

> **Jared**: Yeah, me too. It was all the dev's idea.

Lorna: I know, I know. But your mere presence must've inspired it somehow, cuz it's way different from what she'd submitted originally.

Lorna: Jared? Hello? Where'd you go?????

> **Jared**: I'm here...just debating if I should admit that she'd mentioned having been inspired by my books.

Jared: Now I'm wishing I could take that message back.

Lorna: Are you kidding me?? Why didn't you tell me that before when you sent the updates to me?!! That's actually really sweet. Awwwww. *heart emoji* She's pretty amazing, huh? Your sis did good, huh? Aren't IIIIIII amazing?! Gotta pat myself on the back. Yep.

Jared: ...annnnnd this is why I didn't mention it.

Lorna: *tongue sticking out emoji*

Jared: But yeah, you did real good on this one. Knocked it out of the park, tbh. As always, my little over-achieving sis.

Jared: Also...

Lorna: Wait, you're admitting I was right AND there's more???

> **Jared**: ...yes, I've hired her as a consultant for my next book. Hope you don't mind. It shouldn't detract from this project. But she's got insight that I feel would be highly valuable for making this latest work more rich and believable.

<<extended delay>>

Lorna: I don't mind at all, Jared. I think that's a GREAT idea. And I'm glad it's working out for you two. To work together. As a matter of fact, I was rethinking a few things on this project, anyway, because of a new opportunity that's come up that might change some things. But I hesitated on pausing things since we'd committed to the project. But now...well, do you think that maybe you two could just focus on your project while I hammer out some details on this one? I'm not reneging on the contract. Just wanting to delay it a bit. But I'd compensate her immediately for the time she's put in.

Jared: I can bring it up and see how she'd like to move forward. I think we'd be taking a chance that she wouldn't be as available once you're ready to continue with the project, though. Are you sure you want to risk that?

Lorna: Actually, I just sent
her a message. *cheesy
smile emoji*

Lorna: Now, you two get to
work on that book! I expect
no less than a masterpiece.

Lorna: And I mean that with
all sincerity, Jared. *heart
emoji**kiss emoji**hug
emoji* Love you soooo
much, big bro.

        Jared: And I love you more,
        little sis. *hug emoji*

Chapter 15

✳ ✳ ✳

From: Their Legacy Real Estate
To: TailorMadeFullStackDev

Hi Dear, you've been chatting with my partner for a while and I want to thank you so much for all of the work you've done. It's AMAZING. My partner had mentioned that he will also be working with you on his next book! I'm beyond excited to see the results. That said, I hope you don't mind, but I need to put a pause on this project—but we'll resume it later, if you're available! Just need to tie up some loose ends, first. That said, I have already approved the full amount agreed upon for your work, so you should see that deposited into your account shortly. I know we'll connect again and I truly can't wait for that chance—I hope it's sooner rather than later.

In the meantime, I'll look forward to the day I can work on persuading my brother to allow me a sneak peak of his latest Christian romance.

Til we chat again *wink emoji*

❋ ❋ ❋

Jared re-read his sister's message and tried to parse the feelings that it sparked; he realized that he had been hesitant to highlight the Christian themes of his book to this vendor. His books made his faith apparent. And he'd never shied away from the topic in the past; so the fact that he'd cared to do so now made him pensive.

He realized that he wondered if the woman on the other end might change her mind when his books' global theme was underscored. And as much as he knew that that would say more about her than about him, he made himself come to terms with the fact that he didn't want their conversation to end. And with that, he had to admit something else: he was pursuing this woman; his project was just as much about authenticity as it was about an opportunity to get to know her, personally.

~ Quint Emm Ellis ~

So maybe his sister's comment was timely; his faith and trust in the Lord is everything to him. When Jared indulged in envisioning a life with someone else it was a life and a relationship that was made complete by the one God who was able to fill the gaps that neither spouse could—or should— ever fulfill for the other. If this intriguing, creative and intuitive software developer stayed on the project—and the attraction turned out to be mutual— it was important that they have an understanding of where they each stood now, before allowing either to get more invested.

It'd been a long while since he'd felt this feeling, though. Was it too much to ask that she just so happen to love Jesus, too?

Jared prayed for strength to allow God's will to be done versus forcing his own.. "Help me guard my heart, Lord. But also, help me to recognize what you do and don't want for me...and then grant me the courage to walk toward—or away— accordingly. Also, make things obvious because this is all new to me...dating...I mean, like this, as a Christian man."

He smirked and sent up one more prayer, "Also, if I've already made a mess for myself, please help me out. You know I can be a fool and a babe, but I pray that what the mothers at church say is true: that you watch over both," he chuckled. "Please guide me in representing you well during my continued interactions with this woman. And I pray that you'd help her feel your presence, no matter where she is in her knowledge of you. May she one day know, for herself, the truth of how awesome, how big and how worthy of our wonder and praise you are—if she doesn't already. In Jesus' name, Amen."

* * *

From: RyanJamisonAuthor (official)
To: TailorMadeFullStackDev
Hi there, I see my sister informed you of
needing to pause the dev project. Hope
that doesn't cause an inconvenience. I'm
still onboard for our consulting project,
though, if you are.

From: TailorMadeFullStackDev
To: Their Legacy Real Estate
Of course I am. This is exciting, I've
never acted as a consultant before; let
alone for a book.

And I'm not at all inconvenienced by
the suspension of the dev contract.
Especially given that she was kind
enough to approve the full contract
amount. That means a lot to
contractors.

From: RyanJamisonAuthor (official)
To: TailorMadeFullStackDev
Yeah, I've had a few paying contracts
bail on me in my day, especially as a

Christian author. That sucks, to put it in technical terms lol.

From: TailorMadeFullStackDev
To: RyanJamisonAuthor (*official*)
Yes! And that is a completely technical term *smile emoji*

From: RyanJamisonAuthor (*official*)
To: TailorMadeFullStackDev
Glad to hear we're still on! I have some questions in mind but want to flesh out the storyline a bit more before we get started. I'll keep a lookout for your quote regarding compensation. I'm fine with hourly, weekly, monthly...whatever you think is most reasonable for accounting for both time and effort. Other than that, do you have any questions for me?

From: TailorMadeFullStackDev
To: RyanJamisonAuthor (*official*)
I do, but it's really just out of curiosity, and I hope you don't mind my asking, but Well, you know how you'd mentioned those pivotal moments in our lives...Would it be safe to say that

some of your own foundational moments served as background for any of your books?

From: RyanJamisonAuthor (*official*)
To: TailorMadeFullStackDev
I'd say it's definitely safe to say that—for all of my books. The opportunity for redemption is actually a big theme I find myself heavily relying upon. It's something I'm compelled to share, but also something I continually need to remind myself of. Everyday we have an opportunity to start a new day, a new year, a new life. And nothing can imprison our sense of hope—not our pasts, our failures or even our aspirations—when we're freed to pursue the Lord beyond all else like we were crafted to do.

From: TailorMadeFullStackDev
To: RyanJamisonAuthor (*official*)
"Like we were crafted to do." Yes. I noted those themes of devotion being the spark for breaking free of expectations that had bound the

characters. I can't say enough about how refreshing it is when I am able to find romance novels that are not only well written and align with my faith in Christ, but also echo the reasoning behind that faith...as well as offer tangible—realistic—examples of the rewards and challenges that come with holding on to our faith in Christ. I know I sound like a fangirl, right now. It's just...I mean, I genuinely enjoy your work. So I'm totally on board with supporting it.

Matter of fact, I'd like to offer to consult for free. I just want to help, really. We need more of these kinds of books on the shelves.

From: RyanJamisonAuthor (*official*)
To: TailorMadeFullStackDev
I can't express how glad I am to hear you express all of that! I'm very pleased to know that we can relate when it comes to faith in Christ. And I was actually hoping you really enjoyed my books and that you weren't just being kind. It says a

lot when someone as astute as you've impressed me to be, sees something worth noting in my writing. Also, you are very generous, but I value your time and insight. I'd like to compensate you for lending both to my project. You're really helping me add that level of detail that I desire to offer my readers.

From: TailorMadeFullStackDev
To: RyanJamisonAuthor (*official*)
If this were a dev job, I'd be billing you, believe me lol. But I just have no idea what I'd charge for this. And frankly, it doesn't sit well with me to do so *shrug* I get to be part of a Ryan Jamison novel, and I trust you'll do right by this character as you have others. The bragging rights will be compensation enough.

From: RyanJamisonAuthor (*official*)
To: TailorMadeFullStackDev
How about this, since we both admire one another's work I'll make you a deal: I'll keep fanboying over you...if you keep fangirling over me. I mean, who couldn't

use a little encouragement, right? What do you think?

From: TailorMadeFullStackDev
To: RyanJamisonAuthor (*official*)
You're fan-boying over me??

From: RyanJamisonAuthor (*official*)
To: TailorMadeFullStackDev
Yes, but I am obviously being way too subtle about it. I admire your honesty, appreciate the care and skill you've demonstrated with our project and respect your keen observations. You come off as someone who is intelligent, compassionate, solid and driven. All of that and you love Jesus and don't bawk at a Christian guy who writes romance novels. How could I not be a fan?

From: TailorMadeFullStackDev
To: RyanJamisonAuthor (*official*)
Well, when you put it that way! I'd be a fool not to take you up on that offer lol. Having you as a fan feels great!

Chapter 16

✳ ✳ ✳

Over the next several weeks Jared reached out to Ta'Mara. Initially, his questions focused on her profession, on the terminology, processes and thought patterns that characterize a Software Engineer.

From: TailorMadeFullStackDev
To: RyanJamisonAuthor (*official*)
I think the answer to that is: depends on the dev! Maybe the commonality is an ability to think linearly. You know—'if this then that' type of thinking.

From: RyanJamisonAuthor (*official*)
To: TailorMadeFullStackDev
Hmmm, sounds like the style of thinking I could have used more of in my youth lol. Hey, random question: do you play chess? I was just wondering because that's exactly the kind of outlook that lends itself well to that game.

From: TailorMadeFullStackDev
To: RyanJamisonAuthor (*official*)
Well, I've played chess a few times, but never seriously. I guess I'm actually more of the "Connect Four" tribe. There's actually an online app where you can challenge others—remotely—to different games. I'm kind of addicted to it.

From: RyanJamisonAuthor (*official*)
To: TailorMadeFullStackDev
Really? Maybe you and I could play a round of online Connect Four or something. Haven't played that game in forever! Brings back good memories of me and my siblings when we were kids.

From: TailorMadeFullStackDev
To: RyanJamisonAuthor (*official*)
Aww, that's so sweet. Yeah, that sounds fun, actually. I might even try a round of chess...so you can at least beat me at one game.

From: RyanJamisonAuthor (*official*)
To: TailorMadeFullStackDev

Oooh, that sounds like a challenge if I ever heard one. What's the name of the app? I'll go ahead and sign up now.

From: TailorMadeFullStackDev
To: RyanJamisonAuthor (*official*)
The app is called Not So Bored Games. When you sign up, just search for my handle and hit connect. I'm TailorMade.

From: RyanJamisonAuthor (*official*)
To: TailorMadeFullStackDev
Indeed, you are. But what's your handle?

From: TailorMadeFullStackDev
To: RyanJamisonAuthor (*official*)
Haha ;)

From: RyanJamisonAuthor (*official*)
To: TailorMadeFullStackDev
Did you get my invite to connect?

From: TailorMadeFullStackDev
To: RyanJamisonAuthor (*official*)
Yep! I'm sending you an invite for a chess match! I'm biting the bullet early, I guess. But to be honest, I adore board

games...but I'm horrible at them no matter what it is lol.

From: RyanJamisonAuthor (*official*)
To: TailorMadeFullStackDev
That's fine, I hate a good challenge anyway.

From: TailorMadeFullStackDev
To: RyanJamisonAuthor (*official*)
LOL! Well, I will do my best to disappoint you, then.

From: RyanJamisonAuthor (*official*)
To: TailorMadeFullStackDev
I very much doubt you could do anything to disappoint me...

Except refuse me the honor of playing you in a round of Connect Four after this game.

From: TailorMadeFullStackDev
To: RyanJamisonAuthor (*official*)
I can at least commit to not disappointing you there.

Chapter 17

✳ ✳ ✳

Days passed and they found themselves meandering from game to game, answering each other's moves as they worked, worked out, ate and even relaxed. Somehow, knowing the other was on the other side of their virtual board made them feel a little less lonely in the world.

Eventually Jared asked Tay about her impressions and feelings as it pertained to her role as a woman in the Tech field.

From: TailorMadeFullStackDev
To: RyanJamisonAuthor (*official*)
I'll try to articulate things well. But there are also so many variables, I really don't know where to begin.

From: RyanJamisonAuthor (*official*)
To: TailorMadeFullStackDev
I see. Well, I'm really interested in your perspectives. But I don't want to make you uncomfortable. It'd be completely

fine if you've changed your mind about this arrangement.

From: TailorMadeFullStackDev
To: RyanJamisonAuthor (*official*)
Oh no, it's not that...I'm finding myself more comfortable with the idea of sharing my thoughts with you than I thought I'd be, actually! It's just that, though every perspective differs, the intersection of race and gender are a distinguishing factor in mine. I'm a black female, and my experience will be rooted in that composite identity...not just the parts. I'm not sure I could reliably separate the two even if I tried. Which is why I'd mentioned possibly connecting you with other colleagues, in case you needed different takes on things.

From: RyanJamisonAuthor (*official*)
To: TailorMadeFullStackDev
While I appreciate that, you may have noticed that the majority of my heroines are black females.

So, *we seem perfectly matched, to me.*

From: TailorMadeFullStackDev
To: RyanJamisonAuthor (*official*)
I did notice that. Though your books' leading ladies spanned the gamut of backgrounds, most of those ladies were AA.

Have you had a lot of experience dating black women?

From: RyanJamisonAuthor (*official*)
To: TailorMadeFullStackDev
To put it tactfully, I had a very different life before turning it over to Christ. And it did include my having dated women of different backgrounds, faiths, ethnicities, perspectives.

So, yes, I have dated black women. But my books reflect aspects of my past relationship with one very special woman, who happened to be a black woman.

From: TailorMadeFullStackDev

To: RyanJamisonAuthor (*official*)
Do you think you're hoping to recreate
what you had with her in your books?

From: RyanJamisonAuthor (*official*)
To: TailorMadeFullStackDev
Wow, you are not mincing words here.

*...maybe a little. But I also use my books
to process my relationship with my
family, with the Lord. With my parents,
who have passed away. Writing began as
a tool for me to re-learn how to value
women for the reasons that the Lord
does. In the process it turned into a tool
that also helps me view myself and all of
my relationships from different angles.
It's kind of like I'm being gifted with a
birds-eye view that offers the tools
needed to view situations and people
through a more holy, understanding and
respectful lens.*

*I don't expect to recreate what I once
had in the life I had before. I understand
everything has its season. I've come to
reason that the best way to honor the*

seasons that have passed is to build
really good things upon them. And I look
forward to the opportunity to do so, with
the right person, no matter the shade of
her skin.

But I won't pretend that some shades
don't appeal to my senses slightly more
than others. Are you okay with that?

From: TailorMadeFullStackDev
To: RyanJamisonAuthor (*official*)
Let's just say that I, personally, have no
complaints with that.

Thank you for your honesty. If you're
ever up for it, I'd be very interested in
hearing more of your story some day.

From: RyanJamisonAuthor (*official*)
To: TailorMadeFullStackDev If we ever
meet in person, I promise you I'll share
as much as you want. And would love to
hear more about you, as well.

I do hope we get to meet in person one
day, by the way. I have a feeling we'd
have a great deal to talk about.

The computer screen cast its blue glow upon
Ta'Mara's face as she read and re-read that last
sentence. She ran her thumb across her bottom lip
before taking the lip between her teeth to stifle her
smile. Though a lot could be lost in translation when
communicating with someone electronically, she sure
felt like "Mr. Jamison" was coming on to her. A giggle
escaped her at the thought that she would not only
get to inform one of his heroines but even become a
real life version with him. For just a few moments, she
allowed herself to indulge in all the possibilities. And
then, with one very deep breath, she dragged her
thoughts back to the land of practicality. For all she
knew he could just be an affable guy.

Or a guy with a potbelly, a comb over and mommy
complex. Or a serial killer.

And for all he knew she could be, well, an overweight
(though adorable) workaholic homebody who's only
dated sporadically and who's longest term

relationship ended with her running away like a coward.

Besides that, he was all the way in Oceanside, California. So even if he was flirting it obviously wasn't with any real intent.

"Oh girl", *she thought to herself, "you need to lighten up and enjoy the attention. Lord knows it's been a while...and at least you know you can add 'good taste' to his growing list of appealing qualities."*

From: TailorMadeFullStackDev
To: RyanJamisonAuthor (*official*)
If we ever meet in person, I'm going to hold you to that promise.

She forced herself to hit the send button and commit to the increasingly flirty banter being shared between herself and her client.

Oh boy.

"It's just light flirting...that I won't indulge in beyond this point. Keep it strictly professional, Ta'Mara and don't get silly" she told herself, unconsciously rubbing the goosebumps that'd popped up on both her forearms.

Then she grinned.

Still, she couldn't help but wonder if a trip back to California would be a completely bad idea. She didn't love the last thing that'd happened there, but she adored everything else. And, she realized, she missed it. Didn't hurt that that'd make it a little bit easier for her and her mystery author to meet—if he was serious about that offer, that is. Which he wasn't, she told herself. He probably said all of that precisely *because* they were so far apart that it'd never happen!

Ta'Mara lowered her lids and shook her head, striving to evict all the drama that'd managed to sneak in with the help of a guy she'd never actually met.

For most of what remained of the evening she attempted, and failed, to focus on fleshing out her plans for her freelance business. Finally admitting defeat, she settled herself in bed and streamed a rom-com that ended up watching her sleep.

The following day, Friday, she berated herself for staying up so late. Despite the fact that she'd known she'd be working at home the following day, as the manager she still couldn't take advantage of sleeping in like some of her staff might do.

It was with lids that were still heavy despite four generous helping of coffee, that Ta'Mara spotted the notification on her phone. She couldn't help but grin when she noticed that the notification was from her freelance app.

"He just can't get enough of me," she joked to herself, her grin as wide as a mile is long. The tip of her tongue found the corner of her mouth as she opened the app.

But it wasn't Ryan Jamison who'd written her. It was his partner/sister:

> **From: Their Legacy Real Estate**
> **To: TailorMadeFullStackDev**
> Hi again! Thank you so much for your patience as I waited for a few things to pan out with the project we were working on. I feel confident that things are close to being ready for us all to proceed. But I have just one question for you: would you possibly consider a

very brief visit to really "get to know"
our business and mission? You've done
a spectacular job of interpreting that,
with the help of my brother, of
course—I wouldn't dare leave him out
of the picture. But our little family
business is pretty much my baby—and
I'm totally willing to take care of every
expense to ensure that you get to
experience it fully. For your work.

And I understand that I can't just steal
you away from work; but there's a
three-day holiday right around the
corner and I figure that that could be
perfect timing. Would give me a couple
of weeks to get my plans straight. And I
happen to be throwing a business
soiree that Saturday where you'd meet
a toooon of potential, long-term clients
(to whom I'd talk you up with all
sincerity and all the potency you could
ever want, and more—of course, I'll do
that whether you're there or not, but
still...). What do you think?

Please say yes. Pretty pretty please! I'm dying to meet the female software developer that made my brother eat crow.

Who rules the world? We do!

From: TailorMadeFullStackDev
To: Their Legacy Real Estate
A free trip to California? Uhm, YES!

Ta'Mara chuckled and then deleted her consent before her fingers got tempted to hit the send button. Truth be told, she was beyond tempted but couldn't shake the oddness of the timing. Had her brother mentioned the conversation he and Ta'Mara had had the night before? What if they were a brother/sister serial killer team and this was their M.O. Then again, that'd be a pretty elaborate and potentially expensive set-up.

But really, who does that? Who invites their contractor on an all-expense paid trip to California? Ta'Mara could think of one scenario where that could very likely happen, but she wasn't in that kind of contracting business.

And she didn't even know either of their names...assuming "Ryan Jamison" was a pen-name. The only names that were on their website were that of their deceased parents, and even then the story of their parents' inspiration on the business had only included the couple's first names.

"Yup," she mumbled in a disappointed sigh, "Best to assume they're axe murderers. Brilliant and rich and very bored axe murderers." Ta'Mara stared at the message, reread it and then turned her phone's screen off. Placing the phone face down on her desk she decided that she just wasn't inclined to decline such an adventure on an empty stomach.

She'd do it after lunch.

Chapter 18: the Revelation

It wasn't until she'd tucked herself into bed that she'd mustered up the resolve to send her gracious refusal. As soon as she'd sent it, though, she had a sinking feeling she'd made a mistake. "Oh, Ta'Mara, why do you have to be so damn practical. all. the. time?" she muttered angrily to herself. She went through her ritual of hooking her phone to its charger, placing it on the nightstand, turning off her light and tucking herself in. All the while knowing she was deluding herself; ruminations over her decision would be keeping her wide awake for hours.

It wasn't until she'd tucked herself into bed that she'd mustered up the resolve to send her gracious refusal. As soon as she'd sent it, though, she had a sinking feeling she'd made a mistake.

~ Quint Emm Ellis ~

"Oh, Ta'Mara, why do you have to be so damn practical. all. the. time?" she muttered angrily to herself. She went through her ritual of hooking her phone to its charger, placing it on the nightstand, turning off her light and tucking herself in. All the while knowing she was deluding herself; ruminations over her decision would be keeping her wide awake for hours.

✳ ✳ ✳

The following couple of days Ta'Mara went about her work and after work routine as usual; with the exception of her checking her phone every five minutes.

She still hadn't gotten a response from either of the "could-be-axe-murders" siblings. Which could be a good thing if her fringe scenario was actually true. Maybe her refusal was enough to send them to their next victim.

But Ta'Mara also knew that the likelihood of there having been much danger in the trip was slim. She didn't regret her decision—she didn't think. Well, she understood her decision. What she didn't understand was how she could be so hung up on hearing back from a guy she'd never met and who'd never offered his real name.

"Maybe I should have asked if Ryan Jamison was his real name. Why didn't I ask that?"

They'd continued playing their current online board game, but there was no other communication between them. She almost wanted to scream at the discord that that situation sowed; that of being engaged with someone she was—admittedly, very interested in; while real, significant communication with him seemed to cease.

"Ooh, did you say Ryan Jamison? I loooooove his books," Charlene nearly squealed from the doorway of Ta'Mara's office. "Can you believe that a guy could write such delectably cinnamon-romantic love stories? I can't wait til his next one comes out," she continued, inviting herself in to take the seat opposite Ta'Mara. "I've read every one of his books. Let me tell you it is hard to find good novels like his that doesn't involve me blushing as I read things I know my Jesus loving spirit shouldn't. Not that I don't read those, too. Not gonna lie, but if I had more choices like him...well. I'd be better off. Anyway, what's your favorite? Mine is the one about the highschool sweethearts who grew apart but reunited after bumping into each other at their highschool reunion. I don't know why but it gives me all the feels—maybe it's the idea of second chances. But then, I guess a lot of his books have that theme. "

Ta'Mara just nodded, for once grateful for Charlene's chatty nature. It meant the conversation could, mostly, be one-sided.

When Ta'Mara sensed that the current pause was her cue to respond, she smiled and confessed, with as much casualness as she could muster, "Yeah, I've checked out a few of his books. I do enjoy them. He's an excellent writer. I don't really know if I have a favorite, yet," she lied. From the moment she'd begun "Lover's Quarrel" she knew she'd found a protagonist that she'd remember. She understood the character in a way that she wouldn't have thought possible for a romance novel.

"Oh, keep reading and you'll find one. That man can write his tail off. But I won't pretend like I don't wish he'd clue his audience in on what he looks like. Call me superficial, but not one author's photo after all of these years!? Makes you wonder if he's horribly disfigured or something. Or horribly famous. Like maybe he's some big movie star that can't let it be known that he writes panty droppers."

"Or maybe he's just a regular guy, a kinda butch guy that'd get laughed out of his circle of friends," Ta'Mara offered, drawn into the guessing game. Truth be told, she'd been pondering the same thing herself. "I mean, I'm not sure how many guys would be confident enough to announce to the world that they write…er…'panty-droppers', as you put it." Ta'Mara couldn't help the smirk that plumped her cheek at the crass term.

"Well, with the dough he must be making off all of these by now, I can't see how that income would be embarrassing at all. Nah, I'm thinking it's either a matter of low self-esteem or he's famous."

"Well his self-esteem seems just fine; but famous, that I could see."

Charlene's eyebrow arched as she looked at Ta'Mara. "What makes you so sure about his self-esteem? You said you'd only read a few books but you got all that from those?"

"Uh, well. All of his hero's are kind-hearted and, often, self-assured men. I figure it must take one to know one!" she finished a little too brightly.

Charlene pondered that and then shrugged as she placed both hands on the arms of the chair. "Maybe. Or maybe he's projecting what he wishes he was." She pushed herself out of Ta'Mara's chair. "Ah well, maybe we'll never know. The mystery continues," she concluded. "Well, I better get back to work and let you get to yours. Thanks for the girl-chat, Tay."

"Thank you, too, Charlene." Ta'Mara waved as Charlene headed out of her office.

Maybe we'll never know.

Surely Ta'Mara wasn't considering changing her mind about the trip for such a superficial reason as to get to see what a mysterious author looked like. No, she resolved. She had to finally admit to herself that that wouldn't be the only reason. She'd be going to see if the connection they'd had online existed in real life, as well. She'd go to visit California again, even if it was a different part. But she'd mostly go just to meet the man that'd managed to move her with just words in both his books and in their conversation. She'd go because she'd already been envisioning nights spent laughing, talking and playing board games with this man whom she'd never met. She'd go because she knew she'd wonder for the rest of her life what could have happened.

Ta'Mara picked up her phone and stared at its black screen for a long moment. Taking a deep breath, she turned on her phone, mentally considering all of the safety precautions she would prepare, just in case they did turn out to be serial killers, of course. She'd ask if the invitation was still on the table, and if so, could they at least exchange names and social media so that they could see one another beforehand. That seemed like a fair request.

There was a notification already on her phone from her freelance app. Ta'Mara rushed to open it, glancing up to be sure she wasn't being viewed by her boss. She got up and turned the blinds on her office window so that she'd have a bit more privacy. Sitting back down she opened the message.

> **From: RyanJamisonAuthor (*official*)**
> **To: TailorMadeFullStackDev**
> *My sister informed me of the invitation she'd extended toward you. And it took*

me a while to figure out how to follow
that up. Let me just say, first of all, that
I did not expect her to make such an
offer. I should have known better than
to mention that I'd brought up the
possibility of our meeting in-person.
My sister, once she's got an idea in her
head she runs headlong into executing
it. But I will also admit that I would
have really enjoyed having a chance to
meet you. As I said before, I feel like we'd
have a lot to talk about with one
another.

I wasn't surprised to hear that you'd,
gently, refused. I was disappointed, of
course. But it's completely
understandable given the anonymity
we all have enjoyed in this business
relationship. That said, I hope you'll
reconsider the invitation, perhaps not
now but maybe in the future once you
and I get to know one another more. I
hope you'll also consider me more than
a business associate, one day. To help
with that, let me start by giving you my
real name (but please don't share this,

as I do enjoy my anonymity in that regard).

My name is Jared Iona. Below is everything you could ever need to confirm I'm a real person and probably not a menace to society: my phone number, email address, my social media links (LinkedIn, Facebook).

I want you to know that I would really like to keep in touch with you and I look forward to resuming our chats...to talk about anything we want. If the feeling is mutual, I'd love to start a whole new conversation with you, beginning with your name.

Chapter 19

✳ ✳ ✳

Jared was annoyed at himself. It'd only been a day and he was on pins and needles waiting for his mystery woman to respond to his latest message. But it wasn't only that—she hadn't answered his latest move in their online chess game, either. He knew her to be the kind of person to take her time as she considered her moves, but it'd never taken her an entire day.

Boy, Lor must've scared her off good! he thought, angrily.

It was rare that Jared found himself genuinely pissed off—and even more rare for his ire to be directed at his sister. But when he'd casually mentioned his conversation with their vendor, he had no idea that his sister would take that as an invitation to be so forward with the woman.

Maybe he should have known better, but despite her spontaneous nature, Lor had proven herself more than capable at intuiting people's boundaries.

"Not when it comes to matters of the heart, though, as you should know by my personal track record," she'd responded miserably when he'd confronted her about the direct message he'd spied on their company's shared account.

"That's no excuse, Lorna," he'd growled. "You can't just—insert yourself into my love life like that. I can handle it. I was handling it. We had a great conversation going and now—I don't even know how to respond after that."

"I'm sorry, Jared. I guess, you know, I'm just so excited to see you this way. I love seeing you fall in love. You deserve it. And I—I just wanted to help move things along a bit. I don't know—I just know she feels the same way and I guess I figured you guys just needed an extra loving nudge."

Jared's draw dropped at the observation his sister had just shared. "Fall in love? We're just talking right now, this isn't a romance novel, sis."

At the silence that followed he realized that that wasn't the question he actually wanted to ask. Sighing, he prodded his sister. "How do you know she feels the same way? You haven't even seen our conversations."

Her triumphant grin grated his last nerve. "Uhm, cuuuuz, I'm a woman and I just know."

"Well, that intuition seems to have backfired majorly." Jared ran his hand over his face and closed his eyes. It'd been such a long time since he'd felt this sort of connection with a woman—had had the level of conversations he'd enjoyed of late. It'd been a relief to know he wasn't crazy, that he hadn't been romanticising the feelings he'd once experienced. That there was another woman out there that could make his heart, spirit and mind respond in one accord. The only thing that'd been missing was whether that chemistry remained when there wasn't a computer screen between them. He couldn't lose the opportunity to find out.

"Alright. I'm just gonna give her a couple of days to process things and then I'll try reaching out to her. Try to make things less weird...or at least offer a bit more context. I don't know. I'm a professional author and I have no words coming to mind for how to...say..." he struggled to articulate all of the hope and fear and sense of inadequacy that suddenly descended upon him. It was almost like the last fourteen plus years had never happened, and he was back to that guy who had had no idea how to speak to women, how to broach a conversation.

"Again, I'm sorry. I screwed this one up. But if you let me I can just write her and explain—"

"No, no, no. Leave it, Lor. If this is gonna get screwed up with no chance of return it's gonna get screwed up by me, not you. I love you...but please stay out of this from now on."

"Right. Okay." And it was one of the few times that Jared had ever seen his sister so contrite.

"I mean it, Lor."

"I know, bro. I will do my best," she muttered.

"Lor..."

"Okay, okay, okay. I'm out of it. Handle your business." She walked up and hugged him, and he hugged her deeply in return. "I love you, Jared. And if this lady misses out on you, I'll be heartbroken for you both. But it'll be her loss, most of all."

~ Quint Emm Ellis ~

Jared brought his mind back to the present. He knew his sister had meant well, but he sure hoped she hadn't messed this up, whatever "this" might be.

And for the first time, a thought occurred to him that his mystery woman might have been put off by what she saw on his profiles. Maybe she just was not attracted to him. Or maybe he'd misread cues, which is easy to do when writing one another. Perhaps she had never been interested in him at all, and he was now coming across as a sleeze who would try to leverage a business relationship into something more.

The right next step eluded him. He was almost so desperate as to consider reaching out to his sister for advice. Almost.

Chapter 20: the Aftermath

The next several days were a bit of a blur for Ta'Mara.

Jared.

Jared remained glued to thoughts and her feelings couldn't seem to tear apart the difference between then and now.

Then, she'd be an idiot in love. Now, she wasn't—right?

When she'd read his words her heart hit the brakes, hard. And she found herself rereading the message over and over, as if something would change or her eyes had just gotten it wrong the first, second and fifth times.

The links to his profiles glowed blue on the screen. One click brought her face-to-face with the familiar and wholly unfamiliar. This guy, with the fashionably styled curly locks, wide confident grin, even deeper tan(!) and physique that would have made Ta'Mara bite her lip if her jaw hadn't been on the ground—this guy was not her Jared, she almost gleefully surmised. Except—except for those dimples that still made her want to just place her fingers in them. And his brief stint as a janitor that was boldly listed on his LinkedIn profile. His facebook profiles—and yes, those of the other social media sites that profile linked to presented videos with all the tell-tell gestures that she'd recalled over the years. And his kindness and care for others could be seen in even the superficial level of engagement that these online platforms offer.

Not to mention the friends and family she recognized—and missed— from nearly two decades ago. This was Jared.

This was *her* Jared.

And she really needed to leave the office.

Holding it together long enough to email her team and manager of an unforeseen need to leave early, she managed to gather her things calmly and cast watery eyes downward as she strove to avoid interaction during her exit.

She'd almost made it to the door when the office manager's voice was heard behind her. "Tay, everything alright?"

"Yup! Have a great rest of the day!" Ta'Mara answered far too brightly as she declined to turn around and instead continued her trek to her car.

"You too," she heard, the sound trailing behind her as the door slowly closed behind her.

In her car, she busied herself with getting her purse and files situated on her passenger seat, starting her car and safely exiting the parking lot as tears finally ran their course down her cheeks. She only hoped that no one would notice her weeping at the stop lights.

Once home, Ta'Mara grabbed a bottle of wine and poured herself a full glass. After finishing the glass she took a swig from the bottle and plopped herself down on the couch.

Shame made her slam the bottle down on the coffee table. From the back of her mind came the reminder to use a coaster, which she would have ignored but she would not give *him* the satisfaction of ruining her table. She'd already let him ruin her day and throw professional responsibility to the wind, again.

Somehow the bottle of wine appeared in her hand again and she ground her teeth before setting it down, calmly, on a coaster.

Memories flooded back to the days following that fateful FriendsGiving gathering. At the start of the following week, she'd notified her boss that she needed to take a week of paid leave. Her supervisor had pressed for a reason, given there were several meetings for which she needed Ta'Mara's assistance to prepare. Thankfully, she'd been understanding when Ta'Mara had tearfully explained what'd happened between her and her ex-fiance. It was the first time she'd had to hear herself tell anyone aloud that the wedding was called off.

What Ta'Mara hadn't accounted for during her confession was the fact that the co-worker recruited to take up the slack would get wind of—and share the ordeal with others in the office.

By the time Ta'Mara had returned the following week she nearly drowned in the looks of pity cast her way by both familiar and unfamiliar co-workers. Probably didn't help that her proposal had been on public display at her workplace just as staff had been leaving for the day. Every day she'd left work her eyes had been drawn to that spot and the grief and confusion seemed to froth and foam, ready to spill over once again.

She'd suspended her regular walks for fear of bumping into him once again and making a fool of herself in some way. She'd stopped visiting her favorite places because she always saw and felt the shadow of their first and subsequent visits together.

Her world had shrunk down to her tiny apartment, and even it betrayed her with memories of her and Jared and her own actions that'd nearly cost her even more.

All that had prompted Ta'Mara to consider a change of scenery in the most dramatic way possible that fateful New Year's Day. As grateful as she'd always been to have a small, strong immediate family, she'd never been so grateful as when they'd welcomed her home with hugs, strong shoulders, shared tears and even a few curse words; as well as a place to stay while she'd figured out how to stand on the two legs that'd yet to recover from the rug having been pulled out from under her.

After a month or so she began thinking about the choices she'd made and how she'd do things differently. And it's what led her to take the plunge in switching careers so late in life to something that'd lead to her being able to exercise more freedom in her choice of work hours, location and clients. Not to mention something more financially lucrative so that she'd be able to enjoy that elusive lifestyle as a single woman, as well as finally become debt-free.

And with the help of the Lord she'd achieved most of those goals and was well on her way to achieving all of them, which included re-starting a career as a contractor in earnest.

Speaking of which—that reminded her of the project she'd been working on. With Jared and his sister, unbeknownst to her. What in the world was that all about? How could that be random? It couldn't be, could it?

Ta'Mara recounted the scenario: having been contacted out of the blue, having been awarded the contract so quickly. The whole thing really did reek of a setup. But why? Why now? Why not just be transparent so that she could have promptly ignored him?

What kind of sick game was this? Was his sister in on it, too? Or was she just used as a pawn, a middleman. A wing-woman.

She'd never known Jared to be cruel.

But then she'd've never expected him to be so willing to break her heart those years ago. To break *them*.

Digging the phone out of her purse she navigated back to his profiles, again. He looked satisfied. But why wouldn't he be? He obviously had a satisfying career, looks, friends and the gall to flirt with a woman who's name he claimed he didn't even know. He also had a double-life as a romance author.

Suddenly a thought came to mind. Why should she "respect his anonymity"? After what she went through with him back then. And now!

Another thought crept into her mind, But what if he genuinely did not know he was talking with you? What if the woman he was talking about inspiring his novels is you? What if you two were meant to be together and this is your second chance? What if—

"Ugh!" she grunted. Here she was, again, letting her thoughts and her world be turned upside down by hopes anchored in an unreliable man.

So what if, by some crazy orchestration of events, he was genuinely clueless as to who he was talking with.

At that thought a chuckle flowed out of her. Boy, that might be even sadder than the way she felt right now. Wouldn't he be surprised to find out that he was trying to pick up the baggage he'd unceremoniously dropped a lifetime ago.

And that she'd now come with several additional carry-ons.

Ta'Mara tried to shake that self-disparaging thought out of her head. While she acknowledged having gained back all the weight she'd managed to lose, she'd managed to do so on a relatively good diet and had repeatedly gotten a clean bill of health from her doctor. So at this point, weight loss was a matter of preference for one's outward appearance. She'd thought about pursuing the body she'd once had; but she also was, frankly, not nearly as motivated as she'd been when spurred by a health crisis. And she'd managed to carve out a nice life for herself, and a flattering wardrobe to go with it. Most days, she felt fulfilled with how she moved in the world, with roundness in her cheeks (both sets) and soft, yet defined curves.

Though her dating life hadn't been full, there'd been mutual attraction between herself and the few men she'd invited into her life. Like her, they'd all leaned toward the nerdy style of cute. Not the "hubba-hubba" brand of hot that this new Jared smoldered with. And early on, after her break up, she'd made one mistake in allowing herself to go further than she should have with one such person.

That never happened again, though. Because she was smart enough to realize that even that one time was out of a misplaced sense of spite and entitlement.

And apparently this new Jared came with a lot more baggage himself, in the form of multiple love interests—hmmm, maybe "love" wasn't the right word?

Perhaps "skanks" was a better term.

Ta'Mara shook her head, "Am I jealous?!! REALLY?!!"

Taking one last, long swig of red wine, she settled the nearly empty bottle back down on its coaster, grabbed a throw pillow that sat nearby, and put it to her mouth to muffle the scream she emitted. When she was done, she wiped away tears that'd begun to gather at her eyes for the second time that day.

One last cry, she decided she'd allow herself one final, big cry over this guy. And after that, she would not allow one more display of waterworks over this guy. Not one, ever again. Tomorrow, she'd start her day, go to work, do an amazing job, come home and maybe pick up something to eat on the way before sitting down to work on her plan for starting her contracting career. That was at least one good thing to come of this fiasco. She'd make her plans, drink some tea and everything would be alright.

And with that, she curled up on the sofa and sobbed for all the years she'd denied herself the luxury of doing so.

Chapter 21

✻ ✻ ✻

It'd been a week since Jared had messaged the mystery contractor and he was driving himself crazy with how anxious that made him. He barely even knew the woman, had never met her, and yet he couldn't get their conversations out of his mind. Their connection seemed real to him. How could he have been so wrong? Or what did he do or say that would cause her to completely shut down their interaction?

During his workday, at the gym, at home and during drives in between destinations he debated whether or not he should try messaging her again.

Maybe she'd gotten really busy and had just forgotten to respond...to everything. Or had written out a response and had forgotten to press send. Or—or maybe something happened to her!

He should give her the benefit of the doubt, right? Could she have really been that disturbed by his sister's message? Or by his?

It was a dark day for him when he had to admit that the only person who might have more of a clue as to what had happened would be his sister. Maybe her faulty intuition would actually yield some useful information. Even a piece of their conversation might offer some insight.

He was on his way home from work when he decided to give his sis a call. Using his car's dashboard, he selected her number from his "favorites" list and listened as the other end rang throughout his car speakers.

"Hey Babe, finally! You called. I've been dying to hear how things are going with...uhm...the lady we'd contracted! So?"

"Nothing, Sis. Nothing has happened. And I guess that's why I'm biting the bullet and calling you. I just can't figure it out. I must be out of the game for too long...not that I see this as a game. I just mean, I just can't get a bead on what's going on here. I wrote to her and actually shared my social media links with her so she could see I was a real person and ...you know, to give her something to show that I trust her enough to share those things with her, despite my desire to remain anonymous.

"I guess I just would have at least expected a kind let-down. Or even a 'Stop stalking me creep.'" Jared chuckled humorlessly. "But it looks like she's ghosting me. And...I just...I want to know what you think I should do next, given you've had conversations with her too and, you know. You've got the female perspective, and all."

He was met by silence on the other end of the phone. Finally he heard his sister clear her throat. "So," she began slowly. "You said you sent her links to your profile?"

"Right. That's pretty customary nowadays. But do you think she took it the wrong way or something? I don't know what the 'wrong way' could be but—"

"Oh, no, I'm sure she took it the way it was meant to be taken."

"Lorna, what—I don't like the sound of your voice right now. What do you know that I don't?!"

"You're driving right now?"

"Yeah."

"Call me when you get home."

"Lorna, what the hell is going on?!"

"Oh boy," Lorna said in a sigh. Only continuing after a noticeable pause. "You're gonna want to pull over."

"What the—okay, hold on." After a few minutes Jared found a public park and pulled his car into an open spot in its lot. "Okay, I'm parked. What's going on?"

"You know I love you so much, right, Jared?"

"Lorna, I swear—"

"It's Ta'Mara. You've been talking with Ta'Mara this whole time. And she's been talking with you. And neither of you knew it. Until just now...well, Ta'Mara knew once you told her."

Silence walked back and forth between them for a long time.

"Jared?" No response. "Jared, say something?"

"Lorna, that topic is off-limits, you know that. Especially for jokes." Jared warned between gritted teeth. "I don't find it funny—"

"I'm not joking, Jared. I set it up. I did it. I'm not sorry! But I—I was really hoping it'd turn out better than this. I was hoping you'd get to be with the love of your life again. I never got to meet her but I could hear what she'd meant to you in your voice. And I got to see the aftermath of the breakup when I finally got back from AmeriCorps. Jared, I think she still loves you. And that you love her, too. People change and grow. You've grown. I just figured you both needed a chance to meet who you each are now, to see if there was a place for a second chance."

"You're serious." he announced in astonishment as the realization slowly crept into his bones and every crevice and pore. He crumpled against the back of his seat, inhaling deeply several times before choking out, "You're saying I've been...talking with Ta'Mara all this time? My Ta'Mara?"

"Yeah," Lorna replied, softly.

After another minute of silence Lorna asked, "Hey, so you know I'm in the area with a couple meetings but

I'm cancelling those as we speak. Let me buy you an early dinner and a drink, instead? At our favorite little restaurant? We can talk more there."

"No, I need to figure things out. I'll talk with you later." And with that he hovered over the "end call" button but was halted by his sister's voice.

"Do you want to talk with her again?"

"I'll see you in 15 minutes."

Chapter 22

* * *

Minutes later Jared was being escorted to a booth in the diner that he and Lorna frequented when she was in town. It was a cozy place with red pleather seating and a simple menu boasting hearty servings of home style Americana dinner plates. They liked this place because it was one of those eateries where you could focus on the great food and great companions rather than anything else.

Once seated Jared ordered the most expensive drink on the menu. He didn't plan on drinking it, but he did plan on letting his sister pay for it. While he waited he had time to think about the conversation that he and Ta'Mara had been enjoying and wondering if there had been clues along the way that should've caught his attention.

He had just pulled his phone out to go over the messages when Lorna breezed in and swung into the booth seat opposite him, quickly nestling her huge backpack beside her. Most people in her line of career carried stylish briefcases or satchels. Leave it to his sister to look like she was headed back to high school rather than to a million-dollar deal.

"Okay, so you know you can't strangle me in a public place, right?" she began, bombarding him with as self-conscious of a grin as one might ever get from her.

"I'm not so sure any judge would hold it against me if I did, considering the reason."

"Oh Jared. Are you really mad at me? For caring about you?"

"Correction: For meddling. And for manipulating both Ta'Mara and myself! I can't imagine what she must be feeling right now. I can't even explain what I'm feeling."

"Do you feel a little bit of hope, somewhere in all that mess of feelings?"

The waitress returned with Jared's frothy concoction, at which his sister pointed one very arched eyebrow.

"Keep them coming, please—every 10 minutes" he requested of their server. "Courtesy of you," Jared said matter-of-factly, returning his gaze to that of his sister's as he slid the untouched beverage to the far side of the table, away from him.

"Touché," Lorna replied.

The waitress took their food orders and left them as they resumed their conversation.

"So, I mean, you do feel some hope...? Like you two seemed to really hit it off, again." Lorna pressed.

"Yeah, but the reason why she didn't respond is because she hates me from the first time we hit it off. Or more accurately, for being a complete idiot by breaking off our engagement."

"Well, can't blame her for her reaction, of course. Like you said, it had to be quite a shock for her too. But still, for her to respond so drastically, well I'd say that that's better than ambivalence."

"Not sure that makes me feel better."

"Well, think about it—you can't hate something without having passionate feelings about it...or you know, you. Not to mention, the fact that she's been in possession of your identity for a little while now and, despite whatever she is feeling, she's kept your identity to herself? I'd say that's a pretty caring thing to do for someone you hate."

Jared pondered that.

"Look, all I did," his sister continued, "was try to give you two the chance that you wouldn't have given yourselves."

"But what if we'd figured out who the other person was while online and it all just blew up in our faces—like it did?!?" Jared asked, incredulous.

"Actually, I figured you would! I never even thought it'd even get this far without either one of you somehow letting the cat out of the bag! All I'd figured was that at least it'd get you both talking...and if it was meant to be then you'd continue talking. I mean, I'm not a fairy godmother or anything. I could never make you fall in love. All I could do was provide you two a bit of an opening.

"And if you think about it, it's all pretty...well...miraculous. Do you know how many things had to come together to get us all to this point? (1) I could have never had a boyfriend — ex-boyfriend — who introduced me to that app. (2) I could have been a less curious person and never thought to research the app's female developer. (3) Ta'Mara could've just never signed up on any of the freelance sites I'd checked, or (4) I could've totally missed her since she hadn't used her real name and only used the app's logo."

"*Any* of the freelance sites? Did you search through them all?"

Lorna shook her head with a look of mock consternation. "It's like you don't even know me." She held out her hand to him. "Hi, I'm '*Thorough*'. And you are?"

Jared slapped her hand away and rolled his eyes.

"Anyway, (5) the fact that both of you had reason to avoid using your real names: her as a reasonable precaution, being a single female and all and you...well because you're embarrassed to be a romance writer."

"I'm not embarrassed." He said.

"Go ahead, you know you want to glance around to see who heard me."

Jared glared at Lorna.

She held up her hands on either side of her face in surrender. "Sorry bro. Okay, let me finish!"

"I get it, sis. I get it. This may be the closest you'll get to pronouncing an act of God."

"Truth."

"So," he looked at her. "Now what?" He chuckled at her perplexed look; an expression that rarely settled upon his sister's face.

"I have no idea. I used up all my fairy dust just to get the ball rolling. Seems to me you better start asking the One you believe has more authority in this situation than I or anyone else."

"But you said you could get her and I talking again, that's why I sped over here instead of meeting up with a bottle of something heavy and cold at home."

"Correction: Technically, I just asked a question."

Jared grimaced. She had him on that point. He'd been so desperate for a solution he'd heard what he'd wanted to hear.

"She's probably feeling something similar to what you're feeling, right?" Lorna posed. "Wish you two could just share those feelings with each other."

"I wish we could, too."

"So?"

"So, what?"

"Well? What are you going to do about it?"

"I have no idea, Lor. But I'm going to do something. While she and I were chatting, I knew it was weird to get so close to someone so quickly. But I also knew that talking to her felt like 'home'. And I couldn't just ignore that and let it slip through my fingers again. And I won't."

He regarded his sister. "Look, you know if I'd have known what you were up to I would not have given you the go-ahead to do all of this—" Jared continued, holding up his hand when Lorna began to interject, "But—I'm hoping that one day I'll thank you for this one and only time you interfered with my love life." he said, stressing his point. "For right now, I need you to tell me everything you know about Ta'Mara."

Chapter 23

***

Following his very expensive early dinner with his sister—none of which he'd touched because he'd had no appetite—Jared had picked up the phone to see if Lawrence was available for some guy talk. After getting debriefed by Jared of the situation, Larry conferred with his wife to confirm that he was free for an emergency guys' night out. Jared could hear Darla in the background, "What?! Really?! What are you still doing here, go, go!!"

Larry showed up at Jared's place holding a bag of food from their favorite little hole in the wall located near where Larry and his wife lived: philly steak sandwiches with the works, chili cheese fries and rootbeer floats.

They were halfway through their meal before Jared had started on the topic at hand. Larry had patiently waited for that moment, knowing it'd come when Jared felt ready to tackle it.

"She's in Kansas City. Missouri. It's where her family lives." Jared began, looking at the remainder of his sandwich as if that was the intended listener.

Larry was intentional about not slowing down on his own food intake or otherwise giving away the shift in his focus.

"The moment I'd learned where she was I wanted to do a 'Me Tarzan, you Jane' kind of thing and whisk us off to some island where I'd have the chance to woo her again."

Larry finally chimed in. "But then you thought better of it."

"Of course."

"Because it's hard to find uninhabited islands."

"Bingo."

They both chuckled. When silence fell once again Larry pretended to focus on what remained of his chili fries.

"I know it's been well over a decade since I last saw her...but is it weird that I've missed her every single day? I mean, it's like she was always in the back of my mind, in memory and as a hope. I think the best I'd hoped for, really, was that the Lord would grant me the opportunity to share the same depth of love with another woman, someday. And I'd thought that maybe I'd found that. Turns out it was her all along. I can't get away from her, man." Jared licked his lips. "And I don't want to. I never did. I was just..." he trailed off.

"A downright dumbass," Larry finished for him in as nonchalant a tone as there ever was.

Jared side-eyed him. Then shrugged with a sad smirk.

"But you know what you are now?" Larry continued.

At Jared's look he finished, "You're not a dumbass. You made a mistake, Jared. It cost you a lot. But you're not that same person. And looks to me like you may have an opportunity at a second chance that few get. And no, it's not weird to never forget your first love. None of us do."

Jared shot his best friend a questioning look. Larry went on to explain, "My first love was in highschool.

We were highschool sweethearts. Maria. She was smart, sweet, funny with a dry sense of humor. Our favorite hangout together was this beautiful library that wasn't far from our school. We'd talk about everything. We even talked about our future together. And, well, it didn't work out obviously. I have no regrets about my life now, but I do still catch myself wondering what my life would have been like now if I had chosen to go to college at home rather than out of town."

Jared's mouth dropped open. "You never told me about this!"

It was Larry's turn to shrug. "Never had a reason to, really. But, my beautiful wife knows about it, and that's what matters most." Larry winked and grinned. "And I do like that she's a tiny bit jealous of Maria. Though she'd never have anything to worry about.

"Anyway, my point is that lives take different roads. And yours just happens to be bringing you back to the path you'd thought you'd lost for good. I hope you don't let it pass you by."

"I'm not. But I have no idea what to do next. It's like Ta'Mara turns me all butterfingers again. She's the only woman that can make me feel like a tongue-tied teenager. The best I can think of right now is to board a flight, show up and say, 'Hey, Remember me?'"

"Yes, I do," Larry responded, badly mimicking a high-pitched, womanly voice coupled with an equally abysmal southern twang, "and here's my mace in your face."

Jared chuckled. "That sounds fair."

"What about just writing to her, now that you both know who you're talking to? Right now you have more of the story than she does. And I imagine that's the case with more than just this present situation. Maybe it's time to shed some light on the past, as well."

Jared groaned and bent to put his head in his hands. "Yeah," he bit out. "Yeah," he said a bit more confidently, raising from his bent position and licking his lips as the thought of what he was about to do sank in.

"She might ridicule me. Or yell...well as much as one can yell in writing. Or worse...she might not respond at all, again. But I owe her that explanation. And I can give her at least that much."

Chapter 24

✳ ✳ ✳

Ta'Mara kept her promise to herself. She'd shown up the next day at work and been diligent, only giving in to indulge her stray thoughts a few dozen or so times. That night, she worked and re-worked her plans for her contract business. Throughout the day and night she found herself checking her phone even more than she usually did; and she'd nearly pounce on her phone whenever she heard its notification bell. Each time she'd decided not to acknowledge why she'd been so very disappointed to find it was a friend or family member's text, a new email from a spammer or a calendar reminder.

The same pattern repeated itself over the remainder of the work week. For the weekend she'd planned to stay busy by visiting her mom, going to a movie with an acquaintance followed by dinner, taking a solo trip to the Nelson Art Gallery, and then working to finalize her timeline for building, growing and transitioning full-time into her business as a contract software developer. She'd considered squeezing in a visit to the Kansas City Pet Project to take a look at all the cuddly cats and dogs available for adoption. But in the mood she was in she was worried she'd walk away with half of their stock.

It was Sunday and she was headed out the door to visit her mom when she heard the soft "ping" on her phone informing her of a new notification. She dug in her purse, expecting to see a text from her mom confirming that she was still coming to visit. Ta'Mara chuckled, she knew her mom so well. "Yes, Mom," she said aloud just as her hands found her phone. "I'm on my way," she finished talking to herself, smiling.

Dialing in her phone's security code she was about to hit the icon for her to respond to her mom's text when she noted that the notification was regarding her freelance app, instead. She stilled for a moment. She was being so silly, she knew she'd been wanting something to happen there. And for all she knew it could just be a new potential client. But her heart didn't care what it could be; it began drumming a melody immediately in anticipation.

Ta'Mara walked over to the large chair nearby so that she could settle herself and the purse that still hung from her arm into its welcoming cushioned embrace. Then she opened the app. And looked at the indicator, noting that she had one unread response from Ryan Jamison's account.

She opened the message:

From: RyanJamisonAuthor (official)
To: TailorMadeFullStackDev
Ta'Mara,

I hope you'll read this message through to its end. I would totally understand if you never wanted to hear from me again beyond the scope of this letter. But please hear me out.

You'd never met my sister, Lorna, but you may recall that she'd been away fulfilling an AmeriCorps tour while we were together. Anyway, she's a firecracker. And she's the one that set us up like this. She meant well; she said she'd heard how happy I was with you even in my voice and she'd wanted that for me, for us, again. And as crazy as this whole thing is, I'm actually glad she did it. I've missed you. I miss you. I can't quantify how dumb I was fifteen years ago. And I understand why you never responded to my efforts to reach out to you afterwards. I'm not expecting anything in response to this. Though I'd be lying if I said I didn't hold on to the hope that you'll reach back out to me.

All I want to do here is try to explain what happened. Try to explain why it all happened, even though my reasoning was skewed and selfish. But I just want to try to fill in the blanks of our story, as far as my actions go.

I never told you this, but I'd seen you before, before the day we 'met' at that cafe. The first time I saw you was from my duplex's window. I happened to be looking out when I spotted this gorgeous woman swaying down the sidewalk, about to pass me and my home by. And immediately, something in me seemed to click into place. And I knew I had to meet you, despite my lack of know-how when it came to romance and all that that entailed. I knew I had to take a chance and see if you were available...and possibly even interested in me. So I started trying to jog around the same time, hoping to run into you. I still count that as the best decision I've ever made.

I've never met anyone as honest, empathetic, passionate and yet practical as you. You'd always been beautiful to me, inside and out. I was so awed that someone so balanced and healthy could fall in love with an overweight guy with no career and no charisma. But you did, you loved me just as I was; you helped me see things in myself that I'd taken for granted. And as time went on, a whole lot of others began noting your beauty, as well. As that happened, I'd hear more and more comments about how lucky I was to have you and inferences about how astounded people were that we were a couple.

Unfortunately, I eventually let those sentiments, (that I can now genuinely believe were not made out of malice), get to me; and I let my own insecurities make decisions for me. What I should have done was agreed with each and every one of those comments and married you as fast as I could before you knew any better; and from then on boasted about the amazing woman I'd been gifted with. You wouldn't believe how many times I've wished that that's how things had happened. Instead, I began feeling scared that you'd find someone who was more your equal in terms of your faith in Christ, your looks, and your ambitions. I started thinking that maybe I would hold you back from the better future you could have and that you deserved. And then I even convinced myself that I had moved too fast, that maybe I wasn't actually ready for a relationship—let alone a marriage. I started feeling like I was in last place in some race I'd made up, and that I was destined to finish as a loser. And I took those feelings out on you; I blamed you for how I was making myself feel. And I lied to you when I told you that I wasn't sure if what we had was love. What I wasn't sure of is whether my love for you would remain enough for you. Because,

at the time, I had nothing else to offer
but myself. And I just knew that
everyone who ever saw us together
would wonder how someone so great
could ever settle for someone like me.

So I ran. I pushed you away and I ran
away from my feelings. And I didn't
pause long enough to think about yours.
To consider what you felt. By the time
my friends and family were able to
prod/push/pull me from my
self-focused coma and help me awaken
to see my stupidity, it was too late. I
went to your apartment after I'd learned
you'd changed your phone number.
Someone else was already living there.
That's when I began calling your
parents. Of course, the first time I called
your father squarely put me in my place.
He had quite a few choice words for me
before hanging up in my face. And I
completely respect that. He's a good dad.
And I understood when, a few months
later, your mom explained that you were
moving on with your life and that I

should let you go and stop calling. She
was right. And I tried.

But maybe you were right when you'd
asked if my books were an attempt to
recreate what you and I had. To write
out the possibility that we could
experience a second chance.

Is it still just a fantasy that we might try
again? That this might be our chance to
try to build something stronger and
more resilient from the lessons we've
learned both together and apart?

I'm leaving my number below, if you
want to call me or just write me back,
either way is great. And, Tay, I'll fly to
wherever I have to to see you again, if
you'll give me that chance. Set the date,
the time, the place. And I'm there.

Please, please consider praying about
this...about us. I have. And no matter
what, Ta'Mara, you have been and will
continue to be in my prayers.

~ Quint Emm Ellis ~

With hope, always
<3 Jared.

❋ ❋ ❋

The drive to Ta'Mara's mother's house happened in a daze. She knew she should have waited a bit before leaving, being so distracted as she was now. But he'd said he'd talked to her parents all those years ago. And, that couldn't be true. She'd never heard anything, not in all these years had either of them said anything. She had to ask her mom. She needed to talk with her mother, face-to-face. She let that directive replay in her head over and over so that she could avoid thinking about the offer that had summed up Jared's letter. She could barely think as it was; she certainly couldn't fathom the prospect of exhuming a dream she'd thought she had laid to rest.

Upon pulling into the lot of her mother's complex, Ta'Mara took a few extra moments to breathe, to remember to not be upset if what Jared had written was true, to remember that she'd have every right to be upset—and even a little disappointed—if it weren't true but that wouldn't be the end of the world. That life had gone on before Jared. And it had continued fine without him. That she would be okay, no matter what, because God has done and will do amazing things in and through broken people.

With that, she left the safety of her car and prayed that her emotions would listen to all of those reminders.

Ta'Mara's mom lived in an independent living complex. She'd decided to move there just a couple years ago, shortly after Ta'Mara's father had passed away. Her mom had sold their house and added the profits to the nest egg that'd been left by her husband. It'd allowed her a level of independence that Ta'Mara's mother cherished, though her mother mourned the way that it came about. "I'd trade every penny to have that peanut-headed man back in my arms for just one more minute," she'd say, with a sad smile. "Every single penny."

The house had held too many memories, and her mother had expressed looking forward to entering a space that offered a community of people who understood her. Since then, her mother had carved out a space for herself in the new world that was absent from her husband. She'd made fast, good friends in the community, participated in group events and had recently accepted a role to help lead one of those groups.

As hard as it was for Ta'Mara to lose her father, she'd known it'd hurt in a different and inexplicable way for her mother. So to see her re-learn how to do life on her own, to see her face that challenge with courage, had inspired Ta'Mara. And it'd given her a sense of relief, too. She'd always known her mom for her support and strength. But it'd been this period of time that her mom's resilience had truly shined.

After Ta'Mara had checked in to the main office, she headed out and walked the familiar path to her mother's bungalow. Along the way she waved back at a few residents who'd recognized and greeted her.

Her mom's residence mirrored all of the others, a greige exterior with white trim. A panel of three large windows lined a portion of the front of the house that jutted out from the rest, creating a bay window in the interior. Ta'Mara rapped on the white door and tried to clear her head. "Mom, it's me," she yelled through the door for good measure.

"Of course it is, Baby," she heard on the other side of the door along with the sounds of the doors' locks coming undone. Seconds later, her mother stood before her, her smile lighting up her face as she reached up to her daughter for a welcoming hug. Following their embrace Ta'Mara trailed her mother who led them to the large dining room table, where snacks had been artfully prepared. Always a gracious host, her mother was especially so when her daughter arrived; she always made sure to have some things to snack on on the table and, often, a meal to go along with it in case Ta'Mara arrived hungry. Ta'Mara always managed to arrive hungry because of that fact. Except today.

Ta'Mara couldn't eat a thing. Her stomach turned and roiled at the thought of adding another weight upon it. So she just waited for her mom to finish up whatever preparations she'd been wrapping up in the kitchen before heading out to join her daughter at the table.

Once seated, her mom grinned and patted the hand that Ta'Mara had placed on the tabletop. "Always so glad to see you, hon. I know how busy it is at your workplace. So how are things going, there?"

"Oh, good, thanks Momma."

Her mom frowned slightly, a crinkle appeared in her brow as concern marked her features, "What's wrong? Are you still having issues with that one staff member who's gunning for your job? Boy, I swear some people don't know how to work in a team. Always gotta try to outshine folks and then end up not doing anything worthwhile. I told you what I thought you should do—"

"No, Mom. That's not it." Ta'Mara chuckled at her mom's loving defense. Then she sobered, looking away as her lower lip tucked itself between her teeth.

"Oh my, baby, what is it?" her mother's alarm grew at the tale-tale signs of her offspring's inner turmoil.

"It's—it's about Jared."

Her mother blinked, as if trying to remember something.

"Jared. He and I, well, have...re-connected, kind of. Just in writing, for now. But, well it's a long story but he said he'd spoken to you...and dad, all those years ago. He said he'd called? A few times, actually, after I'd moved back here?"

It was her mother's turn to bite her lip as she looked away and suddenly found a need to alight from her chair and putter in the kitchen.

"Well, it was a long time ago, honey. There was so much going on. You know your dad was just starting to get those migraines and we had no idea what was going on there. There was just so much going on. And you," her mother returned to stand behind her chair, with her hands on its back as her watery eyes stared into that of her daughter's. "You were so...broken. So heartbroken. So...spirit-broken. Our number one priority as parents in this world was—and is—you. We just wanted to give you time. To think, and to heal so that you could figure out what you wanted to do next and—"

"Mom, mom, there's no need to explain. Really. I understand why you might've turned him away during those first few weeks. I do. I can't say that I don't wonder what would have happened if I'd known. Would things be different? I don't know but, I-I get it. I don't blame you. I probably would do the same." Though Ta'Mara couldn't deny the hint of hurt that had begun to flower in her heart.

Her mother's sigh of relief was audible. "But," Ta'Mara continued, "He also mentioned that he'd reached out several months later. And I know that by that time I'd started working and..."

"You're father and I just couldn't bear the thought of seeing you go back to that dark place; we saw you beginning to live again, have dreams and plans! We—were afraid of the possibility that he'd take that away from you again. We were probably wrong in keeping that from you, but I can't say we'd've made a different decision, hon. Even now. We haven't been perfect parents...but we were parents—and I am a parent who fiercely loves her child."

Ta'Mara nodded at her mother's quiet and heartfelt statement. She felt a little overwhelmed with the weight of the fuller picture she was now receiving of that period of time; a long ago era consisting of her focusing on taking just one more breath and not letting her sorrow misguide her into thinking that the pain would last forever.

And it hadn't. But she couldn't deny how vivid and fresh the memories of that period were. If she weren't careful, she could find herself being drawn back through time, reliving the script of her past.

Even worse, she already felt the tug to be pulled into a non-existent present—into parallel worlds comprised of "what-if's". What if she'd known about his call? Would they have sorted things out? Would both of their lives look drastically different? Would she be happier?

She shook her head and swallowed the lump that'd formed in her throat.

"Oh baby," she heard her mother's soft comfort. "Did we do the wrong thing?" she asked, revealing the uncertainty of her earlier declaration.

Ta'Mara looked down at the surface of the table and bit her lip as tears strained against the back of her eyes. "I don't know, Mama. I—", inhaling deeply and closing her eyes she exhaled and was able to raise her eyes to meet her mom's. "I think you did what any good parent would do. I think you and dad did what you thought was best. I guess, I—I just would like to know what would've happened if things had been different."

Her mom reached across the table and grasped her daughter's hand, "Honey, I take back what I said. If I could change things and do it all over I'd let you know. Your dad and I, all we ever wanted was our baby's happiness."

"Mom, no. It's—I guess what I mean is that I would like to know the "end". Like, now I don't know. At one point, I knew the end of my and Jared's relationship. Now..."

"You still can, hon."

She squeezed her mom's hand. "Yeah, but I'm a little older and a little more—uhm—more to love," she finished with a chuckle. Releasing a loud exhale, her body relaxed as she felt herself finally beginning to come up for air. "Mom, I just have to believe that all things work together for the good of those who love the Lord and are called according to His purpose. Everything. Even the hard things. Even the things we don't understand. Even the things we wish were different." She felt her tears begin to well up in her eyes, but didn't bother to hide them this time.

Her mother's eyes glistened in response. "Honey, you're beautiful. You don't see it, you never have. You did, for a little while, until—well, I just hope that you'll really believe that about yourself, no matter who is or isn't by your side. You're never too old to learn about yourself, youngin'."

"Well, actually, more often than not I think I'm pretty cute," she corrected, with a smile and shrug. "But Jared...well I guess he reminds me of both a very high time in my life and a very low time. It was a time where I'd worked hard to get in the best shape I'd ever been and felt great about everything in my life. And yet I was dumped by the only man I'd ever ventured to love and be transparent with. He'd seen my sweat, insecurities as well as me at my most fabulous; but even at my best I wasn't good enough. It kinda broke me. I can't lie...especially cuz you and dad had front row seats so you already know the truth. But, yeah, with Jared come so many wonderful feelings; but also a horde of insecurities that I thought I'd dealt with, but am coming to find out I hadn't. Did I mention that he's, like, totally fit; practically a freaking model, now?" At her mother's shocked expression Ta'Mara nodded and grabbed her phone, quickly finding the page she'd familiarized herself with in such a short time. "Yeah, I saw his facebook profile...he'd sent the link."

She handed the phone to her mom, who's mouth formed an ')' as she blinked. "Whoa." her mom said.

"Yeah, that's what I said. I was like, 'Who is this?' "
Ta'Mara chuckled, and shrugged. "The adorable,
chunky guy I fell in love with who'd practically left me
at the altar...him, I could actually imagine a 'maybe'
with. This hunk-a-burnin' love, however...he seems
like a stranger—I don't even know him. And I just, I
just don't want to feel all of these not-good feelings of
inadequacy that I'd felt when we broke up. I don't
deserve a repeat of all that. I don't know if I even want
to risk a fresh onslaught of all of that. I know that's
cowardly, and insecure and not very
'independent-woman' of me. I wonder if maybe we
should just let the dead stay dead...and let him
remember what he lost...the fitter version of what he
lost, that is."

Her mother put the phone face down and replaced
her hand atop her daughters, her smile was gentle
and the grasp of her hand firm. "I love you, Ta'Mara.
And I support whatever decisions you decide to make
with your life, because I know you've only grown
more and more rooted in your faith in Christ. But
even if I didn't support your decisions, I'm your
momma, not your boss."

She continued, "But if I was your boss I'd say this: You let Him be your Rock and your Guide," she said, pointing up and above her head, "like no fear can, and like no human ever can—including yourself—and you will come through it all the better for it." She continued, "I love your father, and he loved me, fiercely. But we both knew that the pair of us were nothing without the Lord as the glue. He and I had so many, many chances to grow apart, to choose our individual wants over pursuing maintaining the love that the Lord had given us for one another. We'd even discussed separating, baby."

At Ta'Mara's widened eyes and mouth her mother hurried to finish, "But obviously we didn't. Honey, I can only attribute the longevity and pretty steady health of our marriage to one thing: we put God first and we knew that it was Him that fulfilled all our needs...meaning that it was not up to piddly little me to be everything for my husband, nor the other way around. It's through that realization that we can allow room for the mercy and grace and patience needed to fill the gaps in all the areas that we both lacked.

"It's what also encouraged your dad to embrace being a man who could help do the laundry, cook dinners and such. While I helped out with mowing the lawn and doing minor fix-it projects—-when he'd dine to let me use his tools, that is." Her mother chuckled at some memory.

"We were partners, and we did what needed to be done for the good of the household that God had gifted us with. God is so much bigger than the expectations we place on others and on ourselves. He's all we need. And even now, baby, I mean you saw how long it took me to remember what up from down was when My Love went on to be with the Lord. But it's that same understanding that got me through and gets me through.

"It's understanding the fact that the Lord loved me and your father so much that he decided to show bits and pieces of His love through us; that he gave us to one another so that we could grow in more accurately portraying and sharing the love of God with one another and, as a result, with the world around us.

"Whatever decisions God leads you to make, I believe it will result in your growing in the ability to love Him and to love others more. I don't think it'll result in your feeding or nursing your fears. I think that's how you'll know you're making the right decisions, Hon."

~ Quint Emm Ellis ~
246

Ta'Mara couldn't dispute the soundness of that frank reasoning; and it gave her a new perspective as she considered and prayed about her next steps.

"I really did like Jared, by the way." Her mother finished with a soft smirk. "I did wish he'd have been a believer, honey. I know they say divorce rates among Christians rivals that of the world, but when both parties are constantly seeking God first, well there's not a stronger couple out there, because that right there is a team. That's what makes up the three-stranded cord the Word tells us about. God is that glue, that third strand that holds a team together. If both people in a relationship are looking at the Lord—truly—they can't help but see one another through him...through his eyes. And that makes all the difference when it comes to those moments when you want to punch that person in the throat just for breathing too loud and blinking one too many times. And believe me, those days will come aplenty."

Ta'Mara burst out laughing at her momma's candor.

"But again I can't make decisions for you—at least not anymore. I've said my piece." her mom ran her thumb and forefinger across her lips as if zipping them shut.

Ta'Mara wasn't fooled though and just chuckled.

"Well, about that, Mom..."

With that she shared about how she and Jared had started talking and one of the things he'd been explicit about was his faith. And that, even as a writer, one of the first things that'd drawn her were the redemptive story lines of his novels.

"My, my, a believer and a Christian author, too? I can't—" her mother's hand splayed across her chest in astonishment. "The Lord truly does know what he's doing, doesn't he?"

"Yeah." Ta'Mara agreed with a grin. She didn't mention that her favorite novel of his is a replica of his and her relationship, except with a "Happily Ever After". For some reason, she still wanted to keep that jewel to herself. That was just for her and Jared, for right now.

A question came to mind and Ta'Mara had to ask, "Mom?"

"Yeah, honey," her mother patted her hand and looked at her daughter with love in her eyes.

"So, I'm just curious, you and dad prayed about letting me know about Jared's calls all those years ago?"

Her mother's hand stilled and her lips pursed. "Well, I'm not saying we were perfect, honey. No man is gonna break our girl's heart and then just think he can call and crawl his way back in. No," her mom shook her head as she folded her arms on her chest. "Naw, your dad and I went straight to our heads and our hearts with that one. Bypassed the Lord, God forgive me.

"But no way were we going to make it that easy. You need to come here with some big gestures or something. A phone call?? After what he did? Nope, I need you to orchestrate flash dances, writing in the sky, and a very public apology, at least. And a damn plane ride so you, too, risk getting rejected in person. Nope. I take back my take-back, honey. No regrets. He didn't do right by you then...but that doesn't mean he can't do right by you now. Especially now that he's invited the Lord to be His Lord."

Suddenly her mom's eyes widened and her gaze darted toward the kitchen. Just then Ta'Mara smelled it, too. The acrid smell of burnt food.

"Oh, no! I left your plate of food in the oven too long!" Her mother jumped up from the table, spry as a twenty-something. When Ta'Mara followed in pursuit she arrived at the doorway of the kitchen in time to see her mom waving a towel over a smoldering baking dish that contained what used to be edible parts of what would have been a great, mother-made meal.

Her mother just shook her head, tsk-ing at the meal as if it should feel ashamed at itself for not warning her sooner. "Well," she said over her shoulder as the dish towel continued to swing back and forth over the smokey dish, "Want to order pizza?"

Ta'Mara laughed and agreed, relieving her mom of dish-towel duty as her mom went to grab her cell phone. They spent the rest of the afternoon chatting about Ta'Mara's work, her mom's latest hobby—figure drawing— and the latest soap opera that was happening among her fellow residents. By the time Ta'Mara headed home she knew way too much about her mom's neighbors' business.

Chapter 25: the Offer

✳ ✳ ✳

From: TailorMadeFullStackDev

To: RyanJamisonAuthor (*official*)

Hi Jared,

I've been a bit speechless ever since I found out who I've been speaking with all of this time. And I guess I still am. But I wanted to respond to you.

First off, thank you for explaining everything that's happened in the past. I'll admit that it does help, even after all of these years. And I hadn't known about your attempts to contact me afterwards. I spoke with my mom and she explained her and my dad's reasoning for not passing on that information. You're right, I have great parents. They did what they felt was best for me at the time.

A lot of time has passed between then and now. And yet talking with you was still so easy.

I still have a lot of reservations. I think that's reasonable.

But I don't want to look a gift-horse in the mouth, either. I've prayed about it...and I haven't felt or heard a "no" from the Lord regarding continuing our communication. So, maybe we should just do that, for now.

~ Quint Emm Ellis ~

253

Just write one another...but this time
knowing who we're writing to. What do
you think?

P.s. Here's my email address, so at least
we're not using this platform any more:
tamaratay_h80@gmail.com

✷ ✷ ✷

The chime on Jared's phone alerted him to a new
notification. Glancing over at it beside him on the
couch his heart jumped into his throat and something
fell heavily into the pit of his stomach. It was a
notification from the freelance app. And unless his
sister was playing with fire or some random
contractor was contacting him, it could only mean
one thing. He snatched the phone up and licked his
lips as he tapped on the icon to open the app.

His jaw involuntarily clenched at the sight of
Ta'Mara's moniker on the platform. He had tried to
mentally prepare himself for the worst case scenario:
that even if she did respond it could very well be to
tell him that she never wanted to see—or talk with

him again. Yet, the possibility of realizing that nightmare stilled his hands now.

Even so, the remaining hope he held onto compelled him to open her message and read its contents.

By the end of the brief communication he was grinning so widely his cheeks began to hurt. It wasn't everything he'd hoped, but it was more than he deserved. She wanted to keep talking with him.

It'd been just about a week since the last time he'd received something from her. He marveled at how much had evolved over such a short period of time. And how much he'd been aching to reconnect with her, in any way, each of those days.

He'd committed to placing the situation in God's hands; but it was hard to know if he was actually doing that—he wanted his Ta'Mara. He wanted to hold her again; he wanted the chance to be the man of God for her that he knew he could finally be. And he didn't want to waste another minute.

But he recognized the Lord's hand in all this. And would do his best to rest in His timing, as well.

~ Quint Emm Ellis ~
255

He went to his office to grab his laptop and bring it back to the sofa with him. Opening up his personal email account he carefully typed in Ta'Mara's email address before beginning his response to her.

From: just_jared007@gmail.com
To: tamaratay_h80@gmail.com

Ta'Mara, hello! Thank you for writing me back! I'm sorry for all of the exclamation points but I'm truly thrilled to be writing to you. I have the widest grin on my face right now!!!

I read your response (of course) and I understand. I'm just glad we're talking, no matter what form it takes. I'd love to know about your life. Your work, friends, hobbies. I know we've already shared a lot. But I want to know you. So please share everything. And ask me anything. ANYTHING. I want you to know me, too. I'm an open book for you (no pun intended...you know, with my being an author and all lol).

Also...please tell me that you're single.
I am.
<3 Jared

✳ ✳ ✳

The letters between Jared and Ta'Mara quickly grew too long and frequent to reasonably remain confined to emails. Within a week Ta'Mara had relented, asking Jared to call her at the number that she then provided.

It was a Wednesday night when her phone rang. Noting the out of town area code Ta'Mara gave herself time for a few—several—steadying breaths. On the third ring she finally accepted the call. "Hello?"

Notes of affection, humor and familiarity infused the caller's deep, rumbling response. "Hey Ta'Mara, this is Jared." He cleared his throat. "It's-it's so great to hear your voice, again."

Ta'Mara felt all the tension in her shoulders flow out of her, like a tide. Though foreign in some ways, she knew this voice. "Yours too, Jared. Although I have to admit...I don't recall yours being so low. Did you go through a second puberty while we were apart?"

His chuckle warmed her, "I guess you could say that. It's probably just what fifteen years of living and a career focused on speaking to others gets you. Would you say I have a voice made for radio?"

"Definitely. But not the face for one."

"Oh! Someone's been on my facebook profile. Did you like what you saw, Ta'Mara?" he said, his voice lowered, intimate.

"I'm not going there, Jared. We're just here doing a friendly chat."

"Hey, I didn't start the flirting. But I sure don't mind picking up what you're dropping."

Ta'Mara laughed. He was right! "You got me on that one. My bad. Wasn't meant to be taken flirtatiously—I don't think. Or maybe it was. I was just—being honest."

"And that's something I've always appreciated about you. And it's something I'm so glad has not changed. I want to be honest with you, too."

Ta'Mara felt herself hold her breath; she could feel something weighty in his voice. "Okay," she invited, cautiously. She imagined all sorts of revelations, "I'm gay." "I'm married." "I'm not actually Jared and this has all been an elaborate prank, surprise!"

"Ta'Mara, I'm too old to play games. And frankly I don't want us to waste any more time. I want you to know that my feelings for you have not changed. They haven't waned. And the more we talk the more I want the future for us that I squandered away. I know we're still getting to know each other—again. But I'm already 'all in'. I'm just—somewhat patiently—waiting for it to become clear to you that I'm the man that God made for you. And that you're the woman he made for me. I don't think our getting to this point, right now, is accidental."

Ta'Mara was taken aback, and allowed the silence to extend far longer than she'd intended.

Jared cleared his throat, "Hello?" he prompted.

"I'm still here. I just wasn't expecting you to say all of that. But—"she continued quickly, "I'm glad you did. I don't think our getting to this point is accidental, either," Ta'Mara admitted.

"Can I come see you?" Jared pressed on, encouraged by her confirmation.

Ta'Mara paused, pressing her lips and her eyes together. Jared waited silently on the other end.

"Yes."

"Friday?"

"*This* Friday?"

"The very same," he said, a smile in his voice.

"What about work? And you don't already have plans or something for the weekend?"

"I'll take off from work. They can handle things without me for one day. And as for the weekend, neither of us were socialites and that never—truly—changed for me. I fully understand if you can't take off on short notice, I don't mean to imply that you should drop everything for this. And obviously, you could have plans. So I could come another day—"

"No, no I don't have plans and—I could probably take the day off, actually. Fridays are typically slow for us. It—just seems really fast."

"Baby, we've waited fifteen years. I don't think we could pace ourselves much slower." He chuckled.

"Oh, Jared," Ta'Mara found herself saying, falling into their old pattern and only belatedly noting the term of endearment he'd called her.

"Do you want me to come next week, instead?" He asked, straining to withhold the disappointment that threatened to shadow his question. He'd hoped she was as anxious to see him as he was her.

"I don't know. It's just that—" she exhaled loudly, deciding that there was no use in hiding what seemed an obvious bridge to cross, at least in her eyes. "Things have changed, Jared. I'm not the slim girl I was when you saw me last. I mean, I'm a woman. I'm not the heroine in a book."

"Baby," Jared said, and she could hear the intent in his tone. "I wouldn't expect you to be. You're not the heroine in my books; you're the inspiration for them. All my characters are just a reflection of you. I'm not confusing you with nor comparing you to one of them, Ta'Mara. On the contrary—they could never be you. I was yours the day you walked under my window sill, taunting me with all the curves and determination a man could ever hope to hold as his own. But at the end of the day, at the end of this life, it's you that I want. The woman who made me feel like superman, even while all I held in my hands was a mop. The woman I looked up to. You're my treasure. You're my hero."

There was a long pause. So long Jared began to wonder if the phone's connection had dropped. Just before he was about to say something to check, Ta'Mara responded, her voice husky.

"Jared, we can't—uhm, have sex, you know, when you arrive. On Friday," she dictated, moreso needing to hear her declaration herself than anything else.

She could hear the triumph even in his restrained reply. "Yeah, baby, I know. I know. I will try to be on my best behavior. Promise. I'll email you the details. Can you give me your address?"

"Yeah, sure. But I'll be picking you up from the airport."

"You don't have to do that."

"I know, Jared. I want to." Ta'Mara paused before continuing. "And Jared?"

"Yeah?"

"You can't call me 'baby'...not yet. Okay?"

She heard his sigh and his chuckle. "Yeah, okay ba—. Ta'Mara. Sorry, just slips out. I understand. It'll just make it that much sweeter when I can address you with all the endearment that's in my heart."

"Boy, your flirting skills are on point."

"Oh, no, Ta'Mara. This is not flirting." He exhaled, "This is sincerity; and that's all you're gonna get from me. You know some things about my past...er...dating life. That involved flirting. Flirting is the last thing I want to do with you...I want nothing but every real, deep, true and lasting thing that God has to offer us from this point onward. I hope that confession doesn't scare you. Or weird you out or anything."

"No more than everything else you've said so far," Ta'Mara said, not unkindly. "No, it doesn't scare me. It's really nice to hear you say all of that. But it's also hard for me to—"

"It's hard to believe me. To trust me." He stated, completing the thought.

"Yeah, you know I've never been one to really open myself up to a ton of people. And that whole—thing—between us it didn't help. It's just really hard for me to trust that people, who aren't my parents, will stick around once I begin relying on them."

"I completely get your doubts about people...about me, specifically." He paused, considering his next words. "As much as it pains me to express this, I did say I wanted to be sincere with you." He paused again, before continuing. "I believe that I'm a changed man. I believe with all my heart that I've allowed the Lord to prune and polish my heart, mind and soul so that I better reflect His. But I have my doubts, too, that I'm changed enough to be the type of husband that the woman of my dreams should have. Have I really changed from the insecure, selfish coward that I was those years ago? Or has only my outward appearance and experiences changed?"

"The heart is deceptive above all things, right?" Jared posed, reciting the verse in the Bible. "I mean, it'll get us poor folks to write all kinds of checks that were never meant to be cashed. So it makes sense what the Word says when it encourages us to guard our hearts because it is the well-spring of life. But guarding our hearts can't mean that we hide it away from others. How could we, then, be an effective witness to others of Christ, who sacrificed Himself at the hands of those who hated him? I've struggled with this a lot, as you can tell. I've pondered it and prayed over it. And I think that, maybe, guarding our hearts means that we're to place our hearts in God's hands, for him to restore, refresh, heal and direct—vs placing our hearts and faith in the hands of people. And I don't know how to do one vs. the other, by the way. I'm just sharing what makes sense to me."

"Wow," Ta'mara breathed. "Jared. You've—you're really. I mean, we've always had great conversations. And even recently online it's been amazing to witness your faith. But hearing you speak like this. I don't know." she laughed, a little flustered all of a sudden. She wouldn't admit it to Jared, but hearing him speak so confidently and knowledgeably about the Word of God and his reliance on the Lord was...well it was a turn-on. "Anyway, yeah, I think I get what you mean. Actually," she said, redirecting the conversation a bit, "my mom was saying something similar when talking about her and my dad's marriage."

"And once again, Ta'Mara, I'm so sorry for your loss. I just wanted to say that voice-to-voice versus as a string of black letters on a white screen. I'm very sorry."

"Thank you, Jared. I appreciate that. And I'm sorry, as well, for your loss—of your mom. She was an amazing, genuine, generous woman. And I always felt I could see so much of her in you."

There was a brief pause before Jared responded. "Thank you, Ta'Mara. You don't know how much that means to hear someone say. Especially coming from you."

And right then, hearing the strain in his voice, Ta'Mara wished they were in a place—both relationship-wise and in their proximity—for her to just hug him close; for them to console one another, to mourn and rejoice in the lives of their parents, together.

"Yeah," Ta'Mara said, clearing her throat of the small knot that had formed. "So, my mom, she was trying to explain the same thing you were just saying, earlier. But, I mean, I don't get how you can love someone and not put your heart at risk."

"I don't think it's about not putting your heart at risk, though. I don't think it's about avoiding danger. Because that's a response to fear, right?"

"No, I don't feel like talking about how I'm being fearful and how fear is not of God. I know that...but I mean, it's a rational concern and it can't just be covered over with a band-aid of platitudes."

"I'm not saying it's not a rational fear, at all. I'm afraid, too."

"Of what?"

"Of losing you, again." She heard his voice break at the end of that last word, and her traitorous heart leapt through the phone and landed solidly beside his. He took a deep breath and began again. "I'm afraid I'll say or do something stupid—I'm really afraid of messing this up with you and then...that's it for us," he finished softly. His chuckle followed the silence before he continued, "It's why I pressed so hard to come see you as soon as possible." Jared decided not to mention that he'd actually wanted to come tomorrow but knew that'd really be pushing it. "Because I'm hoping to sweep you so far off your feet that you don't land until you're in my arms to stay."

"Jared," Ta'Mara responded in a near moan. "What are you doing to me?"

"Not nearly as much as I want to, believe me, Ta'Mara." Jared quickly responded, his tone meaningful.

They were both silent for a long while, only their breathing keeping them company.

Finally, Jared spoke. "So, yeah about that best behavior..."

They both laughed at that.

"So, if we're both afraid," Ta'Mara ventured, picking up the topic at hand, "what are you saying we should do? Ignore our fear and act like it's not there? Because I can't do that."

"No, Ta'Mara. And I would never expect you to be untrue to yourself. I think we acknowledge it—like we just have. But then we have to pray to the Lord that he'd help us guard our hearts, in the way he wants us to; a way that frees us to be courageous, to follow His will—not our own. I mean, it's my fears that placed 15 years between us. Think about that. And I know God can make beauty from those ashes...but it's hard not to wonder what would have happened had I been a different man. The man I am now."

The man I am now.

The words reverberated through her. In every word he'd spoken and written Ta'Mara witnessed the man that had grown out of the boy she'd dated so long ago. She wondered to herself if she'd grown nearly as much. "Jared, I agree with you...I just don't know how to practically apply it. Do you?"

"No clue."

At that they both laughed.

"Well," Ta'Mara said, still laughing. "Lord help us both, then."

"I am in agreement with that prayer. Amen and amen."

And that was the first prayer she and Jared had ever prayed together.

Chapter 26

✳ ✳ ✳

As soon as the "cellphone" light came on on the landed plane Jared checked his message. He was greeted with a recent text from Ta'Mara, informing him that she was running approximately seven minutes behind but she would meet him at baggage claim. He couldn't help the grin that reached his lips. He had no doubt that she would be just about seven minutes late, exactly. His Ta'Mara. He loved that woman. Even though he knew that, in years to come, her pragmatism would be a point of contention for them both. He sighed, oh how he hoped for those years to come. He promised himself he'd remember how he felt right now; whenever they were in the middle of an argument or disagreement or whatever they'll call them, he'd remember this moment where even that possibility was uncertain. And how he'd looked forward to the day when he could argue with the woman he loved. As well as love the woman with whom he argued.

A notification popped up on his phone just as the seatbelt sign turned off on the plane and all the passengers began rising up and gathering their luggage from the carry-on. This chime was from his sister. When he checked Lorna's text thread he rolled his eyes at the um-teen messages displayed from her on his phone.

> Text 1: Call me as SOON as you land.
> Text 5: As SOON as you land
> Text 8: You should be landing soon.
> Text 9-12: CALL ME

He answered with a quick response:

> **Jared**: *We just landed...mind if I get off the plane, first?*

> Text 13: no rush.
> Text 14: kidding, soooooo rush. Hurry up!!!!!

He chuckled at his sister and stepped out into the aisle to gather his items. As he strode down the airlock he called his sister since he knew he had a few minutes before Ta'Mara would arrive.

"So you want to gloat some more sis? Go right ahead. I would not be here were it not for my wonderful sister."

"You sound sincere, Bro. Are you okay?"

"Yeah, I'm more than okay. I'm about to see Ta'Mara. And yeah, I am sincere. I was calling fully ready to give you a hard time, but I'm in too great of a mood to ignore the fact that I owe you. Big."

"Crap."

"What's wrong?"

"I was so ready to rub this in your face some more and you went and ruined my moment."

Jared guffawed at that.

"Sorry-not-sorry. Hey, I can't stay on, though, sis. I need to get my head in the game. Ta'Mara will be here in a few and I don't want to be completely slack-jawed when I finally see her again."

"You think a few minutes can help you with that?" she joked.

"Nope, but I've got to give myself at least some chance at feigning a level of cool, calm composure."

Lorna's whooping laughter was all he heard as she ended their call with a quick, "Call me later, I want details!"

He hadn't checked-in any luggage so he didn't pay any mind to the conveyor belt, instead he scanned the doors for any sign of Ta'Mara, checking his phone on occasion to see if she'd followed up with any additional texts.

A feeling tugged at him, and he found his gaze drawn somewhere to his right. Right to the spot where Ta'Mara stood, staring back at him.

His smile broadened as his feet moved of their own accord toward her. Her smile was everything that he remembered. The smooth mahogany of her skin, the soft roundness that took him all the way back to his twenties—to the first and last time he'd ever ached to meet a stranger. To meet her. His Ta'Mara.

That same ache pulled at him now; to meet her, know her and make her his. When he was a few feet away he began to slow, taking the last couple of steps that brought him just within a respectable distance for acquaintances. He knew he wasn't alone in this feeling. He could see it in the glow on her face, the plumpness of her lips and gaze in her eyes. But for now, he wouldn't want to risk losing any of the ground they'd gained by forcing his hand too much, too soon.

"Ta'Mara," he rumbled.

Her smile faltered as she licked her too dry lips and her eyes had the nerve to bat. "Jared, it's, it's—" her words faded as she found herself searching for the words she'd rehearsed before and during her drive to the airport. "Uhm, it's..."

He nodded, "A little bit overwhelming?" he offered. At her nod he gave a small smile. "Agreed," he allowed. Walking forward and to her side, Jared placed a hand gently on her back to guide her around so that they began walking forward together. "Should we find your car? I actually don't know which direction we should be headed. Is this right?" He pointed toward the sign that directed patrons toward the public parking lots.

She nodded, and looked away, annoyed by her flustered response in the face of his composure. Why did he seem so comfortable? So in control? While she was still acting like she was an inexperienced twenty-something? Oh, yeah. Because he's "dated" half of California, she mused.

Today, she wore her favorite dress overcoat. Its large lapels flowed down her chest like flower petals. Their billowy shape framed her body; while her dark skin set off the light coat's bright white color, which complimented the freshness of her pink shirt tucked snugly into fitted dark blue jeans.

She'd shaped her hair so that her bangs created a bouffante in the front while the remainder of her hair was gathered into a natural faux hawk. It was one of the looks that made her feel most daring, powerful and alluring.

She glanced at him, his inky curls swept back, their waves artfully cresting atop his head with one lock escaping to grace his brow. His gold wire-rimmed glasses accented a square jaw sporting a tempting salt and pepper five-o-clock shadow. Brown eyes, just a few shades lighter than her own, watched her as she found herself caught in naked admiration.

"Yeah, that's it," she responded more curtly than she'd intended as she swung her gaze before her and quickened her pace. She took the lead as they walked through the terminal, into the elevator and finally through the parking lot to her vehicle. The whole time they remained in silence, quietly sneaking glances at each other in intervals beneath the yellow glow of the parking lot's lamplights.

She gestured toward her car, "That's me," and began toward the driver's door, only to find her hand gently grasped from behind as Jared tugged her to a stop. Ta'Mara turned to him, a question in her eyes.

Jared moved to her, foregoing keeping the distance he'd intended. Grasping her hands in his he searched her gaze.

"Ta'Mara," he breathed, his lips curving as he drank in the feel of her name on his lips and her hands in his. Jared inhaled deeply and let out the breath loudly before tilting his head. "Look, I realize how unique this meeting is. There are no words that can properly express how amazing it feels to be right here—in this parking lot," he smirked, before continuing softly and inching in a little closer, "with you, right now. I never thought I'd see you again, and yet..." He licked his lips, his eyes darting from point to point around the landscape of her face, lingering on her lips before making a slow trip back up to her eyes. "I don't think we can avoid feeling awkward," he said, heavily. "But I just wanted you to at least know where I stand. And that I hope we can continue to be as clear and honest with one another as we have been, so far."

Ta'Mara had to admit that his admission did make her feel better. It's like he knew what she was thinking and feeling. It'd be an uncomfortable thought—if she wasn't feeling so relieved, instead. She smiled, nodding in agreement as she spoke. "Awkward is an understatement," she conceded with a grin, not bothering to remove her hands from his. His warmth felt like a balm that spread from his hands, to hers and throughout the rest of her body. She sighed, though her smile remained as she gazed up at him. "This is so weird. I feel like I'm dreaming or something. Just—the past several weeks feel surreal. And now we're here, together?" She shook her hand and found her hand moving of its own accord, freeing itself from his grasp so that it lay flat against his cheek as if to assure herself that he was real.

He placed his hand over hers, nuzzled his face against her palm and turned his lips to place a small kiss in the valley of her palm.

The sound of a car passing behind them on its way out of the lot pulled them out of the bubble that'd formed around them. Ta'Mara blinked and began returning her hands to her side. Jared smiled and let her before reclaiming both hands and bringing them to his lips.

"Thank you for being so open with me. It means a lot that you're trusting me with that." He inhaled deeply before lowering their hands and releasing hers.

"Shall we?" He gestured to her car.

She nodded, still feeling the discomfort of the awkwardness that was rightful for their meeting; but also feeling a prevailing sense of peace that she so vividly recalled during her time with Jared in their younger years. Being with him felt like coming home, even after over a decade. A smirk drew itself upon her lips as she noted his familiar bow legged stride to the passenger side of her car. She pressed the key that unlocked the doors for them both and proceeded forward to begin the drive that would take him to his hotel.

Chapter 27

✳ ✳ ✳

Settled in the car, Ta'Mara set the route in the map on her phone and placed the phone in its holder. She could feel Jared's eyes on her every movement.

Looking at him, she pursed her lips. "What? Do I have something on my face or something?"

Jared's eyes widened, a grin as wide as a horizon on his face. "You're just so beautiful. Just as amazingly astonishing as the day we met."

This wasn't the first time Ta'Mara was thankful that her dark complexion hid her blush.

Ta'Mara rolled her eyes and shook her head. "I look a little different than I did when we first met. And definitely from when we last saw each other."

She'd turned to look out her rearview mirror to prepare to back out when she felt a warm, heavy hand fall on the one she'd placed on her gear shift. Her eyes flitted first to Jared's hand on hers then to the eyes that bore into hers with so much intensity she found it difficult to keep his gaze.

But she managed to.

"Ta'Mara—"

"Jared, are we ever going to get out of this parking lot," she joked, forcing a smile on her face before removing her hand from under his to adjust the position of her phone.

A beat of silence played, followed by Jared's agreement, "Yeah. Yeah, I guess that'd be a good start, huh?" He chuckled emptily.

She echoed his hollow laugh as she backed them out of the space and headed them in the direction of his hotel.

The plan was to take him to his hotel where he'd get himself settled before they headed out somewhere for dinner. He'd planned the entire trip, except for Sunday, where he would attend service with her at her mom's congregation and she'd give him a mini-tour of the River Market area before he headed back out that night. He'd asked if there were any activities she'd like to do before then so that he could plan around that. She'd only had one other request for their Saturday morning.

The hotel was located in downtown Kansas City, not far from the River Market. For much of the forty-five minute drive the music playing softly from the radio station filled the silence; Jared kept his gaze out the window, seemingly deep in thought.

Already, Ta'Mara felt the absence of his chatter, of his warmth. If only she hadn't blurted out that unneeded retort to his compliment. She'd learned long ago how to accept compliments graciously. And it's not like she didn't think she was attractive. But there were situations where her realism and recognition of where her looks did not align with the generalized standard of beauty bested her hard-won confidence. And this was one of those moments.

And who wants an insecure woman, on top of it all? She couldn't help but think to herself. All of a sudden she felt like a hot mess. Could she fake the confidence she usually felt the rest of this trip? Maybe this whole thing was a mistake. Was she going to lose him, now, because the tables were turned? You don't have him, anyway. So just enjoy the trip and don't put any expectations on it beyond enjoying yourself and, hopefully, getting needed closure.

She could feel her imperceptible nod at the thought, and awaited the mental shift her pep talks usually resulted in. But when she glanced over at Jared, sitting so close to her—when she could smell the scent of soap and him and know that he was so close, close enough to be missed again. She knew. She knew she was already setting herself up to be a wreck if anything less than the opportunities to make up for lost time resulted from this trip.

Still, she figured it was good advice. And maybe it'd help her loosen up if she could pretend that she really felt that way.

When they pulled up to the hotel Jared turned to her with the first words he'd had since they'd been in the parking lot.

"Ta'Mara," he said, unbuckling and opening his door, "Let me get your door for you, okay?"

Before she could respond he was out the door and hurrying behind and around her car. But when he tried to open the door it didn't budge.

"Oh!" she said, giggling as she unlocked it and Jared swung open the door. Taking her hand after she'd swung her legs from under the driver's wheel, he helped her out of her seat. One of the car attendants came around to their side and handed Ta'Mara a ticket.

Jared told the attendant that he'd grab his own luggage from the backseat. He tipped the gentleman who then hopped in the car and pulled away as Jared and Ta'Mara walked toward the hotel's glass doors, with Jared's hand resting lightly above the small of her back.

Once he'd checked in they found their way to the elevators that the desk manager had pointed them to and were soon on their way up to Jared's room. Since this was one of the pricier hotels in the city Ta'Mara was admittedly curious to get a peek at what warranted the hefty price tag.

And she wasn't regretting the feel of Jared's hand on her back, either.

They stepped off the elevator on the 8th floor and made their way to his door which sat neatly in the middle of the long hall. Jared slid his key card into the door and with a click, they found themselves entering the room. It was expansive, but comfortable, with windows leading out to a view of the city. A rectangular, inset electric fireplace which spanned several feet along the wall opposite the bed. A work desk was positioned in front of the window and the bed faced the windows, with it's back against another wall. Ta'Mara couldn't help but envision a night spent here: from the bed, you could have the fireplace crackling on your left with the rain hammering against the window before you as you viewed the twinkling lights of the city at night. That, plus room service, sounded pretty incredible. She pretended that she hadn't envisioned being in that bed alone.

Jared had already shed his bag on the sitting chair that sat on the far side of the window, opposite of the desk. He was now walking slowly towards her.

"Niiiice," she finally said aloud. "When you travel, you do it right, I see." She said, sticking her tongue between her teeth as she teased.

"I won't deny knowing what I like and going after it." Jared responded, his gaze steady on hers as he stopped only inches from her. He bit his lip as he raised his hand to run one finger from her temple, to her cheek, along the bottom curve of her lip. "You know one of the things that I'd always found most attractive about you, Ta'Mara?"

Ta'Mara shook her head, a warmth enveloping her at his touch, his nearness, the liquid sound of his hushed tone directed toward her.

"You never really knew how gorgeous you are," he answered, his hand dropping to land on one of her hips. "And apparently you still don't." He inched closer, his other hand coming to rest on her other hip. He lowered his head until his lips were a hair's breadth from hers. "Can I show you how beautiful you are to me?" He breathed against her mouth. Her slight nod was enough to bring her upper lip into brief contact with his, before he followed her gesture with a nod of his own. "Good," he whispered before closing the miniscule gap between them and taking her lips with his own.

He started the kiss lightly, gradually deepening his exploration of her mouth; a groan escaped him as she returned his gesture, opening her mouth to his.

When he finally parted their lips, he leaned his forehead upon hers as they both sought to catch their breath. Then he kissed the top of her head as his eyes slid to the bed that was far too accessible.

"I may not have thought this out as fully, or honestly, as I should have," he said, chuckling.

When he felt her stiffen he continued quickly, "Because, I should have known how tempting it'd be to have you alone in this room with me." He leaned back enough for them to be able to look each other in the eye. "But I wanted to show you that this is real. I'm for real. And I don't want either of us making the same mistake I made so long ago in thinking otherwise."

He felt her relax again. And with a sigh she leaned her forehead against his chest. "I'm that obvious, huh? Am I making this harder than it has to be, Jared?"

His hand stroked her back and she felt the rumble in his chest as he replied, "No, bab—Ta'Mara," he said, catching himself. And Ta'Mara felt herself regretting that he had. "I get it and you were right. You are right. We should take things slow. I just wanted to skip past the parts where either of us wonder about what the other is feeling towards us, now that we're finally here in-person. Was that—was that okay?"

"Jared, that was more than 'okay.'" She grinned up at him.

"Careful woman," he said, his head already leaning toward hers.

"But—" she said, before his lips landed. He groaned, and finally managed to step back a bit, giving them both space.

"What we had was so long ago. I just," she paused and looked away as she searched for the words. Returning her gaze to his, she continued, "I just don't want us to make decisions that are based off of a movie we saw over a decade ago. You know what I mean? Who's to say that movie is still relevant, today?"

He placed his hands in his pocket and shrugged as he asked, "Should we disregard the movie, totally, then?"

"No, of course not. But we can't ignore how things have changed outside of it, either. Neither of us have the excuse of age to be that naive, anymore. Change isn't always bad. But change is always...different. I don't want—"

"You don't want me walking out on you again, like I did in the last movie."

"Who's to say I wouldn't be the one walking out?" she quipped, tilting her head with a smirk.

"Touché. Who's to say, indeed." He paused, taking in every aspect of her expression. Finally, he let out the breath he hadn't realized he'd been holding, and allowed his shoulders to relax as he freed his hands to hang by his side. "Listen, I want to see you. I want to continue to get to know who you are, now. And I just don't want to delay in doing so; because I've already spent so many days regretting letting you go. So, tell me what you want. And we'll figure out together how to go about this, with our eyes wide open"

"And our lips apart."

"I don't know if I can promise that," he said, slowly inching toward her again.

She laughed, backing up and watching him trail her until her butt hit the closed door. "Good, because I don't think I can either," she admitted. With that, she let him kiss her again until they were both breathless.

Chapter 28

❋ ❋ ❋

Ta'Mara caught sight of her grin reflected in the window of the rental car she and Jared were riding in. He'd insisted on chauffeuring her around for their "date weekend" as he'd named it. She bit her lip at the memory of his hurriedly pushing her out the hotel door following their last kiss. He told her he just needed a minute to 'freshen up', preferably while she was far, far away from him. So he'd met her a few minutes later in the lobby downstairs. From there he'd led her out of the hotel, to the car that he'd scheduled to be delivered for his use.

Their first stop turned out to be a cozy little cafe situated in a shopping area in Kansas City's Waldo area, The Neighborhood Cafe. Ta'Mara had turned to Jared in surprise, and a question in her eyes, "This is my favorite spot!"

"I know," he said, a shy grin appearing on his face. "You'd mentioned it once a few weeks ago while we were talking about our favorite hangouts. Thought it might be a great way to start the day, with breakfast from our favorite spot."

Ta'Mara laughed, preparing to exit the vehicle, "Jared, you don't have to adopt it as your favorite, too, especially since you haven't even tasted the food, yet."

"It's my favorite for another reason." He watched her. "It's the place I'll remember as the site of our second first date."

Ta'Mara looked away for a moment as she processed what he said. Then, returning his gaze and his shy grin she agreed, "Huh, I guess it is."

Later, as they were finishing up their food their conversation wandered over to Jared's career path. And Ta'Mara asked, "So how is it that you can just take off from work so easily? I mean, I'm a manager where I'm at but they keep pretty good tabs on how much vacay we request. It's one of the reasons I've been wanting to get into freelancing. It's not the most stable thing but you get a lot more autonomy. And I value that," she concluded, returning her gaze at the plate on which she was now pushing food around.

Jared responded, "Well, my work is driven by projects and in between there can be significant lulls. But even within projects there's a kind of ebb and flow; because maybe we're awaiting feedback from clients or from other parts of our department. There's a pretty clear 'go' time and in-between that there's a lot of room for flexibility. Besides that, I don't ask for much time off, and my boss and I have a good rapport. He knows that when I'm requesting time off, I need it—and I guess there's not a culture of micro-managing in my company, anyway. Which I'm thankful for."

He picked up a fry and chewed on it thoughtfully. "But honestly, even if things were different I would be here, now. What I do is okay, I'm good at it. But it's not a passion, it's a living. I'd trade any job for being here with you today." He paused and smiled before picking up a fry "And any day of the week, for that matter." With a wink he popped the fry in his mouth.

Ta'Mara grinned at him, feeling her whole face and body warm at his admission.

"I remember your mentioning in one of your emails that writing isn't your passion, really, either. But neither is writing. So what is your passion, Jared?"

She asked, pushing her plate aside and leaning in to focus her attention on him.

Jared nodded. "Yeah, I don't know what my passion is, really, beyond being a good brother. Being a good representative of those who raised me. Being a good friend. A reliable, hard worker. And one day, a reliable, faithful and loving husband. And above all, being a good steward of this life God's given me, because all that other stuff flows from that relationship. So, I guess in terms of a career, I'm still figuring that out. But in terms of everything else, I feel really fulfilled. Well—" He chuckled, reaching over to place his hand on her hand,"Most everything else. I'm still working on the best part." Ta'Mara looked at the olive toned hand atop hers and resisted the urge to raise it to her lips. Mad at herself for her consistent lack of reserve this morning she managed to draw out enough strength to pull her hand from under his and reach for her plate to move it closer to her, as if to pick at its remains.

Jared sighed and straightened, his gaze still on her. "How about you?" He asked. "I know that you love your job. Is that your passion?"

She shrugged. "Nah, but I think it feeds my passions. I think 'goals' are my passion. And my goal is to be able to work from home, not even be close to worrying about paying my bills; to be able to create and develop things. And to be able to afford to invest in my own personal interests and that of others."

Jared nodded, smirking. "Yes, I could see all of that. You are one of the most goal-driven people I've ever met. You see something, and you have no fear in going after it. I love that about you."

"Well, that doesn't apply to everything in my life," she smirked, glancing up at him. "But to a lot of things, yeah." she acknowledged. "But it seems to me that I could say the same for you, Mr. 'Hey Woman," she said, her voice lowering to its deepest register as she attempted to model his, "I'm gonna travel thousands of miles. Just to see you. For a few days. See you tomorrow!' " She laughed at her own humor.

He burst out laughing, and echoed her "Hey Woman," chuckling. "Well yeah," he chimed in. "I guess I can be goal-driven, too, when given the proper motivation. But I can also admit to still being a go-with-the-flow kind of guy. I'm just putting all my cards on the table and letting you know now that I haven't grown out of that. I've matured a lot, but," he said, tapping the toe of her shoe lightly with his own. "I could sorely benefit from more structure in my life, Ta'Mara." "Uhm, I'm not trying to be somebody's mom," she rapped out quickly. Then with a sharp intake her mouth dropped open as she considered how her words might be taken by someone who lost their mom in the not too distant past. How would she have taken a similar response were it about a father? "I mean, I didn't mean to—"

He waved her concern away. "No worries, Ta'Mara, I know what you meant, and you're right. I had intended that to come off more 'inviting' than 'needy'; but obviously I left my charisma somewhere that's not here." He grinned, rubbing the back of his neck. "I'm usually way better than this when speaking with wome—with others, seriously! I was voted unofficial Marketing guru at my firm for the last two years straight."

"Unofficial—what does unofficial marketing guru mean?"

"It's like those titles you get in highschool, except even less official. The firm I'm at has the annual votes where every person gets a title. No losers, you know, that sort of thing. Mine was Marketing guru."

"For the past two years. So, what was your title before that."

"Oh, it doesn't matter, it really just amounts to a bunch of adults being kids." A deep flush crept steadily up his neck and on his face.

"Oh now I really have to know. What were your titles before then?"

Jared made a face as if it pained him to let the words pass through his teeth. "I'll just say that they were along the lines of 'Most Eligible Bachelor.'"

Ta'Mara narrowed her eyes, " 'Along the lines...'," she repeated. Now her mind would be mulling over what that could be alluding to all day. But seeing his reluctance, Ta'Mara shrugged and decided that maybe it was in both their interests to let it go. "Alright, I'll let you off the hook for now. But I won't guarantee I'm not gonna try to get that out of you at some point; cuz now I'm dying of curiosity! But, okay. Gonna shelf that topic, and go back to the original topic."

"Gladly," Jared agreed.

She paused. "Wait, what were we talking about?" Then by some miracle, she remembered. "Oh, yeah, you were saying how you're still a free-spirit and I was saying how I'm still—not. You know I'd always admired that you had no qualms about living in the moment; being so aware and honoring of whatever you were feeling that you were able to do what was right for you. It was never about doing what everybody else did or what the world around us tells us is the right thing to do. The right way to walk through the phases of life. I just—I just always appreciated that freedom. It's kinda like a super power. As much as I naturally enjoy being thoughtful about what the next steps could bring, I also acknowledge that I can overthink and—just not allow myself to be as present as others seem to be able to be."

They sat in silence for a while as Jared considered what she'd shared with him. He leaned back against the cushion of the booth they sat in and pondered, "Well, I think that's why we all need each other. I mean, in general. People need each other. We help offset one another's weaknesses. That's what I'd meant to allude to earlier with my cryptic come-on, actually."

Ta'Mara's tongue peeked out between her teeth as she teased him. "I knew that. I was just giving you a hard time. But it backfired."

Jared agreed, groaning.

Chapter 29

✻ ✻ ✻

The remainder of their day entailed stops at several spots that Jared had pulled straight from their online conversations: Union Station, Loose Park, Betty Rae's Ice Cream. It was early evening when he finally brought Ta'Mara to the hotel so she could pick up her car and get a few hours of rest in her own home before he'd pick her up for his last surprise trip of the day.

✻ ✻ ✻

Ta'Mara was not one for staying up late. As she'd gotten older she'd found it more and more attractive to be in bed by 9:00 o'clock pm. But here it was, well past her bedtime and she found herself wide awake, looking out the window of Jared's rented sedan wondering where they were headed.

It took a while but at some point Ta'Mara realized the route they were on would bring them past one of her favorite little restaurants located just beyond the city lines. Her family used to come here whenever they were returning from a visit with family in Columbia, Missouri. So many memories came flooding back to her and her heart sped up in anticipation of viewing her family's old haunt, even at 60+ miles per hour. So when Jared slowed and pulled into the restaurant's nearly empty parking lot Ta'Mara's jaw dropped, her gaze swinging to meet Jared's.

"My family used to come here all the time! How did you know about this place?"

"You told me all about it, Ta'Mara."

"Really, I don't remember mentioning anything about my family trips in our emails. That's funny."

"No, it was the first time you'd taken me to your favorite restaurant in LA."

Realization began to dawn in Ta'Mara's eyes.

"You were wearing one of those princess dresses, I think they're called that. It was a burnt red, and it looked great on your complexion. It was also one of the first times I got to see you in something other than your sweats. Although I loved seeing you in your sweats, too, don't get me wrong."

Ta'Mara could feel the tears knocking at the back of her eyes.

"You told me about how your father and mother had made this their tradition before you were born, when they'd visit your mom's side of the family out-of-town. And then after you were born, it became a place that held so many wonderful memories of seeing your mother and father reminisce and joke with one another. And meet-up with staff that'd been in the restaurant for years."

Jared shrugged and offered a soft smile. "This is my way of showing you that I want to share those kinds of memories with you, too. If that's okay."

Ta'Mara looked at Jared, overwhelmed by the day culminating with this gesture. "Jared, I—I don't know what to say."

"How about, 'Jared, I'm starving. Let's eat!'?" Jared grinned.

Ta'Mara grinned in return and with a nod, they exited the car to head for the doors.

"I'm surprised it's still open," she said, "When I was young they used to close pretty early. I remember we would sometimes find ourselves rushing to make it in the doors and claim a seat so that we'd have enough time to eat before they closed."

Jared opened the door for her and followed her indoors. The place was empty, but for one table with the light above it. Candles and white linen adorned the tabletop, alongside the same large white plates and simple glassware she remembered from her youth. An older gentleman came out from the door that led to the kitchen, wiping his hands on a towel and grinning from ear to ear at the couple before him.

"Ah, I see you've made it after all." He came over and gently picked up Ta'Mara's hand to place a very light kiss on the back. Ta'Mara could only smile, wide-eyed as she was at the scene before her. "Mr. Potter! I, uhm—Jared?" She threw a questioning glance up at Jared, who had come to stand beside her.

"You're beau here," the older man said, jerking his chin toward Jared, "Has reserved a table for you two. And only for you two." The man winked at Jared. "And I can see why." He turned back to Ta'Mara. "I can already tell that you've grown into a charming young woman. I remember you from when your parents would bring you in. It's been a long time, but who could forget that smile. I hope you still like our sweet potato pie a la mode. Sally, my wife, you remember her. She made a whole pie special for ya'll. She's just so tickled at the idea of a young man courting a woman like one should. And I gotta say, I am too. Nice to see."

He clapped Jared on the back before walking toward their table, the expectation being for them to follow.

Ta'mara felt Jared's hand apply gentle pressure on her back as he guided her beside them behind Mr. Potter.

Once seated, and after Mr. Potter had asked about her parents before returning to the kitchen, Ta'Mara just looked at Jared for a moment. "You reserved the whole cafe?" she laughed.
"I wanted you to myself, what can I say?" Jared grinned. He reached across the table to place his hand on hers. She turned her hand, palm up, to meet his. His grin widened, as did hers.

"I'd give you the moon and stars, if I could, Ta'Mara. I know that's a cheesy line, but I can tell you that I also know how sincere that thought is. I'd give you the world on a platter. But I'm not quite in that tax bracket." Ta'Mara chuckled with him.

"Jared, I can't tell you how special this is. My mom and I—" she looked away, out the window. When she turned to him again tears glistened in her eyes. "After dad passed, neither of us could bring ourselves to come here without him. It was like, we just didn't want to make new memories here that didn't include him, I guess. Or maybe the memories felt like they might overwhelm us. I don't know."

She squeezed his hand. "Thank you, for helping me enjoy those memories, while still knowing that there's room for new ones."

Mr. Potter was warm and inviting throughout the dinner service he provided them. And ever the professional, he moved in and out of the scene smoothly, filling their glasses without ever interrupting the flow of conversation. With their pie nearly finished, Ta'Mara found herself regretful to see the night coming to a close. But then a familiar tune began playing over the cafe's speaker system, the volume increasing as the strains of one of her favorite songs filled the space.

She looked at Jared who was looking at her, slightly nodding to the orchestral melody of Ron Sexmith's "Whatever It Takes".

Jared slid out of his seat, his hand extended toward hers as he began mouthing the words to her. She took his hand, allowing him to guide her into the aisle of the cafe where he held her close, moving them both to the rhythm of his serenade.

She could feel the timber of his voice reverberate throughout her body as he began to quietly sing to her. He'd always had a nice voice, but over the years it'd deepened and his control of it strengthened. Ta'Mara could feel herself melting in his arms as he recounted the song's promise, that the singer would make certain to find the path that'd bring these two lonely hearts together.

The song that followed was her other Sexsmith favorite, "Right About Now". She knew what was coming from the first strands of the R&B-like offering; and she drank in the sight of Jared watching her as he hummed the first line leading up to the chorus and then began singing along as Mr. Sexmith confessed, to his audience of one, how much he needed their love.

~ Quint Emm Ellis ~

When the chorus returned, Ta'Mara found her courage, and her voice. Breathily, she introduced hers, entwining her voice with Jared's. And if her harmony was a bit off, no one seemed to mind.

In the background Ron didn't skip a beat as Jared and Ta'Mara sealed their serenades with a variety of kisses.

***

“I feel like I was supposed to make this way more difficult than I have,” Ta'Mara said, laughing, as she and Jared walked hand in hand to her front door an hour later.

“Make ‘what’ more difficult,” he asked, teasing. “My wooing you?”

“Exactly,” she responded, chuckling. “I'm just—amazed at how much thought you put into everything. I'm...moved,” she admitted. “Obviously,” she said, raising up their clasped hands between them as evidence, the coffee and cream of their fingers interwoven.

"Good," he remarked as they stopped to stand before her entrance. "Then my work here—has just begun." He raised their clasped hands to glide his lips across her thumb and the back of her hand before lowering their hands and releasing hers.

He pointed his chin in the direction of her door. "I'm just gonna make sure you get in alright."

Flustered, Ta'Mara realized that that was his way of prompting her to get her keys out. Honestly, she'd been preparing herself for another heat missile of a kiss! Turning around to face the door, she tried to reason to herself that he was being a gentleman. But once inside, facing him with the door ajar, she couldn't deny that she still hoped he'd lean in for a goodnight kiss.

Instead, he began walking backwards towards his car. ""Mālama pono, Ta'Mara," he said, gently, still facing her. And with that, he turned and walked into the night.

"Mālama pono, Jared," she said quietly, knowing he hadn't heard her; but knowing too that he felt it, all the same.

That night, as he prayed, he asked the Lord to watch over her. He asked God to help Ta'Mara guard her heart. No matter what that looked like—even if the results didn't favor Jared's own desires. And that, in the same way, the Lord would help him guard his, as well. He asked the Lord to give him the wisdom needed over the course of their next few days together, and in whatever may come to follow. Jared confessed that, as much love as he felt for Ta'Mara, that he knew that the Lord loved her so much more; so Jared prayed that God would give him the kind of love needed to protect, care for, appreciate, value and respect Ta'Mara the way the Lord desired of him. And he asked the Holy Spirit to soften both their hearts toward the Lord so that He could preside over their relationship and guide it into one that aligns with God's will, vs. their own.

He prayed for Ta'Mara's personal relationship with Jesus Christ as their Lord and Savior, that it would continue to grow and be strengthened as time went on. He prayed that the Lord would lend her his wisdom when it came to daily life decisions, whether it be at work, on the road, or even in the grocery store. And that the Lord would also keep her eyes on the Lord, even in those times when she falters, misses the mark, sins; Jared prayed that Ta'Mara would maintain and nurture a contrite Spirit, the willingness to repent and the fortitude to always get back up; that she would walk in the identity and peace and hope and joy that was rooted in the One who knows her best and loves her most deeply.

Then Jared prayed, again, for the Lord's reinforcement of strength; because his own meager reserves of restraint were already wearing thin.

Chapter 30

✳ ✳ ✳

The next day Jared arrived to pick Ta'Mara up at nine o'clock sharp and waited patiently in his car until she joined him at ten after.

"Sorry," she said as she settled her belongings in her lap and twisted to secure her seat belt. That done, she relaxed into the seat and turned to Jared with a grin, "It takes time to look this good." She then chuckled, though she was speaking truth. She'd planned her outfits the same night that she and Jared had decided he'd make the trip down to Kansas City. Yet yesterday and today she found herself scrapping her plans for her hair, makeup and wardrobe. Today, she wore one of her nicer pairs of fitted jeans, despite the fact that she was aware that they'd be going trail walking later. At the last moment she'd decided to sacrifice practicality for pretty. But she felt great in it, the t-shirt she'd selected with the flannel long-sleeved shirt over it, its shirt tails tied loosely in the front. All of that topped off with her well-worn "rugged" boots, as she called them.

"You're well worth the wait." He said, in all earnestness, reaching over to grasp her hand. She covered his hand with her own and found herself biting her lip as she stared at him, watching as he turned to check for traffic before pulling them away from the curb and starting them on their way.

She caressed the hand he kept casually on hers and mused aloud, "Is it just me or does this feel eerie how comfortable this is—it almost feels like no time has passed at all."

A chuckle rose from him and she watched as a grin spread across his face, as well. "Yeah, actually, I'm pretty blown away, myself. But in the best way. It's always felt 'right' with you and no matter what else has changed, I'm very glad to see that that hasn't." They slowed to a stop at a light and he took that moment to look over at her. "I still can't believe I'm not conjuring up some really amazing, hyper-realistic dream. I swear if I wake up from this...I'm going right back to sleep."

She burst out laughing at that.

✽ ✽ ✽

The car meandered into the parking lot and found it's spot among the small group of other vehicles parked. As Ta'Mara and Jared exited the sound of gravel welcomed them as they began their way across with Ta'Mara leading the way to her mother's cottage.

When Jared had asked Ta'Mara what she'd like him to incorporate into their trip he'd been both pleased and intimidated with her invitation to finally meet her mother, face-to-face. He'd talked with both her father and mother years before through video calls. But there's nothing like engaging with someone in-person. There's nothing more revealing.

He'd been pleased at her suggestion because he already knew he'd love the woman that raised the woman that he's never stopped loving—though he knew better than to outright confess that much to Ta'Mara at this point of their reunion. He'd bide his time.

Conversely, he'd been intimidated by her suggestion because he recognized that, if only for the sake of Ta'Mara's peace of mind and therefore his own, he needed her mother's blessing on their attempt at renewing their relationship. And his last interaction with her parents had, understandably, left a sour note with them when it concerned their beloved daughter. He was a bit nervous as he anticipated the reception he might receive; but no matter if he were received with reservation or open arms, for him the goal was the same: to find a way to convey the change in his nature and the steadfastness of his desire for and admiration of their daughter.

Initially, Ta'Mara had been unsure of her decision to invite Jared to meet her mother so early on in their quest to learn about each other. She wondered if it would be too soon, since she'd be early on in her own assessment of how she felt about him. Would it be wise or fair to place their relationship under the gaze of one who would no doubt approach the prospect of his reemergence in her life with a critical eye, she'd wondered? However, in the space provided by the quiet of this morning she'd had room to consider how quickly she and Jared had fallen into rhythm with one another, prompted by the force of nature that an older, more experienced Jared had become. Maybe she needed an anchor to keep her from drifting off, from getting lost in a sea of emotion churned up by a mix of hurt, hope, familiarity—and lust.

They were both quiet as they checked-in with the office and walked toward her mother's residence.

Finally, she gestured toward the entrance of one of the cottages and threw Jared a quick reassuring smile as they made their way to the doorstep and Ta'Mara rang the doorbell. She then slipped her hand into his while awaiting to hear her mother's voice through the door. Though she promised herself that she'd remain open to considering her mom's observations, even if they were negative, she couldn't deny the way she felt for Jared, nor the bond that'd been dusted off and revealed to be alive and thrumming with life. And she could also tell that he was nervous, and she wanted to assure him that he was not alone in the feelings the past day had brought to the surface, even in this. She wanted to assure him that she was just with him.

"Who is it?" asked her mother, her voice muffled across the barrier.

"Momma, it's me. Me and Jared," she added, squeezing his hand and feeling his grip tighten on hers in response.

The door cracked open and her mothers fair face peeked out. Lavania's eyes met Jared's first, before she looked him over with her lips pressed together as if looking for any loose thread she might spot. Then with a nod she turned her gaze to her daughter and her face immediately softened as she swung the door wide and stepped back to let the pair in.

Jared gestured for Ta'Mara to enter first and he followed behind her, observing as she and her mother greeted one another, hugged and kissed one another's cheek.

When Lavania turned to Jared, she straightened and fell silent. "Mrs. Lawson, " he began, nodding his head in respect toward her. "I'd actually rehearsed some words to say to you at this moment, but I seem to have forgotten them," he said with a chuckle. Mrs. Lawson failed to mirror his mirth. This was going to be rough. "I'm—I'm beyond grateful that you've invited me into your home today. And I really hope that this is just the first of many gatherings to come." He looked over at Ta'Mara who beamed back at him, her smile bright and unheeded.

Lavania looked from him to her daughter and back again, and then, inhaling deeply, her shoulders rose and fell as a deep sigh escaped her. "Well," she said, moving toward the dining room table, "Let's see what you're about, Jared. Come on over and take a seat. I hope you're hungry. I made us all a little something to eat," she continued, walking to the kitchen while Ta'Mara led Jared to the table.

Truth be told, Jared's stomach was too tied up knots right now to fathom introducing food to it, but he wasn't a dumb man. "That sounds wonderful, Mrs Lawson. It smells delicious here."

Once they were both seated Ta'Mara turned to him. "You alright?" she inquired in a low voice, her hand on Jared's.

He nodded. The fact that she'd noted his discomfort and cared went a long way in quelling his nerves. She patted his hand and stood, kissing him on the cheek. "I'm just gonna go help my mom. Be back." He nodded again and she smiled once more before leaving to join her mother.

They returned with Ta'Mara carrying two fully loaded plates and her mom carrying a smaller, less densely packed plate to the table. Ta'Mara set the heftier plate in front of Jared and set the other plate in front of herself. Despite the circumstances of it, she couldn't help but feel buoyed by the fact that she was seated between the two living people who were most significant in her world. But she also realized she had no idea how to get the conversational ball rolling in the right direction—or even what the right direction was for that conversation.

Thankfully, Jared stepped in. "Mrs. Lawson, will you be saying grace or would you like me to do the honors?"

Lavania's eyebrow arched and she tilted her head as she assessed Jared with surprise, and then turned to openly share that look with her daughter who'd responded with a proud smirk. Turning back to Jared, Lavania nodded for him to lead their small group in prayer. They all bowed their heads.

"Dear Father," he began, "Thank you for this day, and for this time together with people we love." At that, Lavania looked up at Jared who's eyes were still closed. Glancing at her daughter she could see that her eyes were open as well, though she'd trained them to remain on the table. But she didn't miss the myriad of emotions splayed across Ta'Mara's face.

"I pray that you would guide our conversation," Jared continued, "and that you would help me not to make a fool of myself in front Ta'Mara's mother." Ta'Mara chuckled at that. "I also pray that you would bless

Ta'Mara's mother and keep her, and continue to bless the relationship that she and Ta'Mara enjoy. May your light shine upon them both. In Jesus' name, Amen."

Jared opened his eyes to find Ta'Mara's mother watching him.

"Alright Jared," she said, nodding. A long, weighty pause hung between the two as Jared held her gaze. With one final nod, she picked up her fork and pointed to her plate with its tines. "Tell me what you think. I've been trying out new recipes from this cookbook I borrowed from a neighbor." She cut into her smaller portions of the breakfast she'd created for them all, breaking some of the tension.

Chapter 31

✳ ✳ ✳

After they'd eaten, the three of them moved their surprisingly light-hearted conversation to the living room where they now sat comfortably. But it didn't take long for the real reason for the visit to surface.

"I'm going to get right to the elephant in the room, Jared," Mrs. Lawson said with authority. "You broke my baby's heart once. So what are your plans for my daughter this time? What are you planning on doing differently?"

"Well," he said with his most charming grin, "I can't lay all my cards out on the table right in front of Ta'Mara."

"Uhm, I'm right here, ya'll. What's this talking about me like I'm invisible." Ta'Mara interjected, more bemused than offended.

"Shhhhh, hon. We're talking," came her mom's easy reply.

Ta'Mara stared at her mom, mouth agape. But then shook her head and relaxed against the sofa's cushion. She'd just sit back and enjoy the show, she guessed. All she needed was some popcorn.

"Jared, if you value my opinion of you at all, you're gonna need to lay your cards out right here. So you, and me, and Ta'Mara can hold you accountable to your own words. So?"

Jared took a few moments to assess Mrs. Lawson's stance, and finally his shoulders slumped as he recognized there was no going around it.

Pointedly avoiding looking at Ta'Mara he addressed Mrs. Lawson. "Ma'am, I plan on marrying your daughter as soon as she's ready to say 'Yes.'"

Lavania tilted her head to assess him once again, and a hint of a smile crossed her lips as she stole a glance at her daughter. The smile made itself more apparent as he could only imagine the expression her mother was witnessing on her daughter's face.

Before Ta'Mara could say anything her mother turned back to Jared.

"And then?"

"And then?" Jared echoed.

"Yes, because there's more to life than getting the girl and a wedding. The real meat and potatoes is what you do once you've got all that. There's a whole big life that follows. There's the mess that follows, along with the beauty...and the fun. It's not like marriage fixes everything. Or anything for that matter, if it's not the right thing to do or if it's just plain ol' broken to begin with. So what makes you think you're ready for marriage, now? Seems you weren't when you two first met."

"You're right. I was a fool. And I won't pretend to be perfected now, but I'm not the same man who takes for granted the gifts that God grants me. I've always remembered the verse that Ta'Mara's father once mentioned during one of our video chats. 'It's the glory of God to hide a matter. And the honor of kings to seek it out.' No king starts out as a king, right? They have to grow and be groomed into the type of person who can distinguish between that which is worth ignoring and that which is worth throwing aside all of their kingdom for. I'd like to think that a king who has suffered great loss at his own hands would not soon forget the cost of his own foolishness."

"So you think you're a king?

"Ma'am, you know the Word as well—if not better—than I. We," he waved his hand to encompass all three of them, "are kings and priests, according to what God says about those who seek His will on earth, and in their own lives, above their own."

"Hmmmm," Lavania hummed to herself, a spark of delight glinting in her eyes. "You remind me of him in some ways. Ta'Mara's father." Her gaze took on a distant look as she recalled moments that only she was privy to. "Yes, that was one of Ta'Mara's father's favorite verses. He and I went through some tough times. And times will get tough whenever you're dealing with two people trying to live one life. But we never faced those times alone. We never turned our backs on one another—we held on to the Lord, even when we wanted to let go of one another. And that's the kind of commitment it takes to make it in a relationship. It takes commitment. It takes courage. It takes love—of God first—so that you can maintain love for your spouse. And Jared, I'm just gonna be straight with you here: maybe it's better to admit if you don't have enough of any of those things to stay the course. I think it's better for everyone involved, in my opinion. And that's just my opinion. But it's rooted in experience. So I hope you'll consider my words."

Jared nodded, allowing her words to sink in and have the space they deserved for both himself and Ta'Mara. Finally, he responded. "I agree with that, Mrs. Lawson. I greatly value your insight and I need to hear it. I'm not here to hide my mistakes or ignore them. I'm here to confront them and overcome them. And I think that takes courage, too. I hope that we can agree on that, as well." Jared responded, holding her gaze.

Ta'Mara's mom held his gaze in return; then a beat later she nodded once. "Hmm," she said. "Well, I've said my piece, you've said yours." She got up then, heading toward the kitchen. "You all want some coffee? I'm going to fix myself a cup. So just let me know."

And that was the sum of that portion of their conversation as far as Mrs. Lawson was concerned. When she'd returned, she asked them about their plans for the day.

* * *

Not too long after, Jared and Ta'Mara stood at the threshold of Mrs. Lawson's door, preparing to set out on their day.

"I'm not fully on board with you, quite yet, Jared," Ta'Mara's mom warned as the couple stood together. "I mean, you all just got together yesterday!" Her lips pressed together momentarily until she glanced over at her daughter; and Mrs. Lawson's demeanor softened. "Time will tell. And I see how happy you make my baby. And that's all I could ever want. I couldn't ask for more than my baby to have someone who loves God and sees her through His eyes. So that right there means the world. But understand," she said, the steel returning to her the gaze that now regarded him, "...this is the last second chance you'll get with *me*."

"I only need one second chance, Ma'am. I promise you that."

"Well, alright." After a beat, she let her gaze soften again. "I hope I'll see you again, Jared."

"God willing—and Ta'Mara willing," he said with a wink cast in Ta'Mara's direction.

That elicited the first real laugh he'd gotten out of Lavania.

"Alright, come here and give me a hug. Just in case I do end up cursing you out after this at least I get my hug while the gettin' is good. Not that I would curse, of course" She smiled at him, her eyes twinkling.

Jared immediately walked to her and bent down to embrace the shorter woman who raised her arms to him. She hugged him then; and he was reminded of his own mother at that moment. When they parted he found himself grinning like a little boy, a little overwhelmed at how quickly he'd grown to value the mother before him. In her eyes, he could see the dawning of genuine affection toward him as well, and in that he felt a sense of relief that surprised him. He realized that he'd not only wanted her blessing for Ta'Mara's well-being, he'd wanted her blessing for his own, as well.

His own family's redemptive view of him had aided in his ability to forgive himself. But it meant something wholly different for Ta'Mara's surviving parent to discern the same possibility of there being a new beginning stored up within him.

He watched as Ta'Mara gave her mother one last, long hug. As they talked softly to one another he mused at what'd brought them to this long awaited moment. So. Many. Years. Filled with disappointment, incomplete pictures, assumptions, yearnings. But also memories—the echoes of two hearts that'd been brought together and had become one, and had remained so. Entwined. That's what they were.

✳ ✳ ✳

They were soon on their way back to the car, their arms wrapped around one another's waists; their hips bumping at intervals.

They arrived back at his car the way they'd left, in mutual quiet. He went over to open the door for her and, once she was settled he ran over to the driver's side and slid himself in. Once inside, he visibly relaxed against the seat, his head on the headrest and eyes closed as he exhaled, "That was rough."

"You're telling me," Ta'Mara agreed, laughing. How was it that even raw, sober moments could hold so much humor for her when she was with Jared? She rubbed his arm, enjoying the feel of his muscle beneath her hand. Maybe too much, so she returned her hand to her lap. "You did good, Jared. You did amazing, actually."

"You think it went alright," he stated, looking at her.

"Yeah, I do," she said, her own astonishment in her voice. "I really didn't know what to expect or envision as the best outcome from this. But, I feel like this is the most," she paused as she tried to find the word. "The most sustainable, reliable."

"Sustainable," he echoed, chuckling at her characteristic pragmatism as he turned the key in the ignition and placed his hand on the gear shift.

"Yeah," she went on to explain, "It's realistic, which makes it a stable foundation that can be built upon. My mom's a romantic, but she's also my Mom. I feel like this was as good of a compromise we could hope for with those two things in mind. She's willing to give 'us' a chance; which makes me feel a little better about falling so—" she hesitated to finish her thought. Maybe there was only so much transparency that she could handle displaying—only so far she could go in placing her heart on her sleeve.

"Falling so..." he prompted.

She shook her head. "I'm just really glad with how things turned out."

He nodded, his gaze seeming to devour her before he turned his attention back to the rearview mirror.

They weren't there yet; they weren't in the place they'd once been where she'd been so open regarding her feelings about him. They were getting there, and he wouldn't push it. But his heart strained in his chest at the premise of hearing her express her feelings toward him now.

Patience, he told himself, yet again. It'll be that much sweeter when we get there.

Chapter 32

Their day continued with a hike on a Missouri trail Jared had googled while he was in California. It wasn't a long trek, about an hour and half round trip. Yet the terrain was incredibly diverse, the well worn path winding under a canopy of tall trees whose fall leaves littered the sky and the ground with yellows, browns, oranges, greens and reds. The path eventually opened up as they arrived at their destination: a man-made waterfall that filled their ears with the magical sound of rushing water. They sat together on a large rock situated near the resulting brook, enjoying the feel of holding one another's hand, breathing in the air made fresh and crisp by the flowing water.

It all was reminiscent of the trips she and Jared would take in Pasadena along the Eagle Rock trail. She inwardly laughed at the pair they'd made when Jared had initially accepted her invitation. They'd had to stop several times for Jared to catch his breath. She glanced over at Jared now, who was laying down, allowing his feet to dangle over the edge of the rock they were on. His eyes were closed, one arm slung over his face as if he were asleep. But his hand remained loosely clasping hers, occasionally he would squeeze or caress her hand with his thumb. The walk hadn't phased him; and she'd inwardly thanked him for the casual pace she figured he was keeping for her sake. Still, Ta'Mara had had to try her best not to let her huffing and puffing be too obvious. There was no way to hide her sweating buckets, though.

Nothing like exercise to kill her buzz. But the waterfall, no matter how small, had managed to wash away the anxiety that'd crept up on her. Now, she only felt the calm that came with the privilege of being able to shut out the rest of the world for a brief period of time.

She felt Jared's hand lift from hers as he worked himself back into a seated position beside her. He adjusted himself so that his locked arms supported the weight of his upper body, with one arm positioned behind her.

"So I'm curious about something." He waited for Ta'Mara to angle her head his way, his profile still toward her. "Why haven't you said anything about the conversation your mother and I had this morning? I mean, I guess what I really mean is, what did you think about it?"

He turned to look at her now. His eyes met hers, then darted around her face as if he was attempting to record every inch of it to his memory. His eyes lingered a good while on her mouth before slowly raising back up to meet her gaze.

She looked away, turning her head slightly to face the waterfall, instead.

"I—well, it was interesting watching two people I care about talk about me as if I wasn't even there, if that's what you mean." She chuckled and risked a glance back at him.

He tilted his head, studying her before redirecting his gaze to the waterfall, as well before responding. "Look, I'm not trying to push you into anything. I just—I'd just like to get a bead on how what I said struck you."

It was her turn to watch him, now. She noticed the flush rising up his neck and along his cheeks as she did so and tried to understand what this moment must feel like to him. He was asking for a little direction, and she was being elusive.

She licked her lips, inhaling as she sat up a little straighter and regarded her own hands in her lap. She began rubbing the palm of one hand with the thumb of the other hand as she considered her next words.

"Jared, I don't want to disappoint you. But I don't know how I feel about...that."

Jared nodded, still facing the waterfall but his eyelids lowered as he absorbed her honesty.

"By 'that," he said, the word coming out more tersely than he'd wanted, "you mean the possibility of marriage, right? Or, is it the possibility of marriage to me, specifically?"

Whoa, this conversation got real deep, real quick. Ta'Mara's shoulders slumped; she realized this is something she'd been considering for a long time and that the extremes of the past couple days—of the past few hours!—was possibly serving as a catalyst to crystalize her thoughts.

"No, that's not it. I mean, not you specifically. I've been single for longer than most people would care to admit...but you know, I've had the space to learn who I am. What I like, what I like to do. And I actually really enjoy 'me'. And I also value the autonomy that comes with not having to concern myself with someone else's feelings and desires and schedule or expectations. Maybe I even covet that." She grimaced at the admission. "As much as I might've wanted a relationship—I mean, I think I want one as much as anyone else—but I've always wondered if I might lose myself in it." She paused, directing her words at him. "Again."

Inhaling deeply through her nose she concluded her thoughts. "I just hear so many married couples—married women, mostly—talk about the hardships of marriage, the sacrifices made that oftentimes seem unbalanced. I want companionship. I do get lonely," she admitted, shrugging one shoulder. "But I'm also oddly at peace with that...and I don't know how to reconcile both of those feelings. It's just kinda hard to see the benefits for me in the equation at this point in my life, besides sex." She bit her lip and chuckled as she glanced his way. "If I'm real about it, I want all the good stuff," she said, throwing both her hands in the air for emphasis. "But I'm not so sure about the rest. And I don't want to regret such a huge decision. It changes your whole life—as it should. But I don't know if I'm ready to submit myself to what may come from choosing that road, anymore. I couldn't do that to myself or anyone else unless I could promise us both that I believed I was ready and willing to walk through hell and highwater with them. And that they were willing to do the same with me."

Jared had turned to look at her while she spoke. His face remained unreadable throughout.

"Does that sound selfish, or narcissistic or something?" She asked, a bit defiantly. She hadn't meant to sound so defensive; but though she didn't feel a sense of shame regarding her sentiments she could already tell that she valued Jared's insight enough to add weight to his perspective of them.

"What it sounds like, to me," he began, "is that you're just giving me some direction. You're telling me, 'Jared, give me a lifetime consisting of nothing but faithfulness, romantic weekends and plenty of sex and you've got yourself a wife." He chuckled and Ta'Mara laughed with him, her surprise at his remark prompting her to hit his shoulder.

"Whatever," she said through her laughter, rolling her eyes.

"And I say," Jared continued, "You've got a deal. So I guess we've got that settled."

"Lies," Ta'Mara prodded, still laughing.

Jared exhaled. Straightening in his sitting position and finally slumping to match her own relaxed one. "It doesn't matter how it sounds to me, Ta'Mara. I asked you for an honest answer. You gave it to me. I just wish it were different...but you can't fault me for that, right?"

"I mean, I'm not saying I don't want marriage, I'm just saying—"

"—You're just giving me the oldest line in the book, 'It's not you, Jared, it's me.'"

"No, not true. Jared, I'm saying I have no idea what I want, but that's the one thing that I do know. But maybe it's easier for me to come to that conclusion because it's not like I have guys falling all over me, or something. Add to that fact that I'm picky and I've been told that I'm not 'open', whatever that means and 'voila'; my reward is the gift of space to think a lot about this stuff."

Jared nodded. "Well, I know I want marriage, obviously."

"Jared, not that I'm complaining but, you're an attractive, thoughtful, Christian man who wants marriage. How is it that you're not married? With kids, the house, the whole nine yards?"

He looked at her then, long. "I've dated a few ladies at my church or that I've met through Christian functions. It just never really seemed to click. Maybe I'm picky, too, Ta'Mara. Or maybe it's the fact that whenever I've considered my life with someone," he looked at her from beneath his lashes, "I've pictured you. So," he shrugged, "Yeah, it's—it's kinda surprising that we'd be brought together right now and not be in similar places, at least in that general area. I could understand if your reservations were about me, specifically. But that's something I can at least work toward trying to resolve for us—"

"Do you feel like you're wasting your time here?" she found herself blurting out.

"No. No," he responded immediately, reaching over and grasping her hands in one of his. "This has been the best—hold on," and with his other hand he dug his phone out of his pocket to check the time. Placing it down on the rock's surface he continued, "this has been the best Twenty-six hours and eighteen minutes I've had in about fifteen years."

"Aw," Ta'Mara found herself gushing.

"No. I just wish things could be different. I wish I could snap my fingers and you'd say, 'Jared, I'd marry you today.'" He snapped his fingers and waited.

"Nice try, dork," Ta'Mara laughed, nudging his shoulder once again.

He pretended to study his fingers. "Guess I need to get these things fixed. Obviously broken."

"Obviously," Ta'Mara chuckled.

She shrugged. "Maybe it's good that this came out now, versus three months from now, or something. I mean, I wish I had a more definite answer but at the same time, I do care for you." She looked away, her tone softer, quieter.

~ Quint Emm Ellis ~

"I've never stopped caring for you, Jared. And I don't want to be the reason that you miss out on whatever God has for you." She couldn't bring herself to say "whoever" God has for him.

"Oh, don't think this changes anything for me," Jared said, causing her gaze to swing back to meet his. "You're not getting away from me so easily." He pointed his finger in the air, "I'll not be a fool twice," he said, his voice a dramaticized interpretation of a Greek scholar.

She'd forgotten just how much of a goofball Jared was, and Ta'Mara was loving every reminder. "You are so goofy."

"You make me that way, Ta'Mara. I'm straight up stupid goofy over you."

Sobering, he reached out and caressed her cheek, and her eyes fluttered closed momentarily, allowing her senses to hone in on his touch. Her eyes opened to a deep brown gaze that bore steadily into her own.

"I see you, Ta'Mara," he said, lightly grasping her chin. "I see the beauty you were, the beauty you are—and I see glimpses of the beauty you are becoming. And I selfishly want to embrace as much of your honesty, tenacity, curiosity, tenderness and everything else in my life as I can. I want you. So until you tell me otherwise, or the Lord tells me differently, I'm gonna pursue this pearl—and all the grit that she comes with—with the hope that, one day, she'll agree to mix our beauty and mix our grit and work out a life that I believe will be even better than what we could ever produce apart. But at least now I have a little clearer picture of things. You're not just figuring out what's right for us. You're figuring out what's right for you, right? So. That's fair."

Ta'Mara observed the compassion and sincerity in his eyes, felt it in his voice and his touch. At that moment, as her hand rose of its own accord to caress his arm, she wondered if his snap might've worked, after all.

They remained seated on that rock for a while, their hands intertwined between them as they stared into the water and allowed one another time for needed introspection. Other hikers came and went and they greeted them with a smile or a wave, as was customary. But the sound of the waterfall surrounded them in a bubble. And Ta'Mara couldn't remember a time when she'd felt so comfortable in silence with anyone. With anyone other than Jared, that is. She looked over at him, at his profile. This man, whom she knew she still loved, flew thousands of miles to be with her. And she was inclined to believe him to have changed from the boy who's insecurities caused an unimaginable rift between them. This man was the same Jared that'd initially captured her heart; but he was also Jared the writer; the man who'd intrigued her in so many online conversations; the gentleman who unabashedly pursued her now; the man who loved God with understanding, humility and ferocity. Not to mention he was smoking hot. What sane woman—especially Christian woman— would consider any answer other than "yes" to the prospect of embracing a life with him?

Jared turned to look at her then, his eyes blazing with the impact of feeling her lengthy regard of him. He scooted himself just close enough to pick up their clasped hands and bring her fingers to his lips, keeping his gaze on her and her reaction to him. He opened her hand and placed a soft kiss on the skin at the center of her palm, watching as her eyes became hooded. He placed another kiss just below that, and then on her wrist, moving down her arm millimeters, his tongue intermittently darting out as if to taste her.

When he heard and watched her whisper his name in a moan he growled, and had to close his eyes momentarily before reversing the course his lips had made, slowly working his way back up to her palm before enclosing her hand in his, once again, and placing their entangled fingers on his right thigh. If nothing else, he knew that Ta'Mara wanted him physically as much as he wanted her; despite everything else, in that they were in full agreement. And that made things very, very difficult.

He regarded her, a twinkle in his eye and smirk on his face as he asked her, "So, you up for a little afternoon delight?"

Ta'Mara's hooded gaze gave way to a look of wide-eyed shock. "What?!" She snatched her hand from his, her cheeks growing warm, along with every other part of her body.

"Why lunch, of course." Jared said, a full grin taking on his face now. "Whatever else could you think I meant," he said in his best feminine southern drawl, his left hand raising to clutch invisible pearls.

Ta'Mara looked at him sternly before busting out laughing. "You know that was wrong," she admonished, lightly hitting him on his arm. He grimaced as if in pain from her tap, before rising to his feet. He offered his hand to her; and she hesitated, a bit concerned that she might end up pulling him down rather than the other way around. But she quickly banished that thought and trusted that the chips would fall where they should. Placing her hand in his she allowed him to help her up, relieved to find that he was strong enough to do so without much effort. He looked down at her, a soft smile on his face. Suddenly his expression went blank and he whipped his head around to look at the spot where he'd just been seated.

He gently released her hand so that he could check his pockets.

"What's wrong," Ta'Mara asked, concerned.

"My phone." He said, as he turned fully to look back at the empty space on the rock where he'd sat. His shoulder rose in a deep, resigned inhale and exhale. "I think my phone has decided to go for a swim."

Ta'Mara followed his gaze to the rock and her mouth dropped. "Oh no!"

She went over to where he'd sat and knelt down, peering into the water. "Oh, I see it!" After a moment's hesitation she gritted her teeth, pushed the cuff of her flannel above her elbow, and reached into the water, praying that no fish—or anything else—decided to cozy up against her skin at that moment. She'd freak out, she knew it. Thankfully, the clear water showed the phone clearly, but not its depth. The stream bed was further down than she'd thought and she soon found herself repositioning herself to lay down on the rock to reach further. Just as she was about to make her second attempt to reach out Jared was laying beside her, his arm darting into the water and deftly removing the renegade phone from the watery depths.

They both sat back up, Jared's entire arm glistening in the sun from wetness, as did Ta'Mara's hand and forearm.

Jared held up the dripping phone; at which Ta'Mara groaned, "Oh, your phone. Is it waterproof?" she asked, hopefully.

Jared shrugged and shook his head, an incongruous grin on his face.

"Why are you smiling, then?"

"See, I told you that you're my hero!" he said, chuckling. "Risking the waves for me."

"And fish bites," she added.

"Yes! *And* fish bites." They laughed.

"You deserve a hero's reward. What shall it be, Ta'Mara? Your wish is my command."

Ta'Mara thought for a moment. "You don't happen to have a towel, do you?"

"Hmmm. What's your second wish?"

They laughed as they got up and Jared used the span of his tee shirt to dry off Ta'Mara's hand and wrist as well as his own.

~ Quint Emm Ellis ~

* * *

Back at her home they sat out in his car in front of her residence, her head resting against the headrest. "This has been an amazing couple of days, Jared," she sighed. "Thank you."

His head rested against his headrest, as well, as he looked over at her. "Thank you, Ta'Mara. Thank you for giving me a chance to show you who I am, now. For this time together. I don't want to waste one second of it."

"Oh, and you haven't. I think we've done just about everything there is to do in my city," she joked.

"Well, not *everything*."

Ta'Mara's mouth went slack for a moment as she noted the twinkle in Jared's eyes and the mischievous grin on his face. "Boy, you are naughty, Jared."

Jared shrugged. "If only in words, for now, Ta'Mara." he responded.

Chapter 33

✳ ✳ ✳

That evening, after they'd both rested and showered in their respective residences, Jared picked Ta'Mara up for their last evening together. He'd asked her to dress for a night of dinner and dancing. So after much debate, she'd decided to dare to wear a bodycon dress she'd bought for a business award ceremony that'd been held shortly following her promotion. She'd wanted to feel competent and womanly, and that dress did the job. She hoped it'd reinforce the same for her tonight. The dress was a pale yellow with purple and white flowers. The shoulderless design possessed sleeves that hung down, which would help mask her upper arms. The dress fit her bosom, waist, hips and softly loosened into a softer but fitted silhouette starting at mid thigh with the hem hitting her knee. She'd invested in a pair of low heels that were actually comfortable and fashionable enough to go with the dress. After looking herself over in the mirror, spanks and all, she was pleased at the overall effect and hoped to see the same reflected in Jared's eyes.

She had. When he came to her door and she'd opened it he'd stood frozen for several beats, until finally he'd remembered to close his slackened jaw and had taken a visible gulp. "You look amazing," he'd whispered. The muscle in his jaw worked. "Do you realize how difficult you are making things for me, Ta'Mara?" He gazed into her eyes, the storm there drawing Ta'Mara in, even as she nodded. "Good," he said quietly. "Don't stop," he murmured, licking his lips as he offered his arm for her. She paused to don her coat before slipping her hand into the crook of his elbow. She allowed him to lead her away from her home, parting only long enough for her to turn and lock her door.

That night Jared and Ta'Mara enjoyed one another's company at a local club that hosted salsa on Saturday nights. Though neither of them were skilled at the dance, they felt like the center of the room when in one another's presence. The dinner was great, and having an excuse to move together was the highlight of the evening. Ta'Mara did note a couple of questioning glances thrown her way by a black man and even a black woman. But for the most part, she was able to tune out the noise and focus on the one person that mattered to her in the room. The one person in the room that she mattered to.

Is it a surprise, then, that they found themselves lost in a kiss that night as Jared towered over her, her back to the door of her home. His hands skimmed the landscape of her back, hips, butt and thighs, not daring to explore higher. He leaned into her, daring her to retreat against the pressure of feeling him against her. She didn't retreat, with a moan she felt herself attempting to open to him; but the dress was so restrictive she could barely do anything. "This dress is in the way," she found herself declaring in a raspy voice as he leaned down to nuzzle her neck. "But that's a good thing, right?" she asked, somehow unsure at the moment. She could only be thankful that the shrubbery near her front door had missed enough trimmings to shield the two of them from view of anyone who wasn't directly opposite them. "I don't think I'm the best judge of that right now," Jared admitted, as he moved to nuzzle her ear, her cheek before recapturing her lips.

Just then the sound of Ta'Mara's phone broke through their preoccupation. Neither knew how long it'd been ringing, but it soon stopped just as they broke apart at recognition of the intruder. The phone then began ringing, loudly, again.

Ta'Mara looked at Jared and Jared leaned his forehead against hers, "Saved by the bell," he chuckled. The ringing finally stopped, again. And they both sagged against the door, attempting to reel in the feelings that had taken hold of them. The phone began ringing again and Ta'Mara nearly jumped this time. "I—I better get that. It might be an emergency with my Mom, or something."

Jared backed up to allow her room to rummage through her small purse and capture her phone. Her brow furrowed as she looked at the number on the caller ID and then, shaking her head, she quickly answered before the ringing had a chance to stop a third time.

"Hello?" Ta'Mara answered. "Yes, this is her." Then her mouth opened wordlessly and her eyes flashed to Jared, "Yes, yes," she said chuckling, "He's here with me. He's fine." It was Jared's turn to furrow his brow. "Oh I understand, it's okay. It was, uh" and she looked at Jared again, "Perfect timing, actually." She paused, "It's lovely to hear your voice, as well. I'm sorry we never had the chance to meet in-person. But it seems I have you to thank for your brother and me reconnecting."

At that Jared's eyes went wide, "Lor?" he exclaimed, incredulous.

Ta'Mara nodded and dodged his hand when he attempted a swipe at her phone. Giggling, she said, "Nope, this is my phone. Get your own." She laughed, batting his hand away. To Lorna she explained, "I think your brother really wants to talk with you. I'm not so sure he's as pleased with this call as we are." Ta'Mara listened and then burst out laughing at whatever quip Lorna made in response. With that Ta'Mara handed her phone to Jared. "She's ready to speak with you now," she said with a wink.

"Lor," he growled into the phone, "What the h—how did you get Ta'Mara's number?" A beat passed, "How did you get into my author's account?" Another beat. "So you're saying it's my fault because I should make my passwords harder to guess?"

At that, Ta'Mara burst out into another round of laughter.

"Well I couldn't text you back today because my phone is broken—Yes, really—And, last night I just didn't feel like ending a wonderful day and night with a chat with my little sister. I'm a grown man, not a teenage girl.—Yeah, I can appreciate that you were worried, but if I'm ever murdered while out of town I'll be sure to haunt you, how's that? Now can you let Ta'Mara and I continue our last night together before I head back home to strangle you tomorrow?" He smiled at her response. "Yeah, I love you, too. Okay, okay, I'll tell her. Now get off her phone, will you?"

With that and one large exhale he ended the call and handed Ta'Mara her phone. "She says she loves you already."

Somehow, the sentiment he'd passed along hit Ta'Mara deeply.

"Tell her the feeling is definitely mutual. And, I can understand her concern," she said in Lorna's defense. "You're her family, and she loves you. She's just looking out for you."

"Sure, but there's such a thing as healthy boundaries, too," he countered.

Ta'Mara nodded, "I don't disagree with that, at all. But I also have to admit that, at least in this case, her overstep was—a good thing. Right?"

The muscles in Jared's jaw worked and he stared at Ta'Mara, his eyes seeking out her lips again. "I should be responding with a 'yes', here, correct?"

Ta'Mara smiled softly before biting her lip. Finally, she spoke again. "Thank you, Jared, for the best—" she stopped to look at her phone— "thirty-eight hours and forty-two minutes I've had in a, very, long time."

Jared nodded, sticking his hands in his pockets. "Yeah. Yeah, okay." He looked at her for a long moment, silence suspended between them. "I'll see you tomorrow. Mālama pono, Ta'Mara." Like the night before, he waited for her to enter her home. And with the door ajar, she watched from behind it as he walked to his car; enjoying the beauty of his lines, of his stride, and of the person who bore them.

"Mālama pono, Jared," she whispered.

Chapter 34

✳ ✳ ✳

The next morning, they'd agreed that Ta'Mara would do the driving so that Jared could drop off his rental early and they could spend as much of their remaining time together as possible. It meant that they'd arrived a bit late to her congregation's service that morning, but were still able to catch most of the worship segment.

As much as Ta'Mara knew her eyes should be on the Lord, how could she not enjoy the sight of a man who loved to praise God; voice raised, hands held high to the Lord as if in true need of the Lord's presence. Worship was her favorite part of service, and it felt amazing to have someone by her side who shared that love; and showed it. She also admitted, once again, that she found it more than appealing to witness such a display of devotion to God.

The sermon focused on how, throughout the Bible, God points his people toward the hope that can only be found in Him; in the power he has to save us from that which destroys the world around us and us with it.

Afterwards, they discussed the sermon at a nearby restaurant and shared what parts resonated with them the most, the least and where they may have even disagreed with the interpretation offered by the pastor. It felt so good to Ta'Mara to be able to discuss things like this with Jared. He'd always been thoughtful, introspective. To have that lens shed on topics regarding the Bible highlighted another facet of his thought process and philosophical leanings. It was a beautiful way to be challenged or affirmed in her own thinking; and for her to do the same for him. In doing so, they learned more about each other.

"Ta'Mara," Jared said during a lull in their conversation. "I've really enjoyed this weekend. Have you?"

Ta'Mara nodded immediately, his grin mirroring her own. "Very much, Jared."

"So, I know it's a challenge, with us being so far apart. But I want this to work. I'm willing to come up here on weekends, so we can see each other—"

Ta'Mara blinked. "That'd be so expensive! You mean every weekend?"

"Yeah, it's nothing if we get to do this, be with each other. What do you say? Are you okay with that?"

"It's so expensive, Jared."

"Don't worry about the expense. I'm a lowly marketing exec but I save well; and as a silent partner of the real estate company, I'm also pretty well taken care of as the beneficiary of my siblings' hard work." He chuckled. "Frankly, I can't think of a more perfect excuse to actually spend my share of the money than to re-establish a new, stronger relationship with you. So, can I see you next weekend? And the weekends that follow? And if you're willing, I'd love to bring you back down to visit California for any of those weekends. Either way, I just want to see you."

"Okay, Jared. If you're down with it I am too. But-", she continued, "I don't think I'm ready to fly out to California...yet. But I'll keep that in mind, okay?"

Jared's whole face brightened with glee. "Great! Great. Okay, yeah. The invitation remains open. But until then, I'll see you right here in Kansas City. Friday night okay?"

Ta'Mara nodded. "Yep, just send me the details and I'll pick you up."

"Perfect." He reached across the table and held open his hand. She reached her hand out and placed hers in his. And Jared's shoulders seemed to lighten as if questions that had been weighing on him the entire weekend were finally resolved.

Following lunch, they made their way to Ta'Mara's car and silently took their seats. The drive to the airport held a solemn feel. A weight seemed to settle upon Ta'Mara at the prospect of saying goodbye to Jared, once more. Could this really work with there being so much distance—and history—between them? Or were they setting each other up for more disappointment?

Ta'Mara parked her car so that she could accompany Jared to his terminal. They sat together, their hands clasped on their shared armrest as they waited until the very last moment before Jared could safely ensure he'd have enough time to complete the security check and make his flight.

As that moment neared, Jared stood and Ta'Mara did the same, facing him with a tight expression, willing back the tears that she knew sparkled in her eyes.

Jared raised his hands to cup her face. "I'll see you Friday, okay?" She nodded in his hands, even as he leaned down to kiss her. Pulling back he raised his lips to kiss her on her forehead before bending so that their foreheads met.

He pulled back slightly so that he could dig in his pocket. Out of it he pulled a music cassette container, like the kind they grew up with as kids. He handed it to Ta'Mara, who looked up at him questioningly. She turned the container over in her hands and read the names of songs handwritten on the cover. They were all the songs he'd asked to be played at the cafe the night before, plus many more he'd dedicated to her in this "mixtape" he created for her. When she opened the container, inside she found a couple flash drives, as well as an ipod with earbuds.

"To help you remember our first reunion weekend together," he whispered to her. "You can plug the usb in your car, and also have the songs handy when you're at work or—you know—whenever. I also included a drive with some gospel songs I thought you might like. Let me know what you think, okay?" After one last, long kiss and embrace, she placed her hands on his chest and grudgingly nudged him toward the gate. "Go, you're going to miss your flight."

He walked backward for a bit, watching her, "I'll be back," he said,without one bit of irony, before finally turning away to catch his flight.

Ta'Mara stayed and watched until his plane backed out of its gate and lifted off the tarmac.

"Mālama pono, Jared," she said, softly.

✳ ✳ ✳

The songs on her mixtape accompanied her entire
drive home: Leon Bridges' "Coming Home", Ron
Sexmith's contributions, Skip Marley and H.E.R.'s
"Slow Down", even Tevin Campbell's "Can We Talk",
Bill Withers' "Just the Two of Us". And then she cried,
because that man had better come back to her or she
knew she would hunt him down herself.

Chapter 35

✳ ✳ ✳

Phone conversations and texts littered that following week, filling their days and their nights with laughter, shared memories and shared tears. On Friday, when Ta'Mara finally saw Jared exit the airport's gate upon his return to her city she couldn't help but run to him, throwing herself into his arms for the long embrace that ensued.

They repeated that pattern the next week, at which point Ta'Mara agreed to take the trek the following weekend to meet him in California.

When she exited the gate in Oceanside it was not hard for her to recognize her man in the crowd, standing tall and beautiful before spotting her and walking briskly toward her, taking her bag.

"Hey Baby," he breathed, bending down to taste her lips for just a moment before resuming his stance to gaze down at her.

"Hey Baby," she responded in kind, a wide grin on her face to match his own.

"I'm parked over here," he gestured toward the exit with his chin and let his arm fall across her back as she turned to walk with him in the direction of the parking lot.

Once they were in his car, he turned to her and leaned over to kiss her again.

"Mmm, can't tell you how good it feels to have you here, Tay. And I can't wait to show you around Oceanside. Oh, and of course my sister is dying to meet you. She's flying down from a meeting held in 'Frisco tomorrow; I had to stop her from coming early because she was really pressing me to come with me to the airport to pick you up. But I told her that I'm not ready to share you with anyone else, just yet, so she just has to exercise patience."

Ta'Mara's eyes brightened. "Oh, I can't wait to meet her, too! I have to admit I'm a bit nervous to meet the woman who managed all of this. I might smother her in kisses, so maybe you ought to warn her."

"Well, uh, how about you smother me in kisses, instead." He invited, leaning in.

"Mmmm, gladly." And leaning toward him, she did just that.

* * *

They spent the evening dining at one of Jared's favorite local restaurants before taking a stroll by the beach.

"Oh, I miss this. I miss the beach and the smell of that sea and salt."

"I think the beach misses you, too." He kissed the top of her head as he stood behind her on the boardwalk, both of them staring out across the sand to drink in the sight and sounds of the ocean's dark, frothy waves. She leaned against him, her back against his front and his arms wrapped around her. It was a chilly evening, but Ta'Mara felt warm from the top of her head to her big toe.

That night, Jared walked Ta'Mara to the door of the hotel suite he'd gotten her. As she turned to face him, her back to the door, they regarded one another, knowing they shared the same thoughts.

It'd be so easy to give in to their wants, their desires right now. They were two adults, and who would know but them? What person would care, really? And hadn't they waited long enough?

Jared closed his eyes momentarily, breaking their spell. Ta'Mara redirected her gaze to watch the muscles in his jaw work themselves.

"I'll see you tomorrow, Tay," Jared whispered, finally, leaning down to plant a gentle kiss on her forehead. "But you'd better go ahead and get yourself inside that room before I forget that I'm a man of God who's attempting to honor a woman of God."

Ta'Mara bit her lip as she chuckled. But as she saw the gleam in Jared's eyes, and the switch of his focus onto her lips, she hurriedly turned and unlocked her door. Once inside, she bid him "goodbye" as she drank in the image of him and of the look of longing he laid bare, between the narrowing edges of her closing door.

✳ ✳ ✳

~ Quint Emm Ellis ~

The next day they were back at the airport, awaiting the arrival of his sister who would join them between meetings she'd set up. Though Lorna didn't live in Oceanside, it'd become a second home for her since it'd developed into one of their company's hottest real estate markets.

They heard Lorna before they saw her; a diminutive little cherub with a pixie cut running and squealing with arms extended toward them. Ta'Mara stepped aside a bit to give Jared's sister room to grab hold of him; but Lorna surprised her by reaching over and pulling Ta'Mara into the group hug. Though tiny, Lorna had the strength of a petite Amazonian.

"Oh my gosh oh my gosh oh my gosh!" She squealed, jumping up and down, taking her two hostages along for the bumpy ride. "You two!" She stepped back then and beamed at the couple before her. Then she lunged in and resumed her two armed grip on them. "Oh my gosh!" she squealed again. With one final, firm squeeze she released them and stood back, hands on her hip. She looked like an artist taking stock of her masterpiece.

Then, a sniffle and a dab at the eye, followed by a long exhale, and the storm that was Lorna finally seemed to calm. For the moment, at least.

"Ta'Mara," she said, turning to the woman who stood beside her beaming brother. Lorna grasped Ta'Mara's closed hand in both of hers. "You are the best thing that's happened to my brother. I am so so so glad to get to meet you." Lorna looked over at her brother. "Look at him. I've never seen him so—so—full. Just deep and full and...content." She reached one of her other hands over toward her brother. Jared took her hand and he looked over from his sister to Ta'Mara.

Content.

To be surrounded by the women he loved most in his life; who loved him—even if one of them hadn't said as much quite yet. But even so, the word 'content' resonated with him. What had he been before? He'd been happy, often. Grateful, always. But this, this was something wholly different.

"I'm starving," Lorna declared, giving both Ta'Mara's and Jared's hands one last squeeze before letting them go. "Where are we headed for lunch?" she inquired, looking back and forth between the two before her.

"I was going to take you to your hotel, first, Sis. I've got you set up in the same hotel as Tay, as you both requested."

"Great! Of course, you know you're going to regret that." She winked at Ta'Mara. "Are you ready for all of the lovely tales I have to share about my brother in his youth?"

"Yes, and trust, I'll be recording them for future reference." Ta'Mara chuckled along with Lorna as they shared a little bubble of woman-to-woman camaraderie.

"Don't forget I have at least as many stories about you, Lor," Jared warned.

"Yeah, but I'm not dating Tay. And, also, I'm not at all ashamed. So who's going to be more embarrassed?"

Jared quirked an eyebrow and leaned down, whispering something in his sister's ears. Lorna's eyes got so round Ta'Mara thought they might fall out of their sockets.

"You never told me you knew about that!" Lorna gasped in astonishment at her brother who'd resumed his stance with a knowing look on his face. "How did you—"

"A gentleman never tells," Jared responded. "There's a lot more where that came from, too," he teased. "So just be mindful. Keep the stories kosher, sis."

Lorna looked at Ta'Mara and Ta'Mara noted a sly glint in her eye and she couldn't help but smirk at Jared's sister. She had a feeling that Lorna was not one to let any threat restrain her when she had her mind set on something.

Jared's loud sigh underscored his own awareness of the same. "Just don't embarrass me too much?" He said, turning around to get their little group started toward their next destination.

❋ ❋ ❋

They went to lunch after dropping off Lorna's numerous amounts of luggage. Ta'Mara didn't have to worry about awkward conversation during their first time hanging out together. Lorna was such a chatterbox, with plenty of unbelievable and downright hysterical anecdotes to share from just work, alone. Ta'Mara had already been grateful to Lorna, but now she just plain ol' adored her. It was no wonder their company did so well with her as their people person.

They'd finished their lunch and just chatted a bit until Lorna's next appointment, which was soon after. She'd kindly paid for the whole meal, explaining, "Believe me, this right here is a gift to me. I'm so so so happy for you two. I can't wait to meet up with you tonight. Also, brother," she said to Jared, "Have I mentioned that you owe me...big?"

Jared snorted. "Not for a whole couple days, at least."

"Just making sure you don't forget."

Jared wrapped an arm around Ta'Mara's shoulders and turned to look at her, and when she turned to meet his gaze suddenly the world around them diminished.

"Oh, I don't think you'll *ever* have to worry about that," he said, just loud enough for his sister to hear.

"Mmhmm. Ooookay. That's my cue to leave. I'll talk with you both later."

They barely noticed her exit.

✳ ✳ ✳

Afterwards, Jared took Ta'Mara back to the hotel so they could both get ready for that evening. They would be heading to an early dinner and a walk on the beach at dusk before meeting Lorna at a bar located on the boardwalk that offered outdoor seating.

While he had some time, he decided to text Lorna to see what she was up to. Truth be told, he wanted to know how she felt their first day together went.

> **Jared**: *Hey, give me a call when you're free.*

> **Lorna**: Free now. Give me a sec.

A few minutes later his phone rang and his sister's voice spilled over from the other side.

"Oh my gosh, I love her, I love her, I love her. She's perfect for you! You both are so low-key you make me sleepy—or maybe just peaceful or something. I can't tell the difference. I mean, I am at my most peaceful when I'm asleep. I don't mean that as an insult," she continued. "Just saying you two are like the chillest, and cutest couple ever. I can't wait for you to get married. Are you going to live here, Jared, when that happens? Have you talked about marriage? You look like a married couple already—"

"Lor, Lor," Jared interjected, chuckling. "Breathe! First of all, we have talked about marriage. And she just isn't ready yet. Which is fair considering we only officially reunited a handful of weeks ago. So I'm not pushing it. But, she knows how I feel. I've been plenty open about that. Also, not sure how saying any person or couple lulls you to sleep wouldn't be taken as an insult. Except I know you don't always think before you speak, so I know you meant it differently than it came out."

"What!?"

"Hey, like you, I call it like I see it. That's all I'm saying."

"Speaking of which, I was seeing some things myself while hanging out with you two."

"What's that supposed to mean?"

"It means, if you both haven't done the 'do' by now you sure are about to. I know those looks on your faces...and all that touching. You know God is watching you, right?" she snickered.

" Do the 'do'? You mean, 'sex'? How is it I'm able to say the word and you can't."

"I was protecting your innocence."

Jared had to laugh out loud at her retort.

"I'm praying for you, Sis," he said, half joking but in reality, he always prayed for her, his brother, even Ta'Mara before they'd reunited, along with many others. "Anyway, we haven't done anything and we're being very good. Thanks for caring, though, I guess. Not that that should be any of your business," he said in a near growl. "I can guarantee you that I have no interest in *your* sex-life."

"Just trying to help you two avoid the 'oopsey' situation that I see brewing like a storm over both of your heads."

"What situation are you talking about?"

"You know, Jared. 'Oops, where are my lips going? Oops, where are my hands going? Oops, where are my clothes going? Oops where's my pe—"

"I think the whole world gets your point."

"Yeah, and Ta'Mara is about to get your point, too, if you get my drift."

"Loud and crassly clear. We're fine, we've got it under control."

"If you say so, Jared," she said in a sigh that sounded filled to the brim with genuine concern. "I just don't want anything to get in-between you two again. I love seeing my big brother so happy. So content, I mean. You're glowing! The only other times I've seen you glow is after a good workout. And that glow is funky stinky. This one's just—heartwarming."

For his sister to use a term like "heartwarming" indicated how deeply she was touched by what she was observing. And though he'd cherished what he and Ta'Mara have with every fiber of his being, somehow his esteem for what they shared was strengthened all the more.

"I'm going to do everything that's in my power to keep that from happening, Sis. Well…" he chuckled, recanting his answer just a bit. "I'm going to do my best, but the rest I know I have to leave to the Lord."

His tone softened, even more. "But your saying that, Lor, really means a lot to me. I know I rag on you a lot, but I want you to know that I value you, and I value what you're saying. All of what you're saying."

The other end of the line was silent for a moment, and Jared began to wonder if the call had dropped some time during his response.

Then he heard a sniff and an uncharacteristically subdued voice respond. "Thanks Jared. I really needed to hear that."

And Jared was a little floored. What kind of brother had he been all of this time that his sister was moved so much by his genuine expression of esteem for her? He resolved to do better. If he could be as open with Ta'Mara as he had been compelled to be and had pushed himself to be, maybe he could afford to offer at least some of the same to the other people in his life.

Chapter 36

✳ ✳ ✳

In the evening, Jared shared the conversation with Ta'Mara as they walked along the beach, hand in hand. "I don't know if I'm surprised more by her reaction to my compliment—or by the fact that I had no idea she'd respond in such a way. I guess I don't know my sister as well as I thought I did."

Ta'Mara decided to just listen. She had been trying to think of the right words to say to comfort him; and wished she'd suddenly come up with a perfectly crafted response. But she sensed that her being present, being available for him was what was most needed. And she could do that much.

"It was an eye opener," Jared continued. "Actually, this," he used his free hand to gesture between the two of them, "this relationship has been an eye opener. It compels me to be a lot more transparent than I've been in a long time. You compel me," he amended. "And I have a feeling all of my relationships could benefit from a little more of that."

"I hear you," Ta'Mara found herself responding. "For what it's worth, I've really enjoyed witnessing you and your sister interact. It's obvious there's a lot of love and a lot of respect that goes both ways. I don't think you're repairing anything, I guess is what I'm saying—because it kind of sounds like that's what you're thinking. I think what you're talking about, actually, is working to make it something that's even better. I think that's the perspective to look at it from. And that's pretty exciting. I'm excited to see what this realization brings about in your guys' relationship."

Jared stopped their walk forward and turned toward her with a smile so bright Ta'Mara could feel it's glow, and it warmed her from head to toe. "I'm excited for you to see that growth, too, Ta'Mara." He took her other hand. "We do have a good relationship, huh?"

Ta'Mara nodded, not completely certain he was still referring to him and Lorna.

"Thank you, Ta'Mara. I guess I needed to hear all of that, too."

"Of course. We're always harder on ourselves than on others, aren't we?"

He looked away for a quick second before returning her gaze. "Sometimes it's warranted," he finally said, with a small, sad smile.

Ta'Mara squeezed his hands, even as she nodded, and with a warm smile of her own added, "True". She chuckled then, and the light that danced in his eyes in response—the relief that flooded his face made her heart flutter. He squeezed her hands back. "But, we all find ourselves wanting, needing opportunities for a second chance, right? We're all works in progress."

He watched her earnestly, searching her eyes as he asked, "Do you really believe that?"

She smiled, "I really believe that."

"Do you believe that a life, a good life, can be built upon a second chance?"

"I want to. I mean, I believe it when it comes to salvation. That's the whole point of being redeemed; entering into a new life and a renewed relationship. But—if I'm being transparent," she said, chuckling, "Maybe I'm not so sure about how applicable that idea is outside of that. And I know that's an incompatible view."

"It's honest, I wouldn't want any less from you. Does it help that I believe we could build something great on this second chance? That I want to build something strong, enduring and beautiful with God and with you."

"Yeah, actually, it does. I know you've been completely open to me these last several weeks. But yeah, I—I want to believe with you, Jared. I really do. I want you to be certain of at least that much. If it helps, at all."

"I'll take it!" he said, excitedly.

They both laughed at that.

"I'm a starving, parched man, here, Tay. I welcome any hint of relief you're willing to drop in my direction."

Ta'Mara was so tickled by his effusiveness she couldn't help but feel giddy. "Oh, I love you, Jar—"

They both froze. Moments later Jared's chest rose and fell a little more rapidly than it had minutes before, as did Ta'Mara's.

"I—" Ta'Mara tried to get out something but even that tiny little word died on her lips, just in time for Jared to claim her mouth for himself.

He'd kissed her to prevent her from backtracking her words. He'd kissed her to keep himself from echoing them and possibly scaring her away. And he kissed her to show her what he longed to tell her.

When they pulled apart, their faces so close to one another that they felt the other's breath, he allowed a whispered, "Me, too," to pass from his lips and hang suspended between them.

When they finally turned to start their walk back to the car their hands clasped even tighter than they had before. In silence they considered the space they now traveled in—together; and understood that their world had shifted all of a sudden, and for good.

✳ ✳ ✳

Dinner with Lorna was filled with laughter, storytelling and great food.

The bar had a small dance floor located just beyond its seating area, and Jared watched Ta'Mara sway in her seat to the beat of the music. Moments later he stood and offered her his hand as he excused them from the table.

Lorna watched the couple dance and laugh, getting closer and closer 'til finally Ta'Mara was in Jared's arms and the couple just stared at each other, swaying to their own, mellow beat.

"Yep," she said, taking a sip of her drink. "Like I said...Oopsies."

---

* * *

That night after Jared had dropped her off, Ta'Mara went to her room to prepare for bed and the early flight she'd be taking tomorrow.

A knock on the door interrupted her preparations. When she asked who it was she was surprised to hear Lorna's voice.

Ta'Mara opened the door to see the small and mighty woman standing at her threshold, her lip bit and large eyes pleading. "Mind if we talk?"

"Of course!" she responded, opening the door wide for Lorna to enter.

Lorna entered and stood in the middle of Ta'Mara's room until Ta'Mara gestured for Lorna to take a seat in a nearby chair. Ta'Mara seated herself across from her.

"What's up? Anything wrong?" Ta'Mara's heart skipped a beat as she imagined Lorna delivering some news about Jared not having made it home safely after dropping Ta'Mara off.

"Oh no, not at all!" Lorna assured her. "Everything is right, actually. I just wanted to tell you, one-to-one, how much I love witnessing you and my brother interact. It's obvious he cares for you deeply. And that you care for him, too."

Lorna's eyes searched Ta'Mara's and Ta'Mara smiled shyly and nodded.

"And, I think you're aware that I'm not Christian, myself. But I understand and respect that your guys' faith is a fundamental aspect of the relationship you're building."

"Mmhhmm," Ta'Mara invited.

"I also noted that you both are pretty, uhm, affectionate."

Ta'Mara stiffened. Where was this conversation headed?

"And I'm just saying that because I know that my brother really, really loves being with you. And I think you do, too. At least from what I see. I just—"

"Lorna, what are you saying?"

"Doesn't the Bible say somewhere that it's better to marry than to just be hornballs, or something?" Lorna finally blurted.

Ta'Mara blinked, taken completely off-guard by Lorna's question. "Uhm, not quite but I know the verse you're referring to. I guess it could be interpreted kinda like that. But that was also written at a time when women didn't have many options; I'm thinking that was especially true if they weren't virgins."

"So the Bible isn't applicable now that women can have jobs and aren't shunned after having sex with someone?"

Ta'Mara: "No, that's not what I mean, uhm—"

"It just seems to me," Lorna continued with her eyes averted and her brow bunched as she genuinely pondered the verse she'd so badly butchered. "It seems to me that the point, the essence of that—uhm—proverb is that, at least for you who are Christians—there's a need to choose. Are you gonna do what's considered a sin? Or do what's considered 'right' in God's eyes. The point is that there's no in-between. And my own personal experience has been that by avoiding making a decision, you've already guaranteed one."

That actually made sense. And Ta'Mara had no logical retort. But it still didn't feel good to have this perspective brought up to her.

Lorna continued, "Look, I don't have a problem with you and my brother doing the horizontal mambo. But I feel like both of you would have a problem with it. And I know you're still figuring things out for yourself; but if you both love God the way you claim to do, well. I mean, if something did happen, how would it impact you? My brother? Let alone the relationship you're both building. I just—I don't know. I wish you folks didn't make this so complicated by mixing in religion. But it is what it is. So I'm just saying, please, think about what's going on...where you two are headed. For both your sakes. I don't want to see my brother go off on another bender. It wasn't cute in his 20's and it'd be just plain tragic now."

"Wow," was all Ta'Mara could get out, initially. "And you're not Christian, you say?"

Lorna shook her head. "My brother has a saying: 'Even Balaam's donkey spoke righteously once in his life.' He says he reminds himself of that to help him not miss recognizing God showing up in the most unlikely places." She shrugged. "Consider me an unlikely place."

"O-kay. Well, while I appreciate your concern, I don't think it's really your concern, Lorna. Besides that, if we were going to do the 'horizontal mambo' it would have already happened. Believe me. We're okay. You don't need to—"

"That's what he said, too."

"I know. And he's right. You should listen to him, sometimes."

"Damn. Okay, I appreciate you sticking up for my brother."

"And for myself, too. For us both."

"Okay, I'm backing off. I just hope maybe one of you will consider the observations I'm sharing, too." Lorna relaxed in the chair for a moment and finally she got up and, leaning down, gave a still seated Ta'Mara a warm hug.

"I really do like you, Ta'Mara. And of course I love my brother. I wish you both the absolute, mightiest, most wonderful best. Even if I'm not always the best at showing it."

Ta'Mara chuckled and placed her hand on Lorna's back in genuine reciprocation of the physically awkward embrace. "I know you do, Lorna. I can feel it from every fiber of your being. I know it."

With one last squeeze, Lorna straightened and with a small smile she waved. "I'll just let myself out, then." And with that she left Ta'Mara to deal with the echo of their conversation.

Chapter 37: the Acceptance...

Over the next few months Jared continued to fly down to Kansas City every weekend, except for when Ta'Mara visited him in Oceanside every last weekend of the month.

One week she had come down early, on Thursday, so that she could attend an office function with Jared the next day. And the stares she endured, mostly from his female co-workers, could have killed. It was also then that she'd learned what his prior annual titles had been; and she could feel the heat creeping up her neck and face. Again, she found herself thankful for her dark skin tone which revealed little of her discomfort. It was also her first opportunity to be able to view Jared's work and his office; to see the campaigns and strategies and the evidence of his efforts. And to see how modest he'd been regarding his contributions to the company over the years. That weekend, they'd also spent an evening with Larry and Darla, eating take out and laughing while Jared walked them through a two-hour round of Dungeons and Dragons.

Another weekend she'd flown into Los Angeles where Jared met her so that they could reminisce and remember the good times they'd shared there; as well as talk through the not-so-great feelings that those memories brought up. He'd stayed with his brother, Samuel, that weekend; while she'd stayed at the hotel suite Jared had reserved for her. And the following Saturday she, Jared, Lorna and Sam enjoyed an evening out at the movies and dining at the siblings' favorite Hawaiian inspired restaurant, Ono Hawaiian BBQ on Figueroa. Ta'Mara remembered coming to this place a lot with Jared and Sam in the past and couldn't help the grin on her face as, per tradition, all three siblings consumed a double portion of the establishment's famous macaroni salad.

Other weekends, in Kansas City, Jared might join her at the board game meetup that she sometimes attended that was held at a cozy Kansas City restaurant over brunch. It was there that Jared got introduced to table-top role playing games. She stank at every game she played, but she always had the best time, all the same. Ta'Mara especially enjoyed getting to watch Jared interact with everyone; and to see him get into the games. To look at him, one wouldn't think he exactly fit in with the game geeks, such as herself. But his warmth and enthusiasm never wavered.

Each weekend he visited Kansas City they would visit her mom, who had taken to trying out her own variations on Hawaiian dishes to share with Jared.

Otherwise, depending on the location, they'd spend most of their time together hanging out at their respective homes watching movies, playing board and card games. Often, he'd be in the living room and she in the office as they both worked: he on his latest manuscript; she on the small projects she'd sought and been awarded via the freelance app.

And on more than one occasion Jared found himself struggling to foil his girlfriend's attempts at gaining a sneak peak of his latest Ryan Jamison novel. "You'll be the first to read the completed version," he'd insist as he'd shut the laptop or find himself nearly running around the home, laughing as she followed him with a mischievous glint in her eye.

Their routine shifted only during Ta'Mara's monthly 'hair days,' when Ta'Mara needed a Saturday to thoroughly prep her hair for the weeks that'd follow. Jared would hang out at her cottage while she'd go about the hours-long chore of washing, detangling and braiding her hair so that it'd stretch out for whatever style she chose to pull it into for the following days—which was typically a bun unless she and Jared had plans. She'd been relegating her hair care to Sunday evenings since the start of her and Jared's courtship. But she'd quickly found that she really needed to afford herself at least one day to complete this when she wasn't exhausted and had more time.

Jared had found a local Kansas City gym which he joined shortly following their first weekend together. On Saturday mornings he'd complete his reps before he and Ta'Mara were due to reunite that day. So on days when she was due to have her hands full with detangling her dampened tresses, he'd sleep in, visit the gym a couple hours later and arrive at Ta'Mara's home, afterwards. Once there, sometimes he'd set up his laptop and work for most of the day, other times he'd try to fix something that was broken, like her floor lamp that'd gone out months ago. Some days he'd enlist in a round of online D&D or he'd order them some food to eat while they watched a movie together.

He'd been very mindful about stating how much he loved her natural hair, the softness and springiness of it. So once Ta'Mara had even attempted to let him help her with detangling and braiding her hair; but she'd had to shoo him away because they were doing more laughing than hair.

Other Saturday mornings, Ta'Mara even found herself joining Jared's early morning exercise routine. She could admit that she was not nearly as serious about it as he was. Oh, how the tables have turned, she'd think. But she did enjoy letting him guide her in how to properly execute forms.

No matter what they did, though, every weekend it became more and more difficult to say goodbye.

The fourth time Ta'Mara came to visit Jared, they drove up to the hotel only to find that her reservation had not been recorded, and there just so happened to be a record number of people in town for a large convention. All the hotels were booked.

"Well," Jared started, "If you're okay with staying at Hotel Mi Casa, there's always room for you there."

Ta'Mara smiled. "Hotel Mi Casa sounds lovely. Do they offer room service?"

Jared grinned. "They do now."

Once they arrived at Jared's house he led her to the guest bedroom so that she could get her luggage settled. He was thankful that the weekly cleaning service he'd hired a while ago had just arrived a couple days before. So everything was still in order for Ta'Mara's surprise visit.

Jared had intended to take Ta'Mara out for lunch at another local restaurant he wanted to introduce her to. But it felt so good to have the love of his life in his home he felt the urge to stay in.

"What do you think about me seeing if I can get the hotel chef to whip us up something for lunch?"

"Please do. I hope they can accommodate last minute orders!"

"I'm pretty sure they'll make an exception."

Jared cooked them one of his go-to comfort meals: hawaiian pineapple chicken tacos, spam fried rice, wedge salad, and cinnamon rolls.

"Hey," he said as he began to bring their plates to the table. "Don't suppose you'd be up for dinner and a round of Connect Four...or?" he said, wiggling his eyebrows, "Dungeons and Dragons?"

"Hmmm, D&D, no," she shook her head, laughing. He was persistent in trying to get her to play the multi-hour game with him and the online teams he'd join; and she'd even joined in once in a while; however today was not going to be one of those days. "But I might be convinced to play a game of Connect Four and a bit of chess to go along with this delicious homemade meal of yours."

"Deal," he agreed with a wink and a smile before gesturing for her to follow him into the living room as he held both of their plates.

* * *

An hour and a couple board games later they'd eaten and laughed their fill.

"This was so good, Jared." Ta'Mara exclaimed, patting her stomach, still enjoying the taste of her last scoop of fried rice. Growing up, she'd never eaten spam; she'd been taught that it was poor people's food. However, for Jared's family, it was a key flavor in Hawaiian dishes. And Ta'Mara had marveled at how much she'd missed because of her own ignorance.

Jared beamed. He'd felt immense pleasure in watching her enjoy the food that held meaning for him and that he'd made with her in mind. Jared licked his lips, "I'll forward your compliments to the chef," he joked.

"Please do. And where is the tip jar?"

He laughed with her.

Ta'Mara rose and grabbed her plate and then reached for his. He pulled his plate out of her reach and stood up, as well. "Ah ah ah. You're a guest. Let me take that."

She tsked, but begrudgingly handed him her plate but followed him to the kitchen, leaning on the door frame as she watched him place the dishes in the sink and rinse them off. "Well, I'm more than a guest, right? You gotta let me do some things for you, too."

"Oh, you're so much more than a guest, Tay," he supplied softly, turning toward her and leaning back against the sink counter.

She walked toward him then, like it was the most natural scene for him to be leaning against the counter with her in his vicinity. As she closed the distance she could see him swallow and his stance shift.

"Ta'Mara," he said, as she came to a stop just a hair's breadth from him.

"Jared, you're such an amazing man," she said, her voice low as she looked up at him. "Have I told you that?"

Jared shook his head and licked his lips, "Not in so many words, but I know how you feel about me,

Ta'Mara." He watched her, his eyes blazing as he saw the same yearning in her eyes.

"Do you," she taunted, licking her lips in turn.

He leaned down and kissed her, gently at first. And then with a ferocity that was matched by her own.

With a growl Jared bent and picked Ta'Mara up to cradle her in his arms. He stalked to his own room and carefully deposited her on his bed. Looking at her, he admired her from his vantage point. Her breath coming in short, rapid bursts, her eyes dilated and gaze focused on him.

Shrugging out of his soft polo shirt, he tossed it somewhere behind him. "You have entirely too many clothes on, Honey," he said in a gravelly, low voice. "Can I help you with that?"

"Yes, please," Ta'Mara agreed breathily, even as she lifted shaky hands to the buttons of her blouse.

At that sight, Jared stilled, his sister's words inconveniently making themselves very present in his brain, "Oopsey, where did my hands go? Oopsey, where did my clothes go?"

~ Quint Emm Ellis ~

Taking a deep, stabilizing breath Jared laid a hand on Ta'Mara's, halting her clumsy progress. She looked up at him, confused.

"Ta'Mara, I—we don't want this. Not like this. You don't want this."

"I've wanted to play connect two with you for a very long time, Jared. So, I'm pretty sure I want this."

"Are you?" he threw her own question back at her, his concern overriding his normal response to her humorous remark.

"Maybe it's you who isn't sure," she said, embarrassment flooding her as a replay of a similar scene that happened so many years ago ran through her head. "Maybe you never really wanted this, Jared." *Would she ever learn?* She shook her head, swinging her legs over the bed and preparing to make her escape from the realization of how stupid she'd been, again.

Jared placed his hands gently on her shoulder.

"Ta'Mara, do you seriously believe that I don't want you? When you can see, with your very own eyes, that that is definitely untrue."

Ta'Mara gaze involuntarily swung to focus on the bulge in his pants. She licked her lips before biting her bottom one.

"You really should not look at me like that, though, Baby. Not right now," he said, his voice dangerously husky.

"Ta'Mara, I want you. But I want you the right way. Even if that means we have to wait a little—or a lot—longer." He tipped her chin up so that her eyes met his. "And I think you want me, too, the right way. The long term way. The way that we can look back at and know we placed our God first from the very beginning...like we'll need to do continuously. This is—difficult—but I'm okay with us taking the time needed to do this right. Because we won't ever have another 'first time'. I want our memory of it to be something we can both look back on without a single tinge of regret."

Ta'Mara shook her head. So many thoughts whirling around, trying to coalesce into something that she could not yet define. But what she felt, right now, is that this was a mistake; her coming to his house and maybe—maybe more than that. This is the second time she'd neatly dismissed her faith for the possibility of consummating her pre-marital relationship with this man. Add to that that he was a believer himself and she nearly took him with her into what would have turned into something they'd both regretted. She knew that, too. She knew that no matter how great it was, it'd be one point in their union where they knew they'd placed a god above the One True God. And they'd never be able to undo that decision.

"I think, until I know what I want, it's better that we be apart. We've gotten so close, so many times, and—as delayed of a response as it is and I'm sorry for that—I don't want either of us to do something that could jeopardize the health of our relationship with Christ; nor tear down what we've built up so far. I think it's better to allow time for me to figure out what I want—it's not fair to you, Jared. And me either—"

"No." Jared replied firmly. "No." He repeated. "If you wanted to end this relationship because you realized that you don't care about me, I'd let you go. I'd have to, because I love you and I want the best things in and beyond this world for you, even if that doesn't include me. But if you're telling me that you want me to allow you to walk out that door with the possibility of never seeing you again because we love each other and want to show that to each other in the most fundamental, God-ordained way possible between a man and woman, then no. I won't accept that. I'll take cold showers every day. I'll find us chaperones. I—I won't initiate advances, I promise. I'll be the strong one. We are gonna get through this," he determined.

"And this time we'll get through it *together*. I'll do whatever it takes, but I won't lose you over this. Sex is important, but it's not everything. It's not you, Ta'Mara."

"You'd do all that?"

"All that and more." He knelt down before her. "Ta'Mara, what will it take for you to understand that I'd do anything for you? And I'd do anything for *us*."

He sighed, stood and walked to where he'd dropped his shirt. Standing he quickly donned his top, tugging it back into place.

"Here's what I'm going to do," he said, walking over to his bedroom's entrance and turning toward her, leaning against the door jamb with his shoulder. "I'm going to go into the living room and I will find a hotel with a room available."

"Jared, they're all booked."

"The good hotels are. I'm sure I can find myself a room at the less frequented ones, though."

"Wait, you're going to stay in the hotel?"

"Of course. Because we obviously can't stay here together, right now. And there's no way I'm letting you stay in anything that's less than five stars." At her look of dismay he sought to placate her, "It's totally fine, Hon. I actually really like the idea of you making yourself at home here." His eyes twinkled, "Maybe we could plan on adding a bit of decoration this weekend, a feminine touch. What do you think?" He turned to make his way to the living room, still chatting over his shoulder. "You up for a trip to whatever those stores are that offer that kind of thing? Just not IKEA, please. Their maze of aisles are torturous."

As Ta'Mara watched him go the breeze from his ceiling fan caressed her skin and with a start she was reminded of the need to redo the buttons on her shirt. Once everything was back in place she left to join Jared back out in the living room. He was just returning with a steaming mug in his hand which he placed on the table in front of the couch. Looking up at her he smiled, adding "Figured you might like a cup of your favorite tea. Here's fine?"

Ta'Mara smiled and bit her lip, nodding as they both continued to take their seats; she sat on the couch where he'd sat her mug, while he went over to sit, hunched over his phone, in one of the large chairs that'd come with his living room furniture set.

"So I've been doing some searching and I think I've found a good spot that happens to have a vacancy," he mentioned, a deep look of concentration on his face. "I'll give them a call. But I figure, push come to shove, I'll just bunk with Larry for the weekend. It'll give him and Darla a good reason to sneak around like love-lorn teenagers."

"Would you marry me, Jared?"

Jared froze, then blinked at his phone a couple times before looking up at her, his brows knit together. "What? I'm sorry, I think I misheard you."

"No, you didn't. I'm asking you to marry me, Jared."

"Are—are you for real?"

"Yes. Jared, if I'm as honest as you claim I am, I knew my answer even before you snapped your fingers, remember? When we were hiking during our first weekend to gether in Kansas City. If I'm even more honest, you had me the moment I saw you at the airport. I just couldn't let myself fall again.

"But just now, you said you'd do anything for me; for us and for our relationship with the Lord. But you've been saying that for a long time, Jared, both in your words and in your actions." She paused, nibbling at her bottom lip again. "I just had a hard time allowing myself to believe it," she confessed with a small smile.

"But Jared," she continued, "I want you to know that I see you. I've heard you pray for me, for us when you thought I wasn't listening. And I want that, I want you—and I trust you Jared. I don't expect you to be perfect, I don't need you to be perfect. I don't expect you to fulfill a God-sized role in my heart. But I trust that you'll make me a priority, I trust you'll always try your best. I trust that you'll seek the Lord first, in our marriage. And I promise that I will try to do the same; I pray that God will help me to offer the same to you, til death do us part. So, if you're ready for this, I'm done running. I'm done delaying. I'm done depriving us of the good thing that God's trying so hard to gift us with. I want to marry the man I've loved for fifteen plus years."

Jared fell back, resting against the cushion of his chair for support, his hands gripping both arm rests. "Oh my—Tay, I might be having a heart attack right now, Honey. You know I'm old enough, it could happen," he exhaled, but the smile on his face said otherwise.

"Jared, don't joke like that," Ta'Mara said, reaching over to touch his knee.

He leaned forward and placed his hand upon hers. "No joke, I'm so happy I think my heart's about to burst out of my chest. I — wait, look I don't want you to do this because you feel some kind of pressure to do this, at all. I am willing to wait for as long as you need me to. I just want to make sure we're clear on that. No more regrets. For either of us."

"I know, Jared. I don't want to wait anymore. I want to marry you, Jared. And I want to marry you today."

"Today? Like, right now?"

"Yes! Shall I snap my fingers?"

"And, what about your mom? Don't you want her in attendance?"

"Wait...Are you—is it too soon for you? I mean, were you jok—?"

"No, no, I am *completely* serious when I tell you that I am seconds away from booking us the next flight to Vegas before you have a chance to change your mind. But I wouldn't be a dutiful husband-to-be if I didn't prompt you to consider all the things that I know are important to you. Like, how you'll feel about getting married without your mom present."

Ta'Mara considered that and then smiled. "My mom and dad eloped, you know. I think she'll understand. But at the end of the day, this is a decision between you and I. I'll have no regrets, as long as you don't. Plus, I figure we'll still want to have a public wedding later, to celebrate with family and friends. As long as my mom gets to be the planner I'm pretty confident that'll make up for much of any disappointment she might have. And then I'll have two anniversaries to hold over your head for the rest of our lives. How does that sound?"

"Wonderful. Amazing." He rose and walked toward her. Taking her hand he brought her up to him. "I love you so much, Ta'Mara. Somehow, I think I've loved you my whole life; and it feels like heaven to finally be able to tell you." He took a deep breath before exhaling his question, "Okay, so we're doing this. Tonight." He paused. "And you're absolutely, 100% sure about this?"

"With everything that's in me, Baby."

Jared grinned.

Epilogue

✳ ✳ ✳

Jared: "Hours later, we were husband and wife."

Ta'Mara: "And then he flew us right back to Oceanside as soon as the next flight was available."

Jared: "Against your protest."

Ta'Mara: "What can I say, I have a hot husband. What wife would want to wait another couple of hours to—you know—spend time with him?"

Jared: "I'd figured, 'Hey, we've waited this long, we could wait a few more hours to make sure I could get our honeymoon right.' I wanted that for her. And for us. "

Ta'Mara: "He did a fantastic job: Got us a lovely room at a hotel managed by one of his co-workers' friend's. The Penthouse Suite! Come on, now! He must've called in a huge favor while I was in the bathroom or something, cuz it was a complete surprise to me when we pulled up in front of the hotel. And I don't know how he managed it all. I walk in and I hear our songs! The ones on the mixtape he'd made me! Plus a few more that he'd added in that were a bit more, uhm, er—."

Jared: "For married folk."

Ta'Mara: "Exactly. And the room was filled with flowers, and petals scattered everywhere! Candle light all over, and pictures of us that had been posted on our Facebook and Instagram pages or that were still on his phone. He'd had them all printed out—in high quality—and there they were, sitting all nicely framed in various spots throughout the suite; both old photos of us together and and recent photos, too. But then he always claims he's not a planner. This man is a master planner, let me tell you."

Jared: "Like I always say, when I have the right motivation. And my wife, this woman right here, is the best motivation I could ever have."

Ta'Mara: "There was even a dinner waiting for us. Not that we ever got to it anytime soon. We were so tired from all the excitement, the plane rides—everything—that we ended up falling right asleep!"

Jared: "Yeah, but we sure made up for it after we woke up."

Ta'Mara: "Mr. Iona!"

Jared: "I would love to kiss that bashful smile of yours right now, Mrs. Iona."

Ta'Mara: "Well you'll just have to hold your horses, Mr."

Jared: "If I must."

Ta'Mara: "So. That's our story. That's how we got together. Uhm, Jared relocated to Kansas City so that we could remain close to my Mom. Honestly, I'm not sure who she loves more at this point, but I'm pretty sure it's him! I can't blame her, though. It's been eight years since we said 'we do' and this man still makes me feel like a newlywed. I don't know how I got to be so blessed with you, Jared, two times in my life but believe me when I say that I am so so thankful for both times."

Jared: "I'm the blessed one, Ta'Mara. God allowed you to see something in me that compelled you to risk loving me, not once but twice...and the second time was after you knew better! I know I married someone who is far better for me than I deserve. In my book, you'll always be my hero, Baby."

Jared and Ta'Mara had spent much of the past hour or so gazing at one another as they'd recounted the story of their life apart and together, apart again and finally...together. Now, the two turned in their seats, hands clasped between them as they faced the small cadre of singles and couples who had asked for their tale. The light from the bonfire they all sat around sparkled against the tears that shone in the eyes of many encircled around the large flame. Ta'Mara gave a watery sniffle and wiped at her own eyes, and then leaned over and wiped that of her husband's before giving him a kiss on his cheek.

"So," she said, breaking the silence once she'd turned her attention back to their small group, "Who's next?"

Whatever It Takes

---

* * *

About The Author

Help others find the books they enjoy;
please share your impressions by leaving a review on Amazon!

~

"If there's a book that you want to read, but it hasn't
been written yet, then you must write it."

\- Toni Morrison

Quint Emm Ellis enjoys penning plots centering
around unabashedly nerdy, introverted,
cinnamon-roll mantic, passionate, fallible women
who happen to be black, who happen to be Christian,
and who happen to love an uplifting and, possibly,
inspirational story.

When not writing a story that she couldn't find elsewhere, she enjoys listening to audio books, watching movies, finding great deals and spoiling her cat and dog rotten, (in different rooms because they don't yet get along). Her dream is to one day be able to afford to be able to walk around in loose pajama pants all day and geek out while mastering niche crafts like music production, film editing and electro etching.

Want free excerpts or news of upcoming books? Join the mailing list at **http://eepurl.com/hOuuyT**

Book Club Questions

General Questions

1. What is the significance of the title? Did you find it meaningful, why or why not?

2. Would you have given the book a different title? If yes, what would your title be?

3. What were the main themes of the book? How were those themes brought to life?

4. What did you think of the writing style and content structure of the book?

5. How important was the setting to the story? Did you think it was accurately portrayed?

6. How would the book have played out differently in a different time period or setting?

7. Which location in the book would you most like to visit and why?

8. Were there any quotes, passages or Bible references / verses that stood out to you? Why?

9. What did you like most about the book? What did you like the least?

10. How did the book make you feel? What emotions did it evoke?

11. Are there any books that you would compare this book to?

12. Have you read any other books by this author? How would you compare them to this selection?

13. What do you think the author's goal was in writing this book? What ideas were they trying to illustrate? What message were they trying to send?

14. What did you learn from this book?

15. Did this book remind you of any other books that you've read? Describe the connection.

16. Did your opinion of this book change as you read it? How?

17. Would you recommend the book to a friend? How would you summarize the story if you were to recommend it?

18. Was the book satisfying to read? Why or why not?

19. If you could talk to the author, what burning question would you want to ask?

About the Characters

1. Which character did you most relate to and why?
2. Who was your favorite character? Why?
3. Which character or moment prompted the strongest emotional reaction for you? Why?
4. What motivates the actions of each of the characters in the book?
5. Did the characters seem believable to you? Did they remind you of anyone you know?
6. Were the characters clearly drawn and depicted?
7. If the book were made into a movie, who would play each of the lead characters?
8. What were the power dynamics between the characters and how did that affect their interactions?
9. How does the way the characters see themselves differ from the way others see them?

10. Were there times you disagreed with a character's actions? What would you have done differently?

11. Which character would you most like to meet in real life?

About the Plot

1. What scene would you point out as the pivotal moment in the narrative? How did it make you feel?

2. What scene resonated with you most on a personal level? (Why? How did it make you feel?)

3. What surprised you most about the book? Why? Were there significant plot twists and turns? If so, what were they?

4. Were there any plot twists that you loved? Hated?

5. Did the author do a good job of organizing the plot and moving it along?

6. What was your favorite chapter and why?

7. What (if any) questions do you still have about the plot?

8. How did the author build the tension?

9. Did the ending answer all your questions? Did you think it was believable or too farfetched?

10. What aspects of the story could you most relate to?

11. Were you rooting for the couple to get together all along? Why or why not?

12. Did the plot make sense or were there some gaps/liberties taken to help get the couple together (or keep them apart)?

13. What songs did you think of while reading this book? (For extra fun: make a playlist!)

About the Ending

1. How did you feel about the ending? How might you change it?

2. How have the characters changed by the end of the book?

3. What do you think will happen next to the main characters?

4. Have any of your personal views changed because of this book? If so, how?

Made in United States
Orlando, FL
01 August 2023

35668480R00235